The Gecko In The Corner

By Nick Russell

West Bend Public Library
630 Poplar Street
West Bend, WI 53095
262-335-5151
www.westbendlibrary.org

Copyright 2017 © By Nick Russell
All rights reserved. No part of this book may be reproduced in any form or by any means, electronic or mechanical, including photocopying, recording, or by any information storage or retrieval system, without permission in writing by the publisher.

Nick Russell
1400 Colorado Street C-16
Boulder City, NV 89005
E-mail Editor@gypsyjournal.net

Also By Nick Russell

Fiction

Big Lake Mystery Series
Big Lake
Big Lake Lynching
Crazy Days In Big Lake
Big Lake Blizzard
Big Lake Scandal
Big Lake Burning
Big Lake Honeymoon
Big Lake Reckoning
Big Lake Brewpub
Big Lake Abduction
Big Lake Celebration

Dog's Run Series
Dog's Run
Return To Dog's Run

John Lee Quarrels Series
Stillborn Armadillos
The Gecko In The Corner

Standalone Mystery Novels
Black Friday

Nonfiction
Highway History and Back Road Mystery
Highway History and Back Road Mystery II
Meandering Down The Highway; A Year On The Road With Fulltime RVers
The Frugal RVer
Work Your Way Across The USA; You Can Travel And Earn A Living Too!
The Gun Shop Manual
Overlooked Florida
Overlooked Arizona

Keep up with Nick Russell's latest books at www.NickRussellBooks.com

Pain. A depth of pain he had never experienced before. A depth of pain he had never known existed. The beating had been terrible, but it had only been the start. At some point he had passed out and his tormentors had stopped hitting and kicking him and had waved an ammonia ampule under his nose to bring him back to consciousness. Then they brought out the pruning shears.

They didn't take off his left pinkie finger all at once. That would have been too quick. And too kind. Instead they had removed the tip, then used the same ammonia ampule to revive him while they took off another section. He had passed out a third time, and once more they had brought him around, the acrid smell of the ammonia ampule doing its job, awakening him so he could experience the agony as they finished the job.

***

How long had he been driving? Hours only, but it seemed like days. He wanted to stop and sleep but he knew if he did they would find him. Not those two, they were dead. But Torres had more where they came from, and he knew that whoever he sent for him this time would be even more brutal.

How much further? Could he make it before fatigue and pain and loss of blood took their toll and his abused body finally gave out like an old jalopy that had been pushed to its last mile before finally disintegrating into a heap of rusted metal and rubber and glass, with its oil and gasoline and grease spilling out onto the blacktop, just like his blood was leaking out of him? He looked at the GPS, finding it hard to focus his eyes. Three more miles. Three more miles was nothing. He could do that. He had come so far already, what was three more miles? Three more miles might as well have been the distance from the Earth to the Moon. If he could just pull over and rest for a few moments. Just close his eyes and rest.

No! He knew if he stopped he would never move again. It was only three more miles. He could make it.

John Lee Quarrels Series

The Gecko In The Corner
Chapter 1

WHEN HE FIRST SAW THE GECKO on the wall in the corner of his bedroom a week earlier he was going to catch it and put it outside. But it had been too fast for him. Three times he had tried to snatch it and three times it had scurried out of his reach. Frustrated, he had gone into the kitchen and found a plastic flyswatter.

"Don't kill it," Beth Ann had pleaded.

"I'm not gonna kill it, I'm just gonna knock it out so I can throw it out."

"Don't do that, John Lee. They're good luck."

"No, rabbits feet are good luck. I've never heard of lizards being good luck before."

"I bet rabbits don't think their feet are so lucky, if people are always killin' 'em so they can hang them on those little chains."

"I never thought about that," he admitted. "Hold still, you little bastard."

John Lee slapped at it with the flyswatter and missed. The gecko ducked behind the corner of his dresser.

"And even if they ain't lucky, they eat bugs. Long as he's here you won't have no bugs in your house."

"This is Florida, Beth Ann, there are always going to be bugs in the house. And so what if he eats them all? I've got a lizard in my house instead of a bug. Is that any better?"

"Just leave him and come back to bed. I promise I'll take your mind off of it."

"I don't like Magic watching us in bed. I damn sure don't want a lizard watching us."

"Come on, John Lee. Come back to bed."

So he had, and Beth Ann had had been right. It only took a few minutes for him to completely forget about the gecko.

Since then he had come to grudgingly accept the freeloading lizard. Mostly because he couldn't catch the damn thing anyway. So they seemed to have come to an agreement of sorts. As long as the gecko kept the insect population in control and minded its manners, John Lee would think of it as a living bug zapper. But the first time he found it in his bed there was going to be hell to pay.

Magic, his 100 pound protection trained German Shepherd, had not been as quick to welcome their new roommate. But over time the dog stopped growling at the gecko, though he followed it with his eyes whenever it moved.

John Lee was asleep when the dog growled, waking him up. But it wasn't the noise he used to signal his displeasure with the gecko. This was a lower, deeper growl. One of warning. One that there was trouble nearby.

The red numbers on the digital clock on his nightstand said 3:28. He swung out of bed and walked into the darkened living room. Beside him, Magic growled again.

"What is it, boy? Somebody out there?"

He peered through the wood Levolor blinds. It had rained earlier and the moon and stars were hidden behind the thick clouds covering the sky. Even so, he managed to see the dark shape of a strange vehicle in his driveway.

Going back into his bedroom, John Lee pulled on a pair of jeans and a dark blue T-shirt and slipped his feet into tennis shoes. He went to his spare bedroom and retrieved his Bushnell Lynx night vision binoculars and returned to the front window. The car was still there, a silent trespasser.

Kneeling down at the bottom of the window, he pushed the blinds up enough to be able to see out and trained them on the car. The green tinted image showed somebody inside, sitting behind the wheel, unmoving.

John Lee called the Somerton County Sheriff's Office and when the dispatcher answered, he said, "This is John Lee. Who's on duty tonight?"

"Maddy and Barry."

"Are they busy?"

"Maddy's working a one car accident out by the EZ Rest. A couple of kids ran off the road and into a ditch. No injuries. Barry's at the Harris place. Tom caught a couple of kids siphoning gas from his pickup and was holding them at gunpoint. Did you need something, John Lee?"

"I don't know. There's a car parked in my driveway."

"Do you want me to see how soon I can get somebody out there?"

"No, not yet. I'm going to go out and check on it, see what's up."

The dispatcher's name was Tony Ramsey and there was concern in his voice when he said, "Don't do that, John Lee. Let me see if I can call somebody at home to give you some backup."

"It'll be okay," John Lee assured him. "I've got my dog and he's pretty good backup. I'm taking my radio with me. If you don't hear from me in ten minutes, call out the cavalry."

"You think it's somebody from... well, you know?"

"I don't know, probably not. Probably just kids necking or something."

Months earlier John Lee had killed a man in an on-duty shooting. Though the Florida Department of Law Enforcement had ruled the shooting justifiable, the man's father had sworn to get revenge. Since he was the richest man in the county, he certainly had the resources to send hired guns to get even with the deputy.

"I really wish you'd wait and let me call somebody."

"We'd both feel pretty dumb if all it is is a couple of teenagers making out. Hang tight, Tony, I'll be back with you in just a couple of minutes."

John Lee tucked his .40 Glock pistol into his waistband behind his right hip, picked up his 12 gauge Remington tactical shotgun and a high-intensity LED flashlight and went to the back door of his house. "Come on, Magic, let's go see who's visiting us at this time of night."

He scanned the back yard with the night vision binoculars, looking for anybody who might be waiting in ambush. Seeing nothing, he eased out the door, giving Magic the command to stay close at his side. He went to both back corners of the house and looked through the binoculars again. Nothing. Moving at a crouch, he crossed the open side yard, every sense alert to danger.

Keeping to a line of trees at the far edge of his property, John Lee and the dog made their way toward the front. He hoped there were no snakes around. John Lee hated snakes, and feared them more than he did any bad guy with a gun or a knife.

He moved stealthily until he could cross behind and approach the strange vehicle from the rear. The person inside had not moved. Holding the flashlight away from his body with one hand and resting the shotgun on the trunk lid, John Lee pushed the button to turn on the light.

"Show me your hands!"

Nothing.

"I said, show me your hands. Get them up in the air where I can see them!"

He thought he saw the head make a slight movement, but not much.

"Show me your damn hands or I'm gonna shoot!"

When there was no response, John Lee left the shotgun and drew his pistol. He eased his way up to the side of the car. The man inside still hadn't moved. John Lee looked at the man through the window. Thinning brown hair, maybe early to mid-50s. It was hard to say because his face was covered in blood. The driver's window was down. He knocked on the door with his flashlight and the man managed to turn his head enough to look at him.

"Are you John Lee Quarrels?" The voice was weak, not much more than a tortured whisper.

"That's me. Who the hell are you?"

"I'm your father."

The Gecko In The Corner

Chapter 2

JOHN LEE HAD NEVER KNOWN his father. Herb Quarrels had been a sailor from Ohio that his mother had met while on spring break in Pensacola. The two had partied for three days and then he had returned to his job at the Naval Air Station there and Lisa Marie came back to Somerton County with a cheap promise ring on her finger and no idea that a new life was growing inside of her. When she missed her period she had called him in tears, and to his credit he had borrowed a friend's car and driven the 300 miles to her home to do the right thing.

Unfortunately, though the two 18 year olds may have been mature enough to make a baby, they weren't ready for the responsibility or commitment that marriage demanded. They moved into base housing at the Naval Air Station, and when Herb shipped out for sea duty less than two years later, Lisa Marie came home with her baby in tow. Six months after that, when Herb came back to reclaim his wife and child, Lisa Marie was no longer interested in married life. With her parents, a freethinking couple who had placed few restrictions on her more than willing to help care for little John Lee, she couldn't see herself returning to the drudgery of being a full-time mother and wife.

Herb hadn't been all that disappointed, and the divorce was amicable. He had only visited a time or two after that, though he faithfully sent a monthly check to help support his son.

Now, looking at the battered and abused man sitting at his kitchen table, there were a lot of questions John Lee wanted to ask him. Why had his father shown up at his place unannounced in the middle of the night after a 30 year absence? How had he found John Lee in the first place? And perhaps the most pressing question, what the hell had happened to him?

But first he had to attend to the man's injuries.

"No, don't call an ambulance or anything," Herb said, the mere effort of speaking obviously causing him pain. "I don't want to go a hospital. I just need to clean up a little bit and rest."

"You need medical attention."

"I'm okay," Herb told him. "It's not as bad as it looks."

"I sure as hell hope not," John Lee said, "because it looks pretty damn bad. You need to be in an ER."

"No," Herb said shaking his head.

"You don't have a lot of choice in the matter," John Lee replied. "You're half dead."

"Don't you have some bandages here or something? You're a cop. Don't you keep a first aid kit in your car?"

"Yeah, I'm a cop, and I've got a medical kit. But I'm not a doctor. You need more help than I can give you."

The other man started to stand up on shaky legs. "Never mind. I'm sorry to bother you. I'll just go."

"Sit down before you fall down."

"No," Herb said, shaking his head. "I can't go to an ER or hospital. And no other cops."

"Okay, you win. Sit down and let me see what I can do."

"Do you have a garage?"

"A garage?"

"Yes. A garage? Do you have one?"

"No, I don't have a garage. Why do you care if I have a garage?"

"Can't have my car sitting out there."

"What the hell are you involved in?"

"It's nothing. All a big mistake."

"Who did this to you?"

"Muggers. Tried to carjack me."

John Lee reached for his handheld radio. "Where did this happen?"

"Please... please, no cops."

"I am a cop, remember? And how the hell did you know I'm a cop anyhow? Or how to find me? I think the last time I heard anything from you I was, what, five years old?"

The Gecko In The Corner

Herb was weaving in his chair and looked like he might pass out at any moment. Magic barked from the front room and John Lee left his father sitting there for a moment while he went to check on what had alerted the dog. There was another car in his driveway, its headlights on, and he was reaching for the shotgun he had propped up next to the door when he had brought his father into the house when he heard a voice calling out to him.

"John Lee? It's Maddy. Everything okay?"

He turned on the porch light and watched the tall blonde woman approaching.

"Tony called me on my cell phone," Deputy Madison "Maddy" Westfall said as she came up onto his porch. "He said you called in and said there was a strange car in your driveway and asked who was on duty. Then he said you called back again and told him everything was okay, and not to make a notation of either call. But he said you sounded like something was wrong."

"Thanks, I appreciate it. But I've got it handled."

"Am I interrupting a sleepover or something?"

John Lee had known Maddy all their lives and considered the attractive woman one of his best friends. Probably his very best friend. Over the years a teasing sexual tension had grown between them, but wary of hurting their relationship, neither had acted on it. But that didn't mean John Lee lived a celibate lifestyle. Not by any stretch, and Maddy seemed to take delight in busting his chops whenever she could.

"Yeah, or something," he told her. "Come on in."

He led her into the kitchen, Maddy stopping to pet Magic along the way and ruffle the dog's ears. If the big German Shepherd loved anyone in the world nearly as much as he loved John Lee it was Maddy, and he looked at her with adoring eyes.

When she saw Herb sitting at the table Maddy did a double take at his appearance. "My God, what happened?"

"He says he was mugged by carjackers."

"Are you okay, sir?"

"I told you, no other cops," Herb said, an edge to his voice in spite of his injuries.

"This is Maddy," John Lee told him. "She's my friend. I didn't call her, she came to check up on me. I'm not exactly used to having strangers showing up on my doorstep in the middle of the night. Maddy, this is my father, Herb."

"Pleased to meet you," Maddy said, unsure how to address the issue of a bleeding man sitting in her friend's kitchen at four in the morning.

Herb tried to stand up again, but couldn't summon the energy.

"Just sit down. You're not going anywhere."

Maddy's radio crackled and the dispatcher asked "County 28?"

She held it to her mouth and said "28."

"What's you're 20?"

"I'm at that location we talked about."

"Everything okay there?"

She looked to John Lee and he shook his head.

"Uhhh... 10-4. I'll be 10-7 here for a while if you need me."

"10-4."

She looked at John Lee, and asked, "Now what?"

Herb's head was hanging and he seemed to be asleep. Or maybe he had passed out while he was sitting upright, John Lee wasn't sure which. "Let's see if we can clean him up and figure out what happened to him."

His left hand was swathed in some type of towel that could have been any color, but now was coated in blood. John Lee unwrapped it and when she saw what was inside, Maddy gasped.

"Holy shit! Somebody cut off his finger!"

"Yeah they did," John Lee said.

"What the hell is going on here? Carjackers didn't do that, John Lee!"

"No, they didn't."

The blood had coagulated on the man's hand in the wound where his little finger had been. John Lee cleaned it as best he could, using alcohol and swabs from his medical kit. Herb groaned a time or two, his eyes flickered open twice and then closed again.

John Lee and Maddy had seen a lot of mangled bodies in their time as Somerton County deputies, and many times the victims had been people they knew. They had learned to compartmentalize their emotions so they could deal with the task at hand, whether it be a traffic accident, domestic violence incident, or two liquored up rednecks going at it with baseball bats or knives. Maybe it was because he had never known the man as his father, or maybe it was the circumstances under which he had appeared out of nowhere, but John Lee was able to remain dispassionate as they cleaned Herb's wounds and assessed his injuries.

"Well, he's not pretty, but I think he's going to live. He lost a few teeth, and I think his nose may be broken. His hand's about the worst of it. It looks like whoever beat the hell out of him wasn't trying to kill him."

"No, they weren't, Maddy. They didn't want him dead. At least not right away. This was torture."

"Why would anybody want to torture your father, John Lee?"

"I don't know," he told her, looking at the man who had been part of creating his life but never been a part of it.

"Do you think this has anything to do with what happened with Troy Somerton?"

"I don't know," John Lee said again.

"His father said he was going to get even with you for killing him."

In the wake of his son's death, Richard Somerton had made threats to get even with the man who had killed him, and John Lee wouldn't have been surprised to come under attack by thugs he had hired to extract his revenge. Known as Junior by everybody in the county, a name he despised, the aggrieved man would never stoop so low as to get his own hands dirty with such a task.

"But why do it this way?"

"Maybe he figured since you killed somebody he loved, he'd get even by taking out somebody you love?"

"I could see him sending somebody after me. Or maybe even Mama Nell or Paw Paw. But why this guy? Hell, I don't even know him, Maddy."

"Well somebody sure worked him over, and if it wasn't somebody that Junior sent, who was it?"

"I don't know," John Lee admitted. "But I've got a feeling we're going to find out before this is over."

The Gecko In The Corner
Chapter 3

HERB CAME AROUND SOMEWHAT WHEN they half carried him to John Lee's spare bedroom.

"What? What's going on?"

"We're just putting you to bed, sir," Maddy said.

"No. Can't sleep. Have to keep moving."

The man's words were slurred, and if John Lee didn't know better he would think he had been drinking. But it was fatigue and pain.

"You just get some sleep. It's gonna be okay."

Herb shook his head feebly. "Not okay. Have to go."

"The only place you're going is to sleep. Just close your eyes."

"Can't sleep. They may..."

"Nobody's going to hurt you here, sir," Maddy assured him. "You just get some rest, okay?"

He tried to protest, but didn't have the energy. His head sank back onto the pillow and he was out.

They left the bedroom and Maddy said, "I don't know what's going on, John Lee, but this could get ugly in a hurry. What are you going to do?"

"I don't know," he said, realizing that seemed to be his standard answer to the situation at hand. "Let's just let him get some rest, okay? Once he wakes up, maybe I can figure out what the hell he's got himself involved in."

Maddy's radio crackled again. "28?"

"28 here," she replied.

"I hate to bother you, but I've got a report of a gas drive off at the In-N-Out. Old green pickup headed west away from town. Barry is assisting a motorist with a flat tire on Turpentine Highway. Can you cover it, or should I call someone in? County 12 will be on another half hour.

"Go ahead," John Lee told her. "I can handle things here."

"Are you sure?"

"Yeah. The less people that know about this the better right now. Keep this under your hat, okay Maddy?"

There was concern in her big gray eyes when she looked at him. "Are you sure that's a good idea, John Lee? I mean, I know he's your dad and all, but still..."

"He was never a dad to me. He's my biological father, but that's it."

"Then maybe we should make this official and file a report."

"Not yet, okay?"

"Why not?"

He shrugged his shoulders. "I don't know. I just want to find out what's going on first."

"Whatever it is, John Lee, I don't want it to come back and bite you in the ass. If Flag finds out about this and that you didn't report it, there's gonna be hell to pay."

"Screw Flag," John Lee said, referring to the Somerton County Sheriff's Department Chief deputy. There was no love lost between the two of them, and lately their animosity toward each other had grown considerably. "He can go pound sand as far as I'm concerned."

Maddy was skeptical, but she sighed. "Okay, this is just between you and me. But if you need anything, John Lee, anything at all, you just call me. Okay?"

"I will," he assured her and walked her out to her patrol car.

She got behind the wheel and he closed the door for her, then leaned in the window. "Look, Maddy, I really appreciate this. I can always depend on you."

"You know you can," she said. "I'd better go see if I can find this gas thief. More than likely it's somebody who just spaced it out and forgot to pay."

She started the car, put it in gear, then said, "Call me if you need anything, John Lee. Day or night."

He nodded and she backed out of the driveway, then drove off in the direction of the In-N-Out convenience store. When her car was out of sight he turned back to his house, then looked at the car his father had arrived in. It was some kind of midsized foreign job, and a decal on the back window identified it as being part of a nationwide rental fleet. The sky had turned light and he looked inside. Aside from the blood all over the driver's side and a roadmap spread out on the passenger seat, there wasn't anything else. He rummaged in the glove compartment and found the rental papers, made out to Herbert John Quarrels, with an address in Cleveland, Ohio. The car had been rented for a week and still had four days left to go on the contract.

John Lee had thought about what Herb had told him when he had asked if there was a garage they could park the car in. Something about not letting it sit out. He didn't think anybody was that considerate of a rental car. Whatever it was that this man who had suddenly reappeared in his life had going on, someone had wanted to hurt him. Hurt him very badly. And John Lee didn't think they were finished yet. Maybe it would be a good idea to get the car out of his driveway and away from any eyes that might be passing by.

He didn't have a garage, but there was a rough track through the trees behind his house that went back about fifteen yards. He got behind the wheel of the rental car, which turned out to be a Hyundai Sonota, and drove around the side of his house and into the track. It wasn't a garage, but one would have to be standing in his backyard to see the car hidden in the trees.

With that chore taken care of, John Lee went back into his house to wait for his father to wake up.

***

He had dozed off in his recliner and was awakened by a noise from his guest bedroom. It was full daylight. His eyes were gritty and his head ached. He glanced at the clock on his DVD player. 9 AM.

Herb was awake and moaning when John Lee went to check on him.

"I imagine you're hurting quite a bit."

His father nodded. "Yeah."

John Lee handed him a glass and two pills.

"What are these?"

"Vicodin. Pain pills. You're not some kind of junkie, are you?"

Herb winced as he sat up. He shook his head. "No, I'm no junkie. Don't worry about that."

He was still very shaky and spilled some of the water trying to get the glass to his mouth. John Lee helped him. After he swallowed the pills he laid back down.

"Is there anybody I should call, to let them know you're here?"

Herb shook his head. "No."

"Do you have a wife? Kids? Somebody who needs to know where you're at?"

"No. I just need to get some rest and I'll get out of your hair."

"You're not going anywhere until you tell me what the hell's going on and who did this to you," John Lee said.

But Herb Quarrels wasn't telling him anything. At least not right then. His eyes drooped closed and he was asleep again.

***

John Lee was exhausted and in no shape to go on duty, but fortunately he had accumulated a lot of time off. He called the office and Sheila Sharp, the daytime dispatcher, answered. He identified himself and told her he was under the weather and needed to take a personal day off, maybe two.

"Are you okay, John Lee? What's wrong with you?

Sheila was nice, but a busybody and a gossip.

"It's some kind of stomach thing."

"Oh, have you got the trots? Did you eat at that new barbecue place that opened up next to the Dollar Store? My brother Clifford and his wife ate there the other night, and they both been sittin' on the toilet ever since."

"Yeah, I guess that's probably what it was, bad barbecue," John Lee told her.

"Well you just stay home 'till you're feelin' better. Do you need me to send somebody out with some Pepto-Bismol. Or maybe toilet paper? I don't know how much toilet paper a bachelor keeps in stock. Clifford said that him and Melody went through so much that they was usin' paper towels. Said between the crappin' and the paper towels, both their rear ends was gettin' raw."

"I've got plenty of toilet paper," John Lee assured her. "And Pepto, too."

"Well bless your heart. You just take it easy and get to feelin' better. And drink lots of water, John Lee! When you got the squirts like that you can get dehydrated real quick."

"I'll do that," he promised, then added, "Sorry, but I've got to go again. Catch you later, Sheila."

He punched the button to end the call before she could inquire any further about his condition or offer any other advice or insight into his colorectal state.

He fed Magic and let the dog outside to do its business, then poked his head into the spare bedroom to check on Herb, who was snoring lightly. John Lee stared at the man for a long time, trying to assess his own feelings about him. There was no sense of having suddenly attained a father, and though he wanted to know what had happened to the man, there was no outraged need to hunt down whoever had abused him to get even.

And, of course, there was some curiosity about the man. What was he like under normal circumstances? What did he do for a living? He said he didn't have a family, but he wore a silver wedding band on his left hand. In spite of the cuts and bruises, and the swelling, he could see some resemblance between the two of them. They had the same nose, the same jaw line, and shared their hair color.

"Where have you been all my life?" John Lee asked the sleeping man. "And why are you here now, all beat to hell? What have you gotten yourself into that somebody did this to you?"

But Herb couldn't hear him and didn't answer. John Lee watched him for a few moments longer, then opened the back door and whistled for Magic, who trotted inside and bumped his head against John Lee's leg, asking to be petted. He gave the dog some attention, then went back to his recliner and sat down again, the Glock on an end table next to him.

"I need to get some rest, boy. Keep an eye on things for me, okay?"

Magic settled at his spot in the corner and John Lee fell asleep, secure in the knowledge that he couldn't have a more faithful sentinel watching over him or the man in his guest bedroom.

The Gecko In The Corner

Chapter 4

WHEN JOHN LEE WOKE UP again it was a little past noon, and his stomach was growling. He checked on Herb, who was still asleep, then went into the kitchen and started the coffee maker. Magic was standing by the back door, looking hopeful, so he let the dog out. Opening the freezer compartment of his refrigerator, he took down a box of frozen breakfast burritos and popped two of them in the microwave.

He was staring at the timer as it counted down to zero, when Herb said, "Good morning."

He was standing in the kitchen doorway in just his boxer shorts.

"How are you feeling?"

"I'm going to live. I can't find the rest of my clothes."

"I threw them in the washer but I don't think they're going to come clean," John Lee told him. He went to his bedroom and came back with a pair of jeans and a green T-shirt.

"Try these on."

They were snug, but Herb managed to get into them, grimacing as his bandaged hand went through the armhole of the shirt.

"Ummm... I can't buckle the pants with just one hand."

John Lee helped him, then motioned toward a chair at the table and Herb sat down.

"How do you like your coffee?"

"Cream and sugar if you've got it."

He filled two cups and set them on the table. The microwave had binged, and he took out the burritos, putting them on two paper plates. "Salsa?"

Herb shook his head. "No, this is fine."

They sat across from each other, each staring at the other man.

"I guess you've got a lot of questions?"

"Gee, ya think?"

"Look, I'm sorry to show up on your doorstep like this. I imagine I am the last person you ever expected to see in this world. I just didn't know where else to go."

"Are you gonna tell me what happened to you?"

"It's a long story."

"I've got time."

"Really, John Lee, it's better if we don't get into all of that."

"You lost the right to decide that when you came here in the middle of night all beat to hell and bleeding all over the place."

"Like I said, I'm sorry."

"How did you find me anyway?"

"I've been keeping track, as much as I could. I Googled your name a long time ago."

"I'm a cop. Cops' addresses usually aren't listed on Google or anyplace else online the public can get to it easily."

"I didn't find out where you lived on Google. That took more effort."

"More effort than ever picking up a telephone and calling to see how I was? More effort than writing a letter? More effort than ever coming to see me?" John Lee couldn't hide the irritation in his voice, and was surprised at his resentment of this man who had come into his life. A man he had been aware existed, but never had any real knowledge of, or, if he would admit it to himself, any curiosity about until now.

"I wanted to, early on. But things got complicated."

"I could dial a telephone when I was five years old. It's not that complicated."

Herb looked away from him and said, "I guess I deserved that."

"So why are you here? I mean, I can't remember ever seeing you. All you were was a birthday card with a check in it and another one at Christmas."

"I paid my child support every month, just like clockwork. I sent it to your mother at your grandparents' address."

The Gecko In The Corner

"I'm not talking about money," John Lee said. "Why are you here after all these years with no contact? Why now?"

Herb pushed the half eaten burrito away and started to stand up. "I'm sorry. This was a mistake. I'll get out of here."

"Just like that? You show up in this condition, I get you cleaned up, and then you're just going to leave?"

"I didn't want to come here. Like I said, I didn't know where else to go."

"Sit down," John Lee commanded. "You're not getting off that easy."

"I said I'll go."

"And I said sit down!"

"You can't stop me from..."

"Do you want to bet?" John Lee stood up and pushed his chair away. "I spend my life dealing with drunk rednecks, wife beaters, and everything from thieves steeling the copper wire out of vacant houses to guys cooking meth. If I can handle them, do you really think I can't stop you from leaving?"

Herb sat back down, his head downcast.

"I want answers," John Lee told him. "And don't try to bullshit me, because I've heard it from the best of them."

Herb nodded, "Okay, you win. What do you want to know?"

"Why didn't I ever hear from you until now?"

"Look, your mother and I, we were just a couple of kids. We had no business getting married, let alone making a baby. It was a bad idea right from the start."

"Yeah, I get that. Those things happen. That still doesn't explain why I never heard from you."

"I've got a wife, John Lee. We got married when you were four years old. I told her about you and your mother going in, and she seemed to understand that. At first it wasn't a problem. But as time went on, it became one. I came down to see you... I don't think you were even in school yet, and when I got back home she hit the roof. Said I had no business wasting time and money traipsing off down here when I had responsibilities at home. After that, it was a battle every month when I sent the check for the child support. But I did it, John Lee, I paid every month."

"So what do you want, a medal because you wrote a check every month?"

Herb shook his head, but didn't say anything.

"What happened to you? And don't start with that bullshit about carjackers. Whoever did this to you, they weren't after a rented car."

Before Herb could reply, Magic barked outside. John Lee went into the living room and looked out the window to see Maddy in a tug-of-war with the dog over his rubber Kong toy. He opened the door and she looked up with concern on her face.

"How is he?"

"He's awake. Come on in."

She was wearing jeans and a blue long sleeved Somerton County Sheriff's Department T-shirt, and John Lee couldn't help but admire her form as she came up the steps.

"Take a picture, it'll last longer," Maddy teased.

"Why don't you hold still and I'll make a painting instead," he countered.

"Ummm... body paints?" She laughed and went inside, giving her hips an exaggerated wiggle as he looked at her rear end.

"How are you doing today, sir?"

Herb nodded, and it was obvious to see that he appreciated how good the woman looked, even in his condition.

"I don't know if you remember me, but my name is Maddy. We met last night."

"Vaguely," Herb admitted. "It's all kind of hazy to me."

"I don't doubt it. Somebody had really worked you over."

"Herb was just getting ready to tell me about that when you showed up," John Lee said. "Weren't you?"

"This isn't something I want to involve you in. I've caused enough disruption just coming here. How about I just go on my way and we forget I was ever here?"

"Yeah, you're good about forgetting all about me," John Lee said with an edge to his voice. "But not this time."

"I said I don't want to involve you."

"Bullshit. You involved me when you came here."

"That was a mistake. Can't you just forget about it?"

"Even if we wanted to forget about it, a felony was committed against you," Maddy said. "We're police officers. It's against the law for us to ignore something like that."

"What if I don't want to press charges? Then what?"

"It's the state that would be pressing the charges," John Lee said. "You don't have any choice in the matter,"

"Okay, look, this is getting ridiculous. Here's the truth. I was helping a friend build a deck at his house and the power saw slipped and cut my hand."

"That's the story you're going to go with?"

"That's what happened."

"And how do you account for being all beat up like you are?"

"I got in a fight with a couple of guys in a bar."

"Let me get this straight. First you cut your finger off with a power saw helping a friend with some kind of building project. And then, instead of going to an ER, you went to a bar and got jumped by a couple of guys?"

"Yeah, that's the way it happened."

"Who was this friend of yours you were helping? What's his name and where does he live?"

"Just drop it, okay?"

"And where was this bar at? The one where those guys beat you up?"

"I'm not saying anything else. And I'm leaving. You can't keep me here against my will. I've got rights, just like anybody else, even if you are my son."

"Don't call me your son. You gave up any right you had to do that a long time ago," John Lee said heatedly. "And then, when you show up here like you did, you gave up any right to decide when you're going to leave."

"You're just as stubborn as your mother was, do you know that?"

"Don't talk about her. You gave up that right, too, when you abandoned us."

Herb shook his head in anger. "I didn't abandon anybody. Like I said, we were too young and it just didn't work out. I'd have been happy to stick it out and make it work. She was the one who wanted to end it. She didn't want any commitments. Not to me, and not to you either, apparently, since her mom and dad were the ones that raised you. So don't get all sanctimonious on me!"

"Hey guys, let's calm down," Maddy said, trying to intervene in the head-on collision between father and son that was about to happen.

"No problem, I'm out of here," Herb said, standing up again. John Lee rose to meet him. "Unless you plan to handcuff me and cart me off to jail or a hospital somewhere, step aside."

"I don't think so."

Apparently something else that both men shared was a temper and a stubbornness, and Maddy tried once again to be the peacemaker. And this time what she said seemed to have hit home.

"Mr. Quarrels.... Herb, whoever did this to you had a reason. You know it, and we know it. And whatever that reason is, I don't think they're done with you. So whether you want to tell us what's going on or not, you need to think about one thing. However this happened, whoever they are, they found you and did what they did. And if they found you once, they can find you again. You or somebody close to you that they can use as leverage to get whatever it is they want that you have. You came here for a reason, sir. I think that reason was because you needed a refuge from whatever is happening in your life. So how about you just relax and get some more rest, and we'll take it from there."

The two men glared at each other a moment longer, then Herb nodded and sat back down. "You win, I'm not going anywhere right now. But I'm not going to say anything else, either, so don't bother asking."

The Gecko In The Corner

Chapter 5

THE CONFRONTATION SEEMED TO TAKE a lot out of Herb, and after picking at his burrito another minute or two, he said his hand was throbbing and asked John Lee if he had any more Vicodin. He swallowed two, washing them down with water, and then said to Maddy, "Young lady, I appreciate you coming by to check up on me. And I appreciate you being John Lee's friend. Thank you." Then he shuffled back to the guest bedroom, closing the door behind him.

"Are you okay?"

"No, I'm pissed off," John Lee said. "He shows up out of nowhere after all these years, looking like he does, then he wants to be secretive and not tell me what's happening. He's got no right, Maddy. No right to be here at all, and no right to pull this kind of bullshit."

Maddy, whose own father had died when she was still a teenager, didn't know what to say. Was it better to have a father and lose him than to never know one at all, or was it even worse not to know him and then have him show up under circumstances like these?

They sat at the kitchen table talking, trying to figure out what had happened to Herb and what he was hiding. But whatever his secret was, only he knew, and he wasn't saying.

"You know what else pisses me off?"

"What, John Lee?"

"That he's right about my mother."

Maddy nodded her head and reached across the table to put her hand on his. "I know. We both got kind of shortchanged when it came to parents, didn't we?"

"Yeah, we did."

His mother, Lisa Marie, was a beautiful and vibrant woman who couldn't be tied down to anyone or anything. Not even her child. For as long as John Lee could remember, she was a fleeting presence in his life, occasionally breezing into town for a visit, promising him that this time she was there to stay. He never believed her, because he knew that before too long she would get some wild idea that she was sure would make her life complete and be gone again.

The world was full of adventures and she was always off seeking another one. She had gone to cosmetology school in Tallahassee, then worked as a waitress in a Key West bar for a while, then signed onto a cruise ship, where she served drinks to passengers as they explored the ports of the Caribbean. From there she had moved to New York City for a brief stint, thinking she would get a modeling gig, but that hadn't worked out. Then, because it sounded like fun, she had taken a course in driving eighteen wheelers at a school in Allegan, Michigan. And so it had gone, all through John Lee's childhood.

Not that he had ever felt neglected or unloved. His grandparents had given him a good home, even if it was not a traditional one by any means. His grandmother never wanted him to call her by that title, or by any other name except Mama Nell. Though she had been drawing Social Security for a few years, she was the youngest spirit John Lee had ever known.

There was no question that Nell loved her husband Stanley, and their marriage had always been a good one. But everybody, including Stanley, knew that he was her second choice. Her heart would always belong to another.

When Elvis Presley came to Inverness, Florida in the summer of 1961 to make the movie *Follow That Dream,* 14 year old Nell had seen him riding in the back of his white stretch Cadillac limousine and had immediately fallen head over heels in love with the singer, who was almost twice her age. And when he had smiled that crooked smile of his and pointed his finger at her when she screamed, "I love you, Elvis," she knew he felt the same way.

He had gone on to even greater fame while Nell had stayed a small town Florida girl, and though she had been heartbroken when he married Priscilla six years later, she would always love him. If she couldn't have Elvis, at least she could feel like she had a piece of him when she named her daughter after his.

As for her husband, Stanley seemed to accept the fact that he would always play second fiddle to the man he referred to as Elvis the Pelvis, and he really couldn't complain about the fact that their home seemed to be a shrine to the man, because whenever he was feeling amorous, all he had to do was put on a CD of *Love Me Tender* or *Are You Lonesome Tonight?* and Nell would be putty in his hands.

Stanley was a tall, thin man with a weathered face that came from his years of working as a lineman for Florida Power & Light Company, and a gray ponytail that hung down his back. He had been a young man working for a public utility in Pennsylvania when he had been sent south after a hurricane to help restore power in Florida. And while it was hot hanging off the side of a pole 40 feet in the air, he quickly decided he'd rather do that than spend another winter freezing his rear end off in Harrisburg. Stanley was a hard worker, and when FPL had offered him a job, he had been quick to accept.

Stanley, who acknowledged that he was nothing more than an old hippy, still wore his gray hair in a ponytail and kept busy in his retirement tinkering with a dozen different projects at any given time. He loved building things, everything from three or four greenhouses constructed with PVC pipe and plastic sheeting scattered around his property, to a windmill that he had built and connected to the solar system he had assembled to add wind power. Stanley had given FPL 35 years of his life, and while he had enjoyed his work and the utility had treated him right, now that he was retired he didn't want to give them any more money than he had to. More than half of his and Mama Nell's electric power needs were provided by the sun and the wind.

Besides building things, Stanley was also a gardener. He believed that the fact that he grew marijuana along with tomatoes, beans, and sprouts was nobody's business but his own. After all, it was all about having a self-sustaining lifestyle, right? His deputy sheriff grandson had learned that it was best to just look the other way because John Lee's protests about his activities were a lesson in futility. But out of respect for John Lee's position as a deputy, Paw Paw had at least moved the greenhouse with the pot to the back of the property so it wasn't quite so obvious.

And while John Lee's upbringing may have been unconventional, it had not been touched by tragedy like Maddy's had been.

Madison "Maddy" Westfall had been three years behind John Lee in high school, but even then she had been hard not to notice, with her big gray eyes, long ash blonde hair, and legs to match. Her brother Dan had been John Lee's best friend when they were growing up, and he was always telling John Lee that she had a crush on him. But when you're that age, the span is too great to attempt to breach.

When Dan drowned while swimming in the Suwannee River at seventeen, it had broken his parents' hearts. As so often happens when a child dies, their marriage had not survived the strain. They had divorced and Richard Westfall had moved away. Over time he had taken to drink, and it was only a few years after his son's death that he had driven his car off the road and into a lake somewhere down around Ocala.

Her mother had remarried twice after that, but neither relationship had worked out. She became more and more withdrawn, seldom leaving her bedroom, and never stepping outside the house. Madison had been forced to become the adult in the family while she was still just a girl. She was the one that paid the bills from the monthly Social Security check and an annuity from her father's life insurance policy, she was the one who did the grocery shopping, and she was responsible for the cooking, cleaning, and other household duties. And she had handled it all with a maturity far beyond her years, still managing to graduate at the top of her high school class.

"So what happens now?"

"I don't know," John Lee said. "But I want to know more about this guy. Can you run a background check on him and see what you can come up with? I'd do it, but I'm supposed to be home sick, and you know that if I call it in, Sheila's going to have a million questions."

Maddy nodded her head. "Oh yeah, I forgot. She called me to tell me you had the Hershey squirts and that I should check up on you. Need any toilet paper, John Lee?"

"No, thanks," he told her. "I think I'm good. But then again, maybe not. I have no idea what kind of shit is about to descend upon me with my father here."

If John Lee had no idea what was to come, it wouldn't take him long to find out. And it wasn't going to be pretty.

John Lee Quarrels Series

The Gecko In The Corner
Chapter 6

MADDY HUNG AROUND UNTIL IT was time for her to go home and fix dinner for her mother, and then get some rest before she went on duty.

Herb woke up again while John Lee was watching the 6 o'clock news and came into the living room.

"Need some more Vicodin?"

"You asked me if I was a junkie. I'm beginning to wonder if you're not a pusher."

"I wrecked a patrol car chasing a couple of drunk kids in a stolen car last spring. I got banged up and the doctor gave them to me."

"I think maybe just one will be enough, instead of two."

John Lee gave him a pill and brought him a glass of water. When he was done drinking it, Herb asked, "Mind if I take a shower?"

"Help yourself."

The news was over and *Jeopardy* had come on when Herb finished his shower and came back to the living room with a towel wrapped around his waist.

"Instead of trying to get back into those jeans, let me get you a pair of sweatpants," John Lee said.

Herb stood in his bedroom doorway as John Lee retrieved the sweatpants.

"Did you know there's a lizard up there in the corner?"

"It's a gecko," John Lee said.

"Whatever it is, why is it there?"

"I don't know," John Lee admitted, shrugging his shoulders. "It just showed up one day and made itself at home. A lady I know says having a gecko in the house is supposed to be good luck."

"A lady? Would that be Maddy?"

"No," John Lee said handing him the sweatpants and another T-shirt. "We're just friends, that's all."

"It's probably not my place to say anything about your personal life, but I think you're wrong there."

"What do you mean?"

"There's something between the two of you... I guess some might call it chemistry."

"I said we're just friends. And you're right, it's not your place to say anything about my personal life."

They sat in the living room watching television together, the tension between the two of them hanging thick in the air. There wasn't much conversation. At one point John Lee asked if he was hungry, and when Herb said he was, John Lee microwaved two TV dinners.

They ate in silence, and as John Lee was washing their silverware and the glasses that had held their iced tea, his phone rang.

"John Lee, how you doin'?"

"I'm okay, D.W., what's up?"

"Well, I know you was off sick today, and Sheila said you might need another day."

"Yeah, I'm not sure yet."

"I hope you're up to snuff tomorrow, because you're supposed to testify in that there Byers case in the mornin'. Are you goin' to be okay to make it, or do I need to call Mel Depew and have him asked for an extension?"

John Lee groaned. He had forgotten about the court date. Bobby Byers, known as BB to everyone in the county, had been a loser from the time he could toddle across the yard to the neighbors' house, where he proceeded to kick their aging Springer spaniel in the ribs. People say a child that young can't take pleasure in inflicting pain on another creature, but that didn't seem to be the case with BB. He was happily kicking the old dog and listening to it yelp in pain when it's owner came outside, grabbed him by the arm and took him back to his mother.

The Gecko In The Corner

Instead of thanking the neighbor for returning her child home safely, Linda Jo Byers had immediately gone on the offense, blaming the neighbor for having a nuisance animal and declaring that if little Bobby had kicked it, he certainly had a reason.

And so the pattern was set. BB grew up abusing anything smaller than him, be it dogs, cats, other children, and as he got older, adults, too. And since he topped out at over 6 feet tall and close to 300 pounds, that gave him lots of potential targets. BB had been arrested over twenty times for assault, and he seldom went peacefully. More often than not, his latest victim didn't show up for court anyway, because the few who had done so quickly learned that once he was out on bail, they could expect BB to show up again, and he wasn't going to be happy. But this time around, it looked like the county attorney had a good case. BB had gotten into a fight over a pool game at the Southern Cross bar, something that happened quite often. But this time, the fellow he took on wasn't content to take his black eye and bloody nose and slink away into the night to lick his wounds. Instead, Roger Sowle had called the police and insisted on pressing charges. He had stayed in contact with Melvin Depew, assuring the county attorney that he wasn't afraid to testify against the man who had assaulted him.

John Lee had been one of the deputies who responded to the bar, and it had taken a battle to bring BB in. It cost him a torn uniform shirt and a split lip, but he had fared better than fellow deputy Barry Portman, who had lost two front teeth to BB's massive fist. A fist adorned with heavy silver rings on each finger, not because BB favored jewelry, but because they did more damage to whoever he hit. Between the original victim's testimony, and that of John Lee, Barry, and another deputy who had helped subdue him, it looked like BB might actually get some serious jail time for a change. Authorities in Somerton County didn't take kindly to people who assaulted police officers.

"Should I call, Mel, or are you goin' to be there, John Lee?"

He sighed. He really didn't want to deal with BB's case right now, but he knew he had to be there. It was time the hulking bully got a taste of justice."

"No, I'll be there," John Lee said. "9 o'clock, right?"

"That's right. I'll see ya there."

"Okay."

"By the way, Flag said he expects you to turn in a sick day slip for today, just like everybody else."

"Whatever. I expect I'll come back home after I testify. I'm still not feeling 100%."

"That's fine, you do what you gotta do."

John Lee had hoped the conversation was over, not because he disliked Sheriff D.W. Swindle, but because the man was also his father-in-law, even though John Lee and Emily had been separated for a year now. The sheriff did not approve of his daughter's actions over the past year or so, which included moving in with her female lover, nor did he approve of the fact that he had discovered that his younger daughter, Beth Ann, had been spending nights in John Lee's bed. It was a complicated situation and D.W., who was a traditional father with traditional values, was having a hard time dealing with it. Not that John Lee found it to be a cakewalk, either.

"I talked to Emily today."

"How's she doing?"

"I don't know what's wrong with that girl, John Lee. She keeps sayin' she's gotta find herself. She been findin' herself all this time, and it seems like all she does is get more miserable. I told her she needed to get back home where she belongs and you two need to work it out."

"I hoped that might happen for a long time," John Lee said. "But she seems to be content with the way things are."

"It ain't right, John Lee! It ain't right at all. Both those girls of mine have been a disappointment to me. And you, too!"

"D.W., this isn't the way I wanted things to be, either. It just happened. I don't know what else to say."

The Gecko In The Corner

He noticed Herb watching him as he talked, so he went into his bedroom and closed the door to finish the conversation.

"I know I can't make things happen just 'cause that's the way I want them to be," D.W. was saying. "But darn it, John Lee, this can't go on forever like this."

"You're right about that. Something has to change. And I guess I'm going to be the one that has to change it. I just don't know how, yet."

"Well, you could start by ending whatever the hell it is you and Beth Ann have goin' on."

Before John Lee could respond, D.W. continued, "Oh, I ain't blamin' just you. She made it plain to me and to her mama that she's the one that started it. And when a man's got someone throwin' it in his face like that, well... all I'm saying is it takes two to tango and I ain't blamin' just you."

John Lee really did not want to have this conversation again, because he knew it was pointless. Even though Emily seemed to have moved on, she still showed up and spent the night with him occasionally. It usually happened just about the time he had resigned himself to the fact that the relationship was over, and once again started him hoping that he had been wrong and that there might be some possibility of a reconciliation. But then she would leave again the next day, dragging his emotions through a pit of frustration as she did so.

And the thing with Beth Ann, he knew that was a mistake the first time it happened. Not that he could put it all on Beth Ann. He may have resisted early on, and he still sometimes protested that what they were doing wasn't right, but as D.W. said, it takes two to tango. And while his sister-in-law shrugged off his concerns by saying, "It's just sex, that's all" he couldn't completely accept her casual approach to things because he knew it was wrong. But on the other hand, as he had told his father, he was capable of dealing with all sorts of criminals and lowlifes, so he should be able to deal with a woman Beth Ann's size. It wasn't like she overpowered him and forced him into his bed time and time again.

DW's voice brought him back to the present as he said, "Okay, I'm done preachin' for the night. I know I'm just unloadin' on ya. But just think about what I'm sayin', that's all I'm askin', John Lee."

"I will," John Lee promised.

"You get yourself some rest. I'll see you in the mornin."

John Lee ended the call and went back into the living room.

"Everything okay?"

"Yeah, just work," John Lee said, sitting back in his recliner. "I may be gone when you wake up in the morning. I've got to be in court to testify in a case. I'll be back as soon as I'm done."

"Okay."

They sat in silence a while longer, then Herb said, "We've established that we can't talk about your personal life. What about your professional life?"

"What do you mean?"

"Like I said, I've tried to keep track of what's been going on with you. I read the online edition of the local newspaper here, and I read about you killing that guy a while back."

"Yeah? What about it?"

"Are you okay?"

"I'm not the one who got shot."

"I know that. But that has to be a traumatic experience. Are you okay?"

"This is beginning to sound more personal than professional," John Lee said.

"Damn it, even if I was never a father to you, it doesn't mean I don't care. I'm just asking..."

"No, I'm not okay," John Lee told him. "The man I killed wasn't just some robber or something. He was also one of my best friends when I was growing up. Yeah, he had murdered two people. Two men I cared about. And he was doing his best to shoot me at the time. I didn't have any other choice but to do what I did. I wish it had gone down some other way, but it is what is."

"How do you deal with it?"

"The same way you deal with anything else. Day by day."

Herb nodded, and was silent for a while. Then he said, "I'm sorry you had to experience that, John Lee."

"Yeah. Me too."

The conversation seemed to put a damper on an already strained evening, and it wasn't much longer before Herb said, "I think I'm going to get some sleep."

"Probably a good idea."

As his father was leaving the room he stopped and asked, "By the way, what did you do with my car?"

"I hid it someplace. You seemed to think it shouldn't be sitting out there in the driveway."

"Where did you put it?"

"Don't worry about it, it's out of the way."

John Lee didn't know why he didn't want to tell his father where the car was. Maybe because he figured that if he did, Herb would be gone when he got back. Because while he wasn't very happy to have the man there, he still wanted answers as to what happened to him, and he didn't plan to stop asking them until he had those answers.

John Lee Quarrels Series

The Gecko In The Corner

Chapter 7

SOMERTON COUNTY WASN'T THE FLORIDA of the tourist brochures, with the white sand beaches and young women running around in skimpy bikinis. Located in the northern part of the state, just inland from the Big Bend where northwest Florida curved into the Panhandle, rural Somerton County was far less affluent and more what Old Florida was like long before the neon tourist traps and theme parks further south appeared on the landscape. This was piney woods country, dotted with swamps, bayous, and marshland. Good ol' boy and girl rednecks, along with northern retirees looking for a more peaceful and cheaper way to live out their lives shared the county with alligators, a few black bears, and even an occasional rare panther. Yes, it was hot and humid in the summertime, but the rest of the year was fine, and as the northern transplants liked to say, you don't have to shovel sunshine.

The small town of Somerton was the biggest community in its namesake county, and it wasn't much more than a speck on the map. When John Lee got to the courthouse the next morning, he found a large crowd of people milling about. It seemed like a lot of folks wanted to see Bobby Byers finally get his comeuppance.

John Lee almost did not recognize the defendant when two deputies brought him in. BB's beard was gone and his face was freshly shaven, his hair trimmed, neatly and if his wrists weren't handcuffed and his legs shackled, and he hadn't been dressed in the orange jumpsuit that all County prisoners wore, one might think he was just an everyday working man going about his business.

Melvin Depew read the charges against him, and then spent two hours telling the jury about the night the defendant had attacked Roger Sowle after they got into an argument over a pool game, showed them pictures of the man's injuries taken that night, then went on to recount what had happened when deputies arrived at the bar. He told them how BB had started swinging a cue stick at them as they approached him, and how the deputies had swarmed over him in an attempt to subdue the raging man. There were more pictures, this time of Deputy Barry Portman's bloodied mouth and the stumps of his broken teeth, and of John Lee's split lip.

Next the prosecutor had called the original victim to the stand, and Roger Sowle told of how he had been playing a friendly game of pool with his cousin when BB laid a quarter on the edge of the pool table and said he was playing the winner. Sowle said that had been fine with him, but that after racking up the balls for their game, BB had put a $10 bill down on the table and expected him to match the bet. Sowle said he had told the big man he didn't play for money only for fun, but BB had insisted, and he had finally given in, just to get the game over with. The two players were pretty closely matched in skill, but Lady Luck seemed to have been on his side, and Sowle won the game. But instead of being a graceful loser, BB had accused him of cheating. Sowle testified that he told the big man it wasn't worth an argument, to keep his money, but BB wouldn't let it go and things had escalated from there. The next thing he knew he was picking himself up from the barroom floor, only to be knocked down again. He had managed to escape out the back door and called police.

John Lee, Barry Portman, and Deputy Ross Donaldson then gave their own accounts of their arrival at the Southern Cross and their battle to arrest the defendant. There were no other witnesses, because everybody who had been at the bar that night seem to have developed cases of amnesia and couldn't remember anything that had taken place.

The court recessed for lunch, and while John Lee was in the break room at the Sheriff's Office eating a sandwich from the Subway restaurant across the street a big man with a shaved head and a walrus mustache accosted him.

"I thought you were home with the shits."

"D.W. called last night and said that I needed to be in court this morning for the Byers case."

"Did you turn in a sick day slip for yesterday?"

"Not yet. I just sat down."

"You think just 'cause you're D.W.'s pet that you don't have to follow the rules like everybody else? No, sir. Regulations is regulations, and they apply to everybody."

"I said I just sat down."

"Well you just get your ass up an' you go get a form and you fill it out."

"I'm curious, Fig," John Lee asked, using the nickname he knew Chief Deputy Flag Newton hated, "were you born a complete asshole, or is this some kind of acquired talent that you grew into over time?"

Flag's face turned red with anger and he pointed a finger the size of a breakfast link sausage at John Lee. "You listen to me, boy. I don't have to take that kind of sass from you. I'm giving you a direct order to go get a sick day slip and fill it out. Now, are you going to do it or not?"

John Lee took a bite of his sandwich, chewed, and said around it, "Nope."

Across the table from him, Ross Donaldson smiled and shook his head.

"Let me get this straight," Flag said. "Are you disobeyin' a direct order from me to go over there and get a sick slip and fill it out?"

"I don't have to," John Lee said.

"You may think that, mister, but you got another think coming."

"I don't have to," John Lee repeated.

"Oh yeah?" Flag leaned over so close that John Lee could smell the chewing tobacco on his breath. "And just why the hell do you think you don't have to, when everybody else does?"

John Lee pulled a white sheet of paper from under the Subway bag and held in the chief deputy's face. "I don't have to go get one and fill it out, because I already did."

One of the deputies in the room laughed, and Flag turned his head to see who it was, but they all acted like they were busy with something else and not paying any attention to the confrontation between the two men.

"If you already filled the damn thing out, why in the hell did you say you didn't and start all this bullshit? You tryin' to make me look stupid, boy?"

"No, I'm not trying to make you look stupid, Fig. Mother Nature already took care of that, and who am I to try to outdo her?"

There was a snort and a guffaw from behind him, but Flag ignored it.

"Tell me, I want to know. Why did you say you didn't fill the paperwork out when you already did? What kind of stupid shit is that?"

"You never asked if I filled the slip out, and I never said I didn't," John Lee told him. "You asked if I turned it in, and I said no I hadn't. Here, you want it?"

Flag grabbed the paper from his hand and crumpled it in his fist. "You're gonna push your luck too far one of these days, John Lee. And when you do, you're goin' to be sorry. You can count on that."

He stood up and stormed out of the break room, shoving Deputy Bill Kelly out of his way and throwing the sick slip on the floor. There was silence for a moment, until everyone was sure Flag was out of earshot, and then the room erupted in laughter and hoots.

"Damn, John Lee," Ross said, "I about busted a gut tryin' to keep from laughin' out loud! You do like to poke the hornets' nest, don't ya?"

Bill Kelly bent down and picked up the sick slip Flag had discarded and brought it over to John Lee and dropped it on the table in front of him. "You should probably take that up to Fig's office and turn it in. I mean, like the man said, regulations is regulations."

The Gecko In The Corner

Ross, who had just taken a long pull from his paper cup of sweet iced tea, laughed so hard it spewed out his nose, much to the delight of his fellow deputies.

***

Flag heard them laughing behind him and his fists balled in anger. John Lee thought everything was a big joke, but he was wrong. Like he had told the arrogant little pissant back there, one of these days... then he'd know who he'd been messin' with. And if D.W. didn't like it, that fat bastard could go straight to hell, too.

Every time he put on his uniform and saw the words Chief Deputy on his badge, it ate at Flag's guts. He hated taking orders from his brother-in-law, a man who was not at all qualified for the office he held. An office that Flag himself deserved. He was twice the lawman that D.W. ever thought of being. Three times! All D.W. knew how to do was slap backs and kiss asses. More than once he had thought about running against D.W. in the next election, but he really didn't need the family drama that it would create. His own sister had sided with her husband over her brother when he had broached the subject. What kind of bullshit was that?

Well John Lee could sit there and smirk all he wanted. His time was comin! Yes siree, his time was comin! Sooner or later that smart mouth of his would get him in the kind of trouble D.W. couldn't pull him back out of. And when that day came, Flag was goin' to be standing right there laughing at him. That's right, let's see how the smart ass little prick liked it when it was *him* bein' laughed at!

John Lee Quarrels Series

Chapter 8

200 MILES SOUTH, MIGUEL TORRES glared at the nervous man standing in front of him. Ramon shifted from one foot to the other and gulped air like a fish out of water. Miguel knew the other man was terrified and he enjoyed that. Ramon had good reason to be terrified.

"Where is my money?"

"Uh... I don't know, Miguel," Ramon said, not meeting his eyes.

"What? I can't hear you. And look me in the eye when you talk to me, you worthless turd."

"Umm, I said I don't know."

"That's not a good answer."

"I'm sorry, Miguel. Those two I sent to meet him, they never called and never came back."

"Did you go to the house?"

"Yes, Miguel. They are dead."

"Where is my money?"

"I don't know. They are dead and there is no money."

"I don't care if they are dead or not. They mean nothing. I care about my money."

Ramon shifted his feet again.

"Stop dancing! Do you think you are some puta on stage wearing a G string?"

"No, El Jefe."

The man behind the desk opened a drawer and pulled out a knife, pushing the button and letting the wicked blade spring open. "If you want to be a puta, I can make that happen for you."

"No, Miguel. Please understand, I just.."

"I do understand. I understand that I gave you a job and you failed me. I understand that my money is gone. That is what I understand. But what you must understand, you cockroach, is that I want my money!"

"Please, Miguel. I am working on it. I will find the man and I will bring back your money. That is my promise to you."

"You told me you knew this man. You told me he could be trusted."

"I believed this was true."

"But you were wrong, Ramon."

The nervous man in front of him dropped his head and nodded. "Yes, Miguel, I was wrong. For that I apologize."

"Do you think your apology means anything to me? Do you think *you* mean anything to me just because you are the son of my sister?"

"I can only hope you will give me a chance to prove myself to you."

"I gave you a chance, Ramon. And you failed me."

"I won't fail you again, Miguel. I promise you that."

"Raise your head and look me in the eye when you talk to me!"

Ramon nodded and raised his head.

"Now, repeat what you just said to me."

"I said I won't fail you again, Miguel. I promise."

The man behind the desk sat back in his chair and looked at Ramon for a long moment. Then he nodded his head. "Alright then. I will give you another chance. But you must understand something, Ramon. I am a businessman. As a businessman, I expect a return on my investment. My money is gone and it is not earning me a return. You are the reason that is happening. So here's what we are going to do." He turned to the man with the broad shoulders standing to his left and said, "Jorge, bring her in."

The bodyguard, who looked more Indian than Latino, moved silently in spite of his size as he opened a door in the back of the room. A moment later he returned, guiding a sobbing young woman. Ramon gasped when he saw her.

"Gabriela!"

"Please Ramon, help me!"

He took a half step toward her before the tall man put his hand on the pistol tucked into his belt. Ramon turned to Miguel, tears in his eyes.

"Please, Miguel, I promised you I will get your money back."

"And I believe you," Miguel told him. "This is not about you getting my money. This is about the interest that is due me. The return on my investment I told you about. Do you have the money to give me the return on my investment, Ramon?"

"Please, Miguel," he repeated.

"I asked you a question, Ramon. Do you have the money to give me the return on my investment?"

He shook his head. "No, Miguel. But I promise you I will make this up to you."

"I'm a reasonable man. I ask no more than a bank would if you went to them for a loan. Do you have some collateral you can give me until you can repay me?"

Ramon shook his head. "Please, Miguel. Don't do this."

"Don't do what?"

"Please, leave her out of this."

Miguel shook his head sadly. "I wish I could, my friend. I truly do. I don't care about the woman. What is she? A pair of breasts? A concha? A mouth? All of these I can have from any woman. But this is all you have that is of any value to anybody. So, what can I do?" Miguel shrugged his shoulders. " I must take what I can to ensure the return on my investment."

He turned to the woman and beckoned her to his desk. She shook her head in fright and the tall man pushed her forward. Miguel stood up and took her wrist, feeling her shiver in fright at his touch and said, "Poor little chica, I know this is not your doing, but this man of yours, he owes me. It is my hope that this messy business will all be over soon and you can go home. But in the meantime..."

Gabriella sobbed when Miguel turned his chair to face her. "Please, Señor Torres..."

"Such formalities are unnecessary, my dear. Call me Miguel. We are going to get to know each other very well. Now, take off your dress and show me what you have."

"I can't."

"Oh, you can. And you will."

"No. I can't. You can kill me if you want to, but I can't..."

A vicious backhand cut off her protests and would have knocked her off her feet if Jorge had not held her up. Ramon started to come to her aid, but Laurencio, Miguel's second bodyguard, who looked to be a brother of the first, stopped him with a blow to the stomach that doubled him over and dropped him to his knees.

Miguel ignored them and focused on the woman. "Do not disobey me again or I will have Laurencio cut your worthless husband's throat."

The woman turned at the sound of the click as Laurencio's switchblade opened. He stepped behind Ramon, grabbed a handful of hair and jerked the man's head back, laying the knife's blade along his throat.

"No! Please, Señor Torres, don't hurt him!"

"That is for you to decide. Now, take off your dress."

With hands that she could barely control, Gabriella fumbled the buttons loose and pulled the dress over her head. She kept her head down in shame as Miguel inspected her like one would a thoroughbred horse for sale.

Though his face was impassive, he liked what he saw. Her skin seemed flawless. No tramp stamp tattoo across the small of her back. No tattoos at all. She was wearing simple white cotton panties and a white bra that looked like it came from Walmart. It made her seem pure. Not like the painted whores in their red or black lingerie that worked in his two establishments on the other side of Orlando. He could have any of them on any day, and he did on a regular basis, but this one... this one he was looking forward to getting to know better. Who knows? Maybe he would keep her for a month or two before sending her to one of the whorehouses. Maybe even longer. Of course, there was that promise he had made to Ramon about only wanting to ensure his investment, but so what? Ramon was a dead man already, he just didn't know it yet.

John Lee Quarrels Series

Chapter 9

WHEN COURT RESUMED, IT WAS the defendant's turn to give his side of the story. But instead of trying to explain away the overwhelming evidence against her client, Shirley Jessop, BB's court-appointed attorney, said that yes, he had indeed done all of those things. He was drunk, he was out of control, and he was wrong. But that was the *old* BB. His time behind bars, waiting for trial, had been a turning point in his life. He had found Jesus and was a new man now. The hard drinking, bullying BB was dead, and the new Bobby Byers had been born again, washed in the blood of the lamb.

"All my client asks, Your Honor, is an opportunity to prove to this court and to the community that he has changed. His mother needs him at home. Nothing is going to be gained by incarceration in this case. And though you may judge him differently, Mr. Byers answers to a higher judge, and he knows in his heart that he will never again do the kind of things he is charged with in this case."

Judge Harrison Taylor had been on the bench for over 20 years and had earned a much deserved reputation for fairness and honesty. But he was no fool, and he had a long memory.

"That's interesting, Ms. Jessup. Sometimes I think we ought to just bulldoze down all the churches in this county and build parks on that land, because it seems to me that the real soul saving only happens in the County Jail. In fact, let me look at something here." The judge picked up a piece of paper and studied it for a moment, then said, "I'm looking at notes from the last few times your client was before this court. Last November, Mr. Byers was in here for assaulting somebody in a road rage incident, and he found Jesus while he was awaiting trial back then, too. And then, the year before, he found Jesus while he was awaiting trial for resisting arrest. And I'll be darned if he didn't find Jesus four months before that, right there in jail again!" The judge put down the paper, leaned forward on his elbows, and said, "This Jesus fellow you keep talking about seems to be a mite slippery, Mr. Byers. You keep finding him, and then he seems to get away from you. Or maybe you're the one who slips away from him. Because it seems like the minute you're back out on the street your relationship with him disappears. Here's an idea. I'm sentencing you to eighteen months in prison, less the two months you've already served awaiting trial. Maybe if you spend that much time together, that good influence Jesus has on you might stick." He rapped his gavel and said, "This court is adjourned."

***

Standing in the hallway outside the courtroom, D.W. asked John Lee if he was going to work that night, or take another day off. "I didn't see ya excusin' yourself to hit the bathroom so I'm figurin' you're better now."

John Lee truly liked the sheriff, and he hated lying to him, but he needed to get back home and try to get the answers he needed to resolve things with his father.

"I think I swallowed about half a bottle of Pepto-Bismol," he said. "But I'm still not a hundred percent, D.W. How about I take tonight off, too? Then I've got a regular scheduled day off after that. I'm sure by the time that's over with I'm going to be okay."

D.W. narrowed his eyes just a bit in suspicion. John Lee was as close to a son as he was ever going to have, and he really cared about the boy. But he couldn't help but wonder which one of his daughters might be spending the next two days nursing him back to health. Still, he just nodded his head and didn't say anything.

"Okay, you know best."

"By the way, D.W., me and Flag had a bit of a run in during the lunch break today. I just wanted to give you a heads up."

"What's new? You two are always buttin' heads."

"Yeah, I guess I bring out the worst in him."

D.W. snorted and shook his head. "There ain't no best in him, so I guess worst is all there is."

The two men had never gotten along, and probably never would. Besides the fact that Flag was an overbearing jerk who liked to lord it over the deputies under him, he was also as untrustworthy as a snake. D.W. had no doubt that his chief deputy would stab him in the back in a heartbeat if he thought it would help him get ahead. And on a more personal level, he resented the fact that his wife's hard drinking, heavy smoking brother seemed to have a heart as reliable as an old Detroit diesel engine no matter how badly he abused his body with cigars, red meat, and whiskey, while a heart attack a while back had D.W. eating low fat yogurt and dry toast for breakfast. Life just wasn't fair. He wished his wife had never talked him into hiring Flag in the first place all those years ago. It was the worst decision he had ever made as sheriff.

Maddy appeared in the hallway behind the sheriff and angled her head sideways. John Lee nodded subtly, while telling D.W., "I'm feeling my stomach beginning to rumble again. I'm going to make a quick pit stop, then head back home."

"Well, go take care of business," the sheriff said. "I'll see ya' when you come back on duty."

John Lee walked down the hall, turned left and went past the restrooms, then took the back stairs down. Maddy was waiting outside, seated on a bench in the town square.

"How's your poop chute?"

"The next time I call in sick, remind me to tell Sheila I've got the clap, will you? Three different people today have asked me how my diarrhea is, not counting you."

Maddy laughed. "So what happened with BB?"

"He got religion again," John Lee said. "But the judge wasn't buying it and gave him eighteen months, less time served."

"That ought to keep him out of trouble for a while." She handed John Lee a large envelope and said, "I dug up what I could on your father."

"Thanks."

"Don't thank me too soon. There's not much."

"Give me the *Reader's Digest* condensed version."

"Herbert John Quarrels, DOB June 11, 1960, residence Cleveland, Ohio. No priors, not even a traffic ticket. He works as an accountant for one of those mega car dealerships, married to a woman named Karen, and has an adult son named Jason, who lives at home. No liens or bankruptcies I could find on him, no evidence of cheating on his wife, or anything like that. Just an everyday guy, another face in the crowd."

"Just an everyday guy who showed up at my place in the middle of the night, beat to a pulp with his finger cut off."

"Well, yeah there is that."

Two women walking by stopped to say hello. One of them, a stout gray haired matron, asked Maddy how her mother was doing.

"She's just fine," Maddy assured them. "I think she's going to be back to church in no time at all."

"Well bless her heart," Abigail Foster said. "You be sure and tell her I asked about her."

"I sure will, Miz Foster."

The women walked away, knowing that Maddy had lied to them, and Maddy knowing that they were well aware of it. Her mother was never going to be "fine" again, or even just okay. Her mother's depression was something that was never going to change. It was a fact of life, just like the Spanish moss that draped the live oak trees in the town square, or the summer storms that could bring torrential wind and even tornadoes to Somerton County. She had accepted that a long time ago.

John Lee did not comment, nor did he question the falsehood. It was part of the protocol in the South. Not asking about her mother would have been impolite, and Maddy telling the truth - that her mother had grown even more distant and seldom spoke at all any more, that Maddy had to nag her to do the simplest things such as bathing and brushing her teeth, would have been socially unacceptable. It seemed like every family in Somerton County had a skeleton in the closet, and some of those skeletons were still living, breathing human beings, at least on some level.

"Anyway," Maddy said, returning to the subject at hand, "that's all I could come up with. It looks like your father is an everyday guy who crossed paths with somebody he shouldn't have. Now, as to who that was and why they did what they did, your guess is as good as mine, John Lee."

"Whatever it is, I'm going to find out," he told her. "Even if I have to go home and beat it out of him myself."

"Don't do something you might regret," she warned him.

"What I regret is even going out to check on him when he showed up in my driveway in the first place. I should have just rolled over and gone back to sleep and let him bleed to death."

If John Lee believed that he was going to get his father to finally tell the truth about what had happened to him, it would not take him long to find out that he was wrong.

John Lee Quarrels Series

The Gecko In The Corner
Chapter 10

MAGIC MET HIM IN THE yard for their ritual five minutes of playing, bounding across the grass to catch the heavy rubber Kong and bring it back, then they wrestled for control of it before the dog finally released it from his mouth so John Lee could throw once again and they could start the process anew.

"Okay, that's enough," he told the dog, rubbing the top of his massive head. "Let me get inside and see how our houseguest is doing."

The door was locked and he let himself in. Not seeing Herb in the living room, John Lee assumed that he was asleep, but his bed was empty. He wasn't in the bathroom, or the kitchen, and when John Lee opened the back door and saw he wasn't in the yard, he cursed under his breath. He walked across the yard, and when he saw the Hyundai was gone, he cursed out loud.

"Son of a bitch!"

He was tempted to call Dispatch and put out an APB on the car, but he had not written down the license plate number, and even if he would have, he wasn't sure that was a good idea. He would have to have a good reason for asking for an all points bulletin, and there was no way Flag would miss something like that.

Walking back into the house, he pulled his cell phone from his pocket and punched the speed dial button for Maddy.

"He's gone."

"Gone as in gone, or gone as in dead?" she asked apprehensively.

"Gone as in he's in the wind.

"Damn it. I'm sorry John Lee. Did he leave a note or anything?"

"Not that I'm seeing," he said as he searched the obvious places like the kitchen table, the top of the dresser in the guestroom, and the kitchen counter. Finding nothing there, he went into his bedroom and bathroom, where he came up empty again. "Nope, nothing."

"That sucks," Maddy said.

"Yeah, it does."

"What now?"

John Lee's first instinct was to get in his car and go looking for the Hyundai, but he knew that would be fruitless. Herb could have gone north into Georgia, west into the Panhandle, east toward Central Florida and on to the Atlantic Coast, or south. John Lee didn't know how long ago he had left, but he suspected it had not been long after he himself had departed to go to court that morning. With several hours' lead time, even if he knew where his father was headed, it would be all but impossible to catch up with him.

"John Lee? You still there?"

"Yeah, I'm just thinking. Trying to figure out where he might have gone."

"Any ideas?"

"No."

"Do you think he's headed back home?"

"I don't know. Screw it, I don't care."

"I've got a couple of hours before I go on duty. What can I do to help?"

"Nothing," he told her. "Like I said, screw it. He showed up out of nowhere and he disappeared back into nowhere. I'm not going to worry about it."

"I could come over, just to keep you company."

"That's okay. I appreciate it, but I don't think I'd be very good company right now, Maddy."

"Hey, I'm here for you. You know that, right?"

"Yeah. I know that. You always have been."

"And I always will be," she promised him.

***

John Lee sulked and tried to wash his anger down with beer. He was into his fourth bottle when Magic lifted his head up from the floor, and a moment later John Lee heard a car in the driveway. It was twilight and he went to the door to see who was visiting, realizing that he hoped it was Herb. When he saw the red Toyota pickup he groaned. "Damn it. Not tonight."

Magic barked excitedly and squeezed past him through the door to jump off the porch to greet the attractive woman who climbed out. She smiled up at him as she played with the dog, then walked toward the house.

"What? You're not even going to say hello to me?"

"Hello, Emily."

"Hello, Emily? That's all you've got?"

"Yeah, that's all I've got right now."

She came up on the porch and put her arms around his shoulders and kissed him. Feeling his coldness, she drew her face back. "Wow, what's got you so grouchy? I got a better kiss than that from my cousin Wilbur when he took me to the Junior prom."

"Well, it's the South. I guess you've got to expect that sort of thing," John Lee said.

"Oh, stop it and kiss me proper, like a man should kiss his wife."

He tried to resist, but damn it, the woman knew how to push all of his buttons, and in spite of how angry he was at Herb, and at her, he found himself giving in. Before he knew it they were in his bedroom and she was unbuckling his belt.

"I've missed you, John Lee. I've missed you so bad!"

"I've been right here all along," he told her.

"I want you!"

He wanted to ask if she was back home for good, but he knew better. This was an old tune they had danced to many times before. Emily had moved out and seemed to be getting on with her life. Getting on with her life to the extent that she had been living with another woman for some time now, and made it very plain that they were more than just roommates. He might not see her for a week or two and there would be no contact. If he called her, she always told him she was busy and hung up. But then, she would return out of the blue just like this and spend the night. The first few times it happened he had been hopeful that life was going to get back to normal, but it never had. He never knew what triggered Emily's need to come back home, or why it never lasted more than a few hours. As time went on, he grew less hopeful. But at the same time, he had never turned her away. And he didn't this time, either.

"Damn! I need to thank whatever got you all pissed off at the world," she said afterward.

"What are you talking about?"

"Let's just say you had a certain *enthusiasm* that's been missing lately."

"Maybe it's been here all along and you haven't been around to see it," he suggested.

"Oh yeah?" She leaned on one elbow and put her hand on his chest. "And just who's been getting the benefit of all that enthusiasm, John Lee?"

"That's not what I meant."

"Oh, come on now. I'm not stupid. I know you've had company. A *lot* of company, the way I hear it."

"Maybe you heard it wrong."

"Don't be coy with me," Emily said teasingly, running her fingers through the hair on his chest.

"I don't ask you who you sleep with when you're not here," he said.

"You *know* who I sleep with when I'm not here."

"I'd rather not think about it."

"Really? I doubt that. The way I hear it, every man on earth thinks about two girls together."

"I'm not every man."

"So, who is it John Lee? Who's been getting the benefit of all this enthusiasm of yours?"

"You already asked me that."

"And you didn't tell me."

"If I am sleeping with anybody, it's none of your business. You made it very plain that you're not coming back to stay."

"Let me see if I can guess. How about Maddy?"

"You know better than that. Maddy and I are friends, that's all."

She slapped his chest playfully. "Now be honest, John Lee. She's a pretty girl. You can't tell me you've never thought about doing it with her."

"What I think and what I do aren't necessarily the same thing."

"Okay then, how about that little black girl from Tallahassee? What's her name? Shondra? Something like that?"

"It's Shania. And how do you know anything about her?"

"Oh God, John Lee," Emily said, tweaking his nipple with her fingers. "you of all people ought to know that nobody does anything in this county without everybody else hearing about it the next day. Do you really think you can have an affair with a black girl and keep it secret?"

He pushed her hand away, but she only moved it lower.

"I'm not having an affair with her. We're friends."

"Uh huh. You have a lot of *friends*, don't you, John Lee?"

"Yeah, I do. What's your point?"

He could feel himself responding to her hand manipulating him under the sheet, and he wasn't proud of the fact that she could control him like a puppet on a string.

"In fact," Emily said, gripping him firmly then letting up the pressure just a little bit, only to repeat it, "I hear my little sister is one of your *friends*."

That did the trick. Any effort Emily had made to revive him after their lovemaking session was wasted now. She laughed at his obvious discomfort and pulled up the sheet to look beneath.

"Aww... where did he go?"

John Lee didn't answer, because he couldn't think of a thing to say in a situation like that. He knew what Emily had said about everybody in the county knowing everyone else's business was true, and that it was only a matter of time before she found out about his affair with her younger sister. But he had been like an ostrich with its head in the sand, refusing to acknowledge what was sure to happen.

"Hey, it's okay," Emily said, trying her best to revive the physical evidence of his interest. "I mean, yeah, it's kinky, but who am I to talk?"

"I think maybe you should leave."

"Why? Because I know you're bopping my sister? Geez, John Lee, I've known that for months. At least you're keeping it in the family. Unless you are not telling me the truth about Maddy and your little friend from Tallahassee. Maybe you're spreading the wealth around?"

He sat up in bed and swung his legs over the side, his back to her.

"Like I said, I think it would be best if you go."

Emily scooted over to his side of the bed and ran her fingers down his back.

"You know, John Lee, maybe getting this out in the open isn't all bad. Maybe we can make things work to both of our advantage."

"I don't know what the hell you're talking about."

She reached around and began to fondle him again. "What would you say about an open marriage?"

"What the hell are you talking about, Emily?"

"An open marriage. We could live together, and be together when we wanted, and still have our outside interests. I could still be with Sarah when I wanted to be, and you could be with Beth Ann, or Maddy or whoever, and no hassles. Maybe we could even make it a party, if you get my drift. Not with Beth Ann, that would just be too weird. But I'm sure you've got other friends."

"That's it," he said, standing up quickly. "Get your clothes on and get out of here, Emily."

"Come on, don't be such a prude! I'm serious, John Lee. Living with Sarah, sometimes it gets a little stifling. Maybe this way..."

"So you find living with her stifling? That's interesting, because when we were together you said I was smothering you. Did you ever think the problem was with you, Emily, and not everybody else?"

"I never said it wasn't with me. I've told you over and over that I just..."

"Yeah, I know. You need to find yourself. I've heard it, your dad's heard it, your mother's heard it, everybody in the whole damn world's heard it." He grabbed her by the arm and pulled her from the bed and half shoved her in front of the dresser on the opposite wall. "There, Emily, right there in the mirror. That's you! You found yourself. Now what?"

"Let go of me! Let go of me, John Lee. You're hurting my arm."

He realized how tight his grip was on her and immediately let go, dropping his hands away and stepping back. But if he was appalled by how rough he had become with his wife, Emily seemed to have just the opposite reaction. She looked at him in a way he had not seen in a long time and then grabbed him, crushing her naked body against his. "That's what I want, John Lee. That right there! Stop being the nice guy. Stop being so pussy whipped. Be a man and take me for a change."

That wasn't happening. There wasn't enough Viagra in the world to get a reaction out of him at that point. He pushed her away and went into the bathroom, slamming the door behind him. Emily tried to open it but he pushed in the lock button.

"Come on, John Lee, open the door! We can make this work. Just listen to me."

But he wasn't listening.

"Go away, Emily. Just go away."

She rattled the door twice more. "Jesus, John Lee. Grow up! I'm offering you something most guys would be willing to die for. Talk about having your cake and eating it, too! This could work. I'm telling you, it could work."

"Get the hell out of here," he shouted through the door. "Just get the hell out of here, Emily. And don't come back!"

He got in the shower and turned it on as hot as he could stand, and stood under it as long as he could, hoping the water would wash away everything he was feeling right now. Even after the spray turned cold, he stayed in there, not wanting to ever leave the small bathroom again.

Eventually he did, of course, wrapping a towel around his waist and opening the door, expecting to see Emily still there, and dreading it. But she was gone. Gone like she had been every time. He wondered if she had ever really been there, even when her clothes hung in the closet and she called their place home.

Chapter 11

JOHN LEE WAS GLAD THE next day was one of his regular days off because he had hardly slept all night, going over the whole situation with his father, and then Emily's visit. He had tossed and turned, gotten up and sat in his recliner in the dark living room, and twice he had found himself looking into the guestroom, as if his father might magically reappear. Sensing his restlessness, Magic had watched his every move. The dog didn't like it when John Lee got this way, but didn't know how to comfort him.

He finally drifted off to sleep, but awoke with a start in less than three hours. Magic rose up from the floor to look at him with concern, and John Lee said, "It's okay, boy. Just a bad dream." The dreams had come to him before, ever since the shooting of Troy Somerton. He would replay the whole encounter over and over, and every time he would wake up wondering what he could have done differently. And every time he knew that there had been no other choice. When somebody with murder on their mind is pointing a pistol at you, you shoot first or you die. But the dreams still came.

John Lee took another shower, dried off again and crawled back into bed, noting that it was almost 7 AM according to the digital clock on his nightstand. He slept a little more and woke up again at 8:30 with a headache and a general washed out feeling. He went to the kitchen to feed Magic and make coffee, then carried the carafe and heavy porcelain cup out onto his back deck. It was a chilly morning and he shivered, but didn't have the energy to go back inside and put on a long sleeved shirt. He was into his second cup when his phone rang. Pushing the button to answer, he mumbled, "Hello."

"You certainly sound cheerful this morning."

"I don't feel all that cheerful."

"How can you not be cheerful? It's a beautiful sunny day and you're talking to me. What more can you ask for?"

"There is that. What are you up to, Shania?"

"I was calling to confirm that we're still on for tonight."

"Tonight..."

"Really, John Lee? You forgot?"

"It's been kind of crazy here the last couple of days, I'm sorry."

"My father's birthday party?"

He slapped his forehead. "Damn, I'm sorry. Four o'clock, right?"

"That's right. Will you be there?"

"Uh... yeah. Wouldn't miss it for the world."

"You sound tentative. Is something wrong?"

"No, no. Like I said, it's just been kind of crazy around here."

"Tell me you're not getting cold feet."

"No, of course not. Why would I be getting cold feet?"

"Well, meeting my family for the first time, then us telling them that I'm pregnant and we have to get married. I just thought maybe..."

John Lee knew his mouth was hanging open, and apparently Shania could tell it even from a distance. She laughed, a sound that had almost had a musical note to it, and said, "Damn boy, you are just so easy!"

"I'm easy? I'm not the one who's pregnant and has to get married."

"Then I guess it must be immaculate conception," she told him. "By the way, when are we gonna do the nasty and get it over with?"

Shania Jones was a forensic pathologist who worked at the State Crime Lab in Tallahassee. A tiny black woman in her mid-20s who wore her hair in cornrows, had a beautiful smile and a wicked sense of humor that had kept John Lee on his toes from the moment they met the previous summer.

"Don't write checks with your mouth that your pretty little butt can't cash," John Lee warned her.

"Oh, so you think my butt is pretty? That's nice to know."

"I think all of you is pretty," he told her.

"You haven't seen *all* of me yet. So how do you know?"

"I don't have to see the Grand Canyon to know it's beautiful."

"You better be talking about that big hole in the ground out in Arizona, Mister John Lee Quarrels! I don't know how you and the rest of the good ol' boy rednecks do things over there in Somerton County, but referring to a woman's hooha as a grand canyon ain't going to get you anywhere."

"That's not what I meant. I was trying to say. You know...

He stumbled over his tongue trying to extricate himself from the situation he was suddenly in, much to Shania's delight. He could hear her laughing at his expense.

"Oh, John Lee. What am I going to do about you?"

"I think I'm just going to be quiet now."

"Sometimes that's the best thing to do."

"I wish you would have told me that as soon as I answered the phone."

Her voice changed, the laughter gone, and she said, "Seriously, John Lee. I want you to meet my family. I just know they're going to love you."

"Hey, what's not to love?"

"As Elizabeth Barrett Browning said, let me count the ways." She chuckled and said, "I'll see you tonight."

John Lee set the phone back down on the redwood table next to his deck chair.

"Shit!"

Magic, stretched out in the sun in front of him, looked up with concern.

"It's okay, boy."

The dog lowered his head again.

With everything else going on, John Lee *had* forgotten about the birthday party. He wasn't really looking forward to it. Not that he was against meeting Shania's family, but with the mysterious arrival of his father in his life, and then him disappearing again without a word, the timing was bad. And there was more to it than that. He was sure that Shania's family was wondering about this new person in her life, and just what their relationship was.

That was a good question, and one he couldn't answer himself. Almost from the moment they met there had been some sort of connection between them, a teasing banter and a comfortable friendship, but that wasn't all. There was a mutual attraction, and Shania loved putting him on the spot and watching him squirm as she just had. It had never gone any farther than friendly hugs and an occasional kiss on the cheek in greeting or on parting. John Lee didn't have a Facebook account and had no interest in one, but if he did and had to describe his relationship with Shania, he would have posted that it was complicated.

He seemed to have a lot of relationships like that... complicated in one way or another. Take Maddy. He couldn't remember a time when she hadn't been in his life, and there was nothing he couldn't tell her, or that she couldn't share with him. Many people misinterpreted their close friendship and read more into it, but though they both acknowledged the sexual attraction between them, neither had been willing to cross the line, though they had skated close a time or two.

His marriage to Emily had been in limbo for a long time, and though John Lee had held out hope that things would change and that she would come back home, he had come to realize that it was never going to happen. At least not under terms that he could live with.

And then there was Beth Ann. His affair with his wife's kid sister was probably the least complicated of all. Beth Ann showed up a couple of nights a week, they went at it like randy teenagers, and in the morning there were no uncomfortable silences or regrets. "It's just sex, John Lee," she had told him more than once. "I ain't plannin' to fall in love with you and I know you ain't gonna fall in love with me, either. Sooner or later one of us is probably goin' to meet somebody and get serious. But in the meantime, this fills the need for both of us, and who are we hurtin'?" And though he had been reluctant at first, with hindsight he had to admit that his resistance had been feeble at best.

Yes, life was complicated. Maybe Beth Ann was right. Maybe sooner or later he would meet somebody and get serious. But for now, he would just take it one day at a time and live with the complications. But right now, sitting on his deck drinking coffee in the morning sunlight, John Lee had no idea just how much more complicated things were about to become.

John Lee Quarrels Series

The Gecko In The Corner
Chapter 12

On the 90 mile drive to Tallahassee, John Lee tried to push thoughts of his father and whatever had happened to him away so he could concentrate on things Shania had told him about her family. He remembered her saying that her father had dropped out of school when he was fourteen to help support his family, and that after her parents got married he drove a garbage truck. Meanwhile, her mother had brought in extra money as a hairdresser, working out of their home. Shania was the second youngest of seven children, though she had told him that one brother, Jerome, had been killed in an accident riding in a stolen car fleeing from the police when he was fifteen.

"We never went hungry, and my parents always made sure we had clothes to wear, but it wasn't like we were *The Jeffersons* or had a lot of money to spend," she had said. She added that her parents had impressed the importance of an education on all of their children, and it was a lesson that stuck. All of them had grown up and earned college degrees. One brother was an attorney, another a schoolteacher, and a third was a major in the Army. Her older sister ran some type of community outreach center in Pensacola, and her younger sister would soon graduate with a degree in chemistry. He had once asked Shania how somebody so young had managed to get the education needed for her job and she had laughed, then given him one of her evil grins and said with a shake of her head and an exaggerated accent, "Well Suh, I ain't your average pickaninny. No, Suh! I gots me some brains inside this here pretty lil' head o' mine." Political correctness was never one of Shania's strong suits.

While he knew she was a smart woman, John Lee had not realized just how intelligent she was when they first met. Her IQ was in the genius range. Shania had graduated from high school and started college at age 14, where she quickly outpaced most of her fellow students. When she graduated she could have had her choice of jobs anywhere in the country, and was offered teaching positions at several major universities, but she chose to stay near home and family.

Her experiences in college and medical school had taught her that the intelligence that most people would consider a blessing could also be a curse. Her peers at college were either jealous of her or seemed to consider her some sort of oddity, and many of her professors had looked down on her. She was that cute little freak who really should be home playing with dolls, not learning about the workings of the human body. She left college with a degree and an acquired discomfort around people who shared her education level but nothing else. While she was highly respected for her work, in her mind she was still that strange little girl trying to play with the big kids. Her job at the state crime lab was the perfect fit in many ways. Shania specialized in skeletal reconstructions and spent much of her time alone in her laboratory, where she didn't have to interact a lot with her coworkers.

A more introspective man might ask himself if the attraction Shania seemed to have for him might be partially based upon the fact that they were so different, race aside. John Lee was a simple man, a small town boy with no big ambitions who was, for the most part, content with his life. Truth be told, Shania had asked herself that, though, in medical parlance, the results of such ponderings were inconclusive.

The driveway was full of cars and there was no place to park on the street in front of the tidy white frame house, so John Lee had to drive down half a block before he could find a place to park his Ford pickup and walk back to the house. The yard was neatly trimmed and a porch swing and two rocking chairs were on the small front porch. He pushed the doorbell and a moment later a young woman who could have been Shania's twin opened the door.

"You must be John Lee."

"I have to be," he told her. "I can't get anybody else to take the job."

She laughed and opened the screen. "It's so nice to meet you. I'm Alisha, Shania's sister."

John Lee held out his hand to shake hers, but she brushed it aside and hugged him. "No need to be formal around here, John Lee. Any friend of Shania's is family."

"Who's that you huggin'? Don't tell me your sister's not the only one bring'in a white boy to my birthday party!" The man wasn't a giant, but he was one of the biggest men John Lee had seen in a long time. At 60, Albert Jones was a couple of inches over six feet tall and close to 275 pounds, but there wasn't an ounce of fat on his body. His neck and arms were thick and muscular from a lifetime of throwing trash cans, and his hands looked like they were almost the size of baseball mitts. In another situation John Lee might be intimidated, but the twinkle in the man's eyes confirmed Shania's comment once that father and daughter shared the same wicked sense of humor.

"Now you be nice, Daddy," Shania said, coming into the room and pulling John Lee inside. She hugged him and said, "John Lee, this is my daddy, Albert."

"Nice to meet you, sir," John Lee said offering his hand and watching it disappear into one of Albert's. When men shook hands in Somerton County, especially men shaking hands with a sheriff's deputy, one could expect a bone crushing grip about half the time, as if they had something to prove. But Albert's handshake, while firm and strong, had none of that nonsense. John Lee was glad, because he thought that if the big man really cranked down, he might have to get used to wearing a hook where his hand used to be.

"Don't call me sir, that's what they call my son, the Army officer. Mr. Jones is fine with me."

"Daddy..."

"Okay, how about Albert? Or Al? Anything but "hey you, boy.""

"Daddy! Now you stop that. You promised to behave."

The big man winked at John Lee, then turned to his daughter with a look of innocence and said, "I am be'n nice, Pumpkin. I didn't call him cracker, did I?"

"If it's all the same to you, I really prefer the term Saltine American," John Lee said, giving back as much as he got.

Albert hooted and laughed out loud. "Oh, we goin' to get along just fine, you and me! Ain't we, John Lee?"

"I sure hope so," John Lee said. "Shania has been telling me what a mean old guy you are for so long that I was half afraid to even show up."

"That girl talkin' bad about me again?"

"Oh, not that bad," John Lee assured him. "Why, she said when you're not drunk you're not nearly that hard to get along with."

Albert laughed again and put one of his huge arms around John Lee's shoulder and said, "Come on in the other room and meet the rest of the family."

He led him into a large dining room and said, "Listen up, everybody. This here is John Lee, Shania's friend. John Lee, that incredibly beautiful lady there is my wife, Esther, and the old bat sittin' next to her is a homeless lady we took in just to clean up the neighborhood. We had to get her off the street 'cause she was scarin' little kids and pregnant ladies."

"You watch your mouth, Albert Lee Jones," the woman warned him with a big smile, "or some night when you're sleeping I'm gonna take a baseball bat to you!"

Albert turned to John Lee and asked, "Can you believe a woman that ugly is my wife's mother, and the grandmother of these three beautiful girls of mine?"

"You just ignore that low talking fool," the woman said. "I'm Martha, Shania's grandma."

"Now, that gal there is Yvonne, my oldest daughter, and that's her husband Patrick. And you already met Alisha. Now here on the other side of the table is William, he's the oldest. He's an ambulance chaser, so if you ever need to sue somebody, give him a call. And be sure to tell him I sent you. I get a kickback. The fellow there drinking a beer, that's Jerome, he's the schoolteacher, which explains why he drinks so much. And that one there, that's Major David Jones of the United States Army. He's just back from doing a tour of duty in the sandbox, and now they're sending him to West Point to teach for a couple of years. That pretty lady standing next to him is Tiana. Don't ask me why she married him, it's a mystery to all of us. I'd introduce you to my grandbabies, but none of these slackers have been gettin' the job done."

"I'm your grandbaby," said a little girl of five or six years old sitting on William's lap.

"And I'm one, too," a boy of about the same age said as he came around the corner of the table .

"You are? I don't think so! Have I ever seen you two around here before?"

"'Course you have, Grandpa," the girl said with a giggle.

Albert leaned down and scooped both of them up in his arms and stared at their faces, his eyebrows wrinkled.

"No, never saw either one of you before. I think you must be burglars. It's a good thing we got us a cop here, ain't it, John Lee?"

"We ain't burglars," the little boy said. "You know us! I'm Noah and that's Rachel."

Albert wrinkled his brows again as if in deep thought, then said, "You know what? I think I do remember you two! Didn't I pick you up on my trash route? Yeah, that's right, someone threw you away along with a box of used kitty litter and I brung you home."

"Uh uh," the boy said, shaking his head. "That ain't true, Grandpa."

"It's not?"

"No, sir. We're your grandbabies," Rachel said.

"Grandbabies? I'm too young to have grandbabies!"

"No you're not!"

"Well now, just how old do you think I am?"

"About a hundred."

Albert laughed and squeezed them both and said, "Sometimes I feel like it, that's for sure!"

John Lee shook everybody's hand, welcoming David home and thanking him for his service. He didn't know what he had been apprehensive about. Shania's family were great people and they all made him feel like he belonged with them. They were a big, happy family, everybody talking at once, and there was a lot of laughter.

Dinner was delicious, but enough to give anybody a heart attack. Heaping plates of fried chicken and catfish, mashed potatoes, sweet potatoes, corn on the cob, okra, and three different kinds of pie. And all of that didn't include the huge birthday cake adorned with candles. Albert insisted there were too many of them to blow out alone and enlisted the help of Noah and Rachel, who were happy to assist him.

The afternoon and evening went way too fast, and before he knew it, it was after nine and he still had a long drive ahead of him to get back home. When he made ready to leave there were no handshakes. This was a hugging family and everybody took their turn. Shania insisted on walking with him to his truck, and when he unlocked the door, she asked, "Well, what do you think?"

"I think you have a wonderful family," John Lee told her. "I mean that. I wish I would have grown up in a family like yours."

She smiled broadly and said, "I'm so glad. I know they all love you."

"You think so?"

"Hey, what was it you asked me this morning? What's not to love?"

"Yeah, and then you added something about counting the ways."

"Well, I have to keep you on your toes, don't you know?"

"You do a good job of that."

"Seriously, John Lee, thank you for coming. It means a lot to me." And with that she stretched up on the tips of her toes and kissed him on the lips. That was a first, and totally unexpected. And though the kiss was brief, he enjoyed it.

"You drive safe going home, John Lee."

"I'll do that," he assured her.

The Gecko In The Corner
Chapter 13

He thought about the evening with Shania and her family as he drove back to Somerton County. He had been truthful when he told her that he wished he had grown up in a family like hers. While Paw Paw and Mama Nell had loved him completely and he had never gone without anything he needed, it was still a different way of life. He never had any siblings, and his mother had also been an only child, so there were no cousins. And while his grandparents had provided a sense of home, he had always felt somewhat like an outsider.

Maybe it was because of their rather eccentric lifestyles, maybe Mama Nell's obsession with Elvis, or maybe because they were so much older than any of his friends' parents. For whatever reason, there had never been any question in John Lee's mind that when he was old enough to leave home and start life on his own, he would.

He still had a great relationship with his grandparents, and if the hour were not so late he might have stopped by their house to tell them about his father's sudden visit and quick departure. He would have to do that the next day.

Parking the truck in his driveway, he got out and fussed with Magic for a few moments when the dog greeted him. He was just starting to climb the short steps to the porch when headlights swung into the driveway. He thought it might be Maddy, or maybe Beth Ann, and hoped it wasn't Emily. No, it wasn't his wife or sister-in-law, neither of their vehicles had the bright halogen lights shining on him. It looked to be a big vehicle, maybe an SUV, and when the doors opened Magic let out a low growl. Whoever was coming to visit at this late hour wasn't somebody the dog knew.

"Easy boy," John Lee said, and stepped up onto the porch, keeping his eyes on the SUV.

"Turn off your headlights, I can't see you."

The lights stayed on but two men approached. From their silhouettes, one seemed about average height but the other was both taller and bigger. As they drew near, John Lee put his right hand slightly behind his hip, where his compact .40 Glock Model 27 rested in a Galco inside the pants holster.

The smaller of the two said, "I am sorry to bother you at this late hour."

"What do you need?"

"We just want to ask you a couple of questions," said the smaller of the men, who seemed to do the talking for the two of them. His voice had a Spanish accent to it.

"It's kind of late to come visiting and asking questions," John Lee said.

He dropped his left hand down to Magic's head, feeling the tenseness in the dog. Magic was a good judge of character and he didn't like these two, which was all John Lee needed to know. The men came closer and were almost to the deck.

"That's far enough," John Lee said, pulling the Glock from its holster and holding it by his side.

"Easy señor, we just want to ask you a couple of questions. We mean you no harm."

"Then ask away from right down there. My dog doesn't like you and if you come any closer he's liable to rip your arm off."

"We're looking for a car."

"Does this look like a used car lot do you?"

"We are re-possessors," the man said.

"Well, you're in the wrong place," John Lee told him. "The only car here's my truck, and it's got a clear title."

"Let me explain," the man said, taking another step forward.

Magic growled loudly and John Lee said, "Uh uh. Stay where you're at. Last warning."

The man put his hands up in front of him to show they were empty. "Please, señor, there's no need for violence. We are only doing our job. We just want to find this car and leave. The hour is late and I apologize, but in our business, sometimes that is the only time when we can find the cars we are looking for."

"Well, like I said, my truck's the only vehicle here."

"The car we're looking for is a Hyundai. It is a rental car that was not returned."

John Lee wasn't completely surprised.

"What makes you think it would be here?"

"The car has an electronic locator built into it. The last GPS coordinates we have for it show it to be here. Maybe in your back yard?"

"I told you, there's no car here."

"You are just getting home, señor. Is it possible that someone could have parked the car back there while you were gone?"

John Lee wondered if his father might have returned. But if he had, he was pretty sure these men weren't anybody he wanted to see.

"I think your tracking device or whatever you use is wrong. I'm sure there's no car there."

"But isn't it possible that ..."

"I said there's no car there. You guys need to turn around and get back in your car and leave."

"Señor, if we leave we will have to come back again."

"That's fine," John Lee told him. "But when you do, you come back in the daylight and you bring a police officer with you. Now go before I take my hand off of this dog's head. Because if I do, he's going to eat you."

Through it all, the larger man had not said a word. They stood there a second longer and Magic's growling grew louder. Then the smaller man said, "As you wish, señor. My apologies for disturbing you."

John Lee kept the Glock at his side until they were in their vehicle and had backed out and driven away. He felt the aggressive stance leave the dog beside him and said, "Don't get too relaxed, buddy. I've got a feeling they'll be back."

Knowing it was a waste of time, John Lee still went inside the house to see if Herb had returned, but there was no sign of anybody being there in his absence. Retrieving a flashlight from a kitchen drawer, he went out the back door to the deck and down to the yard, Magic close beside him. He walked across the yard to the track through the trees where he had parked the Hyundai. Nothing there.

Back at the house, John Lee retrieved the shotgun from his Champion gun safe and put it in the bedroom, along with the full-size Glock Model 22 he carried on duty. He started to close the safe, then thought better of it and also took out his Colt AR-15 and a bandolier with six loaded twenty round magazines, loading one of the magazines into the rifle. John Lee always subscribed to the theory that it was better to have plenty of firepower on hand and not need it than to need it and not have it readily accessible.

"I'm going to take a shower," he told Magic. "Let me know if we get any company."

He turned on the water and adjusted the temperature, stripped, and got in the shower. As he stood under the shower spray he remembered his pleasant evening with Shania and her family, but those thoughts were pushed aside by his concern about the appearance of the two strangers looking for the car his father had been driving. He remembered that when he looked at the rental paperwork in the car's glove box there were still several days to go before it was due to be returned. And even if the car was late by a day or two, he didn't think a rental company would be sending out repo men so quickly to retrieve it. No, whoever those men were, whatever brought them out here, had more to do with his father's injuries than with an overdue return on a rental car.

The Gecko In The Corner
Chapter 14

REFERRING TO THE REPORT MADDY had given him on his father, the next morning John Lee called his home in Ohio. A woman answered, and when he asked for Herb, she asked, "Who is this?"

Not sure who he was talking to, John Lee asked, "Is this Mrs. Quarrels?"

"Yes it is. Now, who the hell are you?"

"My name is John Lee..."

"Well, whatever you want him for, Mr. Lee, I haven't seen the bastard in over a week now and I don't care if I ever do."

John Lee started to correct her and explained that his last name was Quarrels, not Lee, then thought better of it. He remembered Herb saying that his wife had not approved of him coming to Florida to visit his son, and that even sending his monthly child support check led to an argument. Whatever marital difficulties his father and his wife had were none of his business, and he didn't want to add to them.

"Do you know if he's out of town on a business trip or anything like that?"

"I said I don't know where he is. He just up and disappeared last week and I haven't heard a word from him since. But wherever he's run off to, it's not a business trip. His boss keeps calling looking for him, too."

"Does he have a cell phone number I could try?"

"I tried calling it over and over. All I get is a message that says the voice mailbox is full."

"Mrs. Quarrels, can you think of anybody Herb has been having a problem with? Some reason he might drop out of sight like this?"

"Who did you say you were?", she asked suspiciously.

"My name is..."

"I don't care what your name is. I said he's not here, and after pulling this stunt, he's not welcome back. If you do see him, you tell him I've already talked to an attorney. If he thinks he can just walk out of here without a word and not call or anything, he's got another think coming!" And with that, she ended the call.

"Well you sure sound like a prize," John Lee said, staring at the phone.

His next call was to the auto dealership where Herb was employed. It took a while to work his way through different levels of receptionists, but finally a man came on the line and identified himself as Anthony Everett, the owner of the company. Figuring he didn't have anything to lose, John Lee identified himself as a deputy with the Somerton County Sheriff's Department in Florida and said he was inquiring into the whereabouts of Herb Quarrels.

"Your name's Quarrels, too? That's a bit of a coincidence."

"I'm his son," John Lee explained.

"I thought his kid's name was James or Jack, something like that."

John Lee glanced at Maddy's report. "Jason. I'm his son from his first marriage."

"Oh, that explains it. I didn't know he'd been married before. Turns out there's a lot I don't know about your father."

"Such as?"

"Such as where the hell he is. He hasn't shown up for work in several days, hasn't called in, his wife doesn't know where he's at, and his phone isn't working."

"Is that like him? To pull a disappearing act like that?"

"No. If he was some flaky salesman or a mechanic, I'd figure he was off on a bender someplace, or shacked up with some broad. But he's an accountant. Everything is by the book with him. Hell, he's your dad, you probably know that already."

"Actually, I don't know much about him at all," John Lee said. "I haven't had much contact with him for most of my life."

"Then why are you calling here now? You doing one of those family search type of things or what?"

"I'm just trying to locate him to ask him some questions."

"Well good luck with that," Everett said. "I don't know what's going on with him, but he's got a lot of explaining to do when he gets back here."

"Is there a problem? I mean, besides him not showing up and not calling or anything?"

"Yeah, there's a problem," Everett told him. "A big problem. About a $5 million problem."

"$5 million is missing? And you think he took it?"

"No. When he didn't show up three days in a row I got nervous. I mean, the man has access to all of our bank accounts. So I started doing some checking, and we've got $5 million more than we should have!"

***

John Lee couldn't remember the name of the car rental company, so he tried several of them at the major airports in Florida, but nobody would tell him anything about their customers, citing privacy laws. He wasn't sure where to go with things from there. He was just a deputy with a small county sheriff's department, not a trained investigator, and he had a strong feeling that whatever Herb was involved in was way over his head. But he didn't know anybody in the department he could turn to without creating more problems. Technically, he and Maddy had both violated the law by not reporting the assault on Herb, and he knew that if Flag found out about it he would pounce on both of them. The chief deputy had been looking for a way to get rid of John Lee for as long as he could remember.

Not knowing what else to do, he decided to go for a ride. John Lee loved to drive and did some of his best thinking behind the wheel. He waved at a couple of people as he drove through town and stopped at the Super Bee to fill his truck's gas tank.

Arley Dawson ambled out from the small office and asked, "How's it hangin', John Lee?"

"To the left last time I looked. How you doing, Arley?"

"Can't complain. Hell, if I did nobody'd listen."

"I guess that's the truth."

"Say, John Lee, need to talk to ya' about somethin'."

"What's that?"

"My neighbor Bill McCoy's got a couple of kids that have taken to runnin' up and down the road on an old motorcycle they cobbled together. Damn thing ain't got no kinda muffler on it and it's loud as hell. Can't hardly hear myself think, let alone watch the TV at night. They're out there making noise 'til midnight or more sometimes. That thing ain't even got any lights on it! I'm surprised one of them hasn't run into the bar ditch and hurt himself by now."

"Did you say anything to Bill about it?"

"Naa, him and me got crosswise a while back 'bout somethin' and we ain't said a word to one another since."

"Really? I always thought Bill was a pretty good guy."

"Oh, he is. I ain't sayin' nothing bad 'bout him. Man's salt of the earth. I just wish those kids of his would stop riddin' that motorcycle!"

"What did you and Bill argue about? You're two of the most agreeable fellas I know. I thought you were pretty good friends."

"We were 'til that argument!"

"Well, what was the argument about, Arley?"

The other man thought for a minute, then scratched his whiskery cheek and said, "Hell if I know, John Lee. I can't really remember."

John Lee was tempted to suggest that whatever the problem was between Arley and his neighbor, maybe it was time to mend fences and get on with life. But he knew things didn't work that way. Not in Somerton County. Right or wrong, people held grudges there. Even if they couldn't remember what the grudges were about.

"Look, I'm off duty today, but I'll mention it to a couple of the deputies and see if they can drive out your way. If those kids don't have licenses or the motorcycle isn't safe, maybe they can have a talk with Bill and put a stop to it."

"I appreciate that, John Lee," Arley said. "But if you could leave my name out of it... like I said, Bill's a good man and I don't want to cause him any trouble."

"I'll see what I can do," John Lee promised.

John Lee Quarrels Series

The Gecko In The Corner
Chapter 15

MAMA NELL AND PAW PAW, whose real name was Stanley, lived a couple of miles from town on five acres that surrounded the big ramshackle house John Lee had grown up in. The yard was guarded by three knights in armor, the Tin Man from *The Wizard of Oz*, and a vicious looking dinosaur with two high foot fins down its back and eight inch long talons. All were made from pieces of scrap metal Paw Paw had welded together during one of his artistic phases.

On this day, his grandfather was up on an extension ladder painting the trim on the front of the house.

"If you'd have called me, I'd have come by to help you."

"Do what? This?"

"Yeah, Paw Paw. There's no reason for you to be up there on that ladder at your age."

"My age? Give me a break, boy. I can still outwork half the men in this county no matter how old they are. You included."

John Lee knew that was true, but said, "I know you can, but you've got those old brittle bones. I don't want you falling off that ladder and breaking a hip or something."

"Spent my life climbing up power poles in all kinds of weather, including tornadoes, so I don't guess I'm going to have much trouble on a ladder."

"Even so..."

Paw Paw climbed down and wiped his hands on a rag. "I'm done anyway. Good to see ya'. Come on in, I imagine Mama Nell can scare us up something cold to drink, and maybe even a sandwich if we look hungry enough. By the way, still got the shits?"

Now John Lee wished he had never called dispatch at all. He might have been better off to just pull a disappearing act from work like Herb had done.

"I'm fine, thanks for asking."

"If you need one, I can probably find a cork around here someplace."

"No, I'm good," John Lee assured him.

"Feast or famine around here when it comes to that. I'm either drinking prune juice to get started, or looking for my own cork to stop."

That was a lot more than John Lee needed to know about his grandfather's elimination problems, so he did not encourage Paw Paw to share any more by replying.

They found his grandmother in the kitchen putting frosting on a fresh batch of chocolate cupcakes.

"I swear, John Lee, I think you can smell my baking from ten miles away," she said in greeting, then put down the butter knife she had been using to apply the frosting and hugged him. "How's your stomach doing?"

"It'll be better when I eat a half dozen of those cupcakes," he told her.

"Did you know that Elvis loved cupcakes?"

"I bet he would have loved yours, Mama Nell."

"Well of course he would have. You sit yourself down and I'll pour you a glass of cold milk. Stanley, go wash up. And hurry back. You know how John Lee is. If you wait too long there won't be any left for you!"

The cupcakes were delicious, and John Lee had polished off his third one before he brought up the reason for his visit.

"What can you guys tell me about my father?"

"Your father? Why are you asking about him? He hasn't been around for years."

"I know," John Lee said. "What do you know about him?"

"You taking an interest in genealogy, John Lee? If you are, you should see Mabel Prichard over at the library," Mama Nell said. "She's really into it. Got a whole shelf of reference books and stuff like that. I bet she can help you."

"No, I'm not getting into genealogy," John Lee said. "I just wondered if you know much about him."

"It's been a long time," Paw Paw said. "What can I say, John Lee? Him and your mother were both kids and things didn't work out. I don't know that either one of them was really to blame. It was just one of those things"

"I'll say this about your father," Mama Nell added, "he always paid his child support right on time. That's more than you can say for a lot of men."

"Do you know why he never came around to visit me?"

"He did when you were real little," she told him. "Then he just stopped coming. I don't really know why. I guess life just goes on and he lived so far away. I can't really say. Why are you asking about him after all these years? You never seemed to show any interest before."

"Well, here's the thing," John Lee said, "he showed up at my place a few days ago."

"He did! Just out of the blue?"

"Yeah, just out of the blue. In the middle of the night."

He told them about Herb's arrival, his injuries, and how evasive he had been about how he had received them, and how his father had left just as mysteriously as he had arrived. Then he told them about the two visitors last night who claimed to be repo men, and what he had learned in his phone calls to Herb's home and the car dealership where he worked.

"It sure sounds like he's mixed up in something shady," Paw Paw said.

"Yeah, it does. And whatever it is, I've got a bad feeling about it," John Lee replied.

"Have you told D.W. about this?"

"No, until I know more about what's going on, I want to keep this as low-key as possible."

"Is that a good idea? I mean, these guys are coming to your house in the middle of the night..."

"John Lee knows best," Paw Paw said. "And besides, D.W. would probably just want to call a press conference or something."

There was no question about it, Sheriff D.W. Swindle did love talking to the media every chance he got. The D.W. stood for Daniel Webster because his mother had wanted him to be a man of words. Unfortunately, most of the words he uttered were hard to understand due to the chaw of tobacco in his mouth. But he was quick to lose the chaw if there was a reporter around.

D.W. was much more a politician than a lawman, and he seemed to have a speech ready for anything and everything that came along. Especially if it was one he could deliver in front of a reporter, or to a group of voters to remind them of what a good job he was doing. And to D.W., a group consisted of anything more than just one person, as long as they were registered to vote.

The sheriff had never really anticipated a career in law enforcement. Actually, growing up he had not given much thought to what he was going to do when he became an adult. Yes, his grandfather, Big Jim Swindle, had worn the sheriff's badge for a decade before an out of work ne'er-do-well named Buster Palmer had gotten liquored up and started beating his wife. When a neighbor called in to report the disturbance, the sheriff went out to their shack on Cass Road to put an end to it. He never got the chance because as he was getting out of his Plymouth squad car Palmer had come around the corner of the house and blown most of his head off with a single shot 12 gauge Stevens shotgun. He then went back inside the house, murdered his wife, and killed himself.

Big Jim's son, James Swindle, better known as Junior, had taken up where his father had left off and served as Somerton County's sheriff for over 25 years before he pitched over dead on his 60th birthday while celebrating the occasion in bed with a 30 year old barmaid named Brenda Davidson. Of course, nobody wanted that scandal to get out, so the official story was that the sheriff had died in the line of duty, answering a prowler call when his heart gave out.

At the time, D.W. was a young deputy with only a couple of years on the job, but he had already decided that life sitting behind the sheriff's desk was a lot better than life in a squad car, and he was more than ready and willing when the county appointed him to fill his late father's shoes. He found that he enjoyed the popularity and being in the spotlight, and while he was more than happy to delegate field duties to Flag Newton and his deputies, he made it a point to get his picture in the paper often enough to convince the public he was on the job. That and kissing a lot of babies, and as many influential asses, assured that he had not lost an election since.

"Look, keep all of this to yourselves, okay? Until I figure out what's going on, I don't want the whole world knowing about it. And do me a favor, Paw Paw. Keep that old shotgun of yours by the door, just in case."

"In case what, John Lee? Do you think someone's going to come around here bothering us?"

"I don't know, Mama Nell. Probably not. But it doesn't hurt to be prepared."

John Lee Quarrels Series

Chapter 16

"I HOPE YOU HAVE GOOD news for me," Miguel Torres said when he answered the telephone.

"We are making progress," Ramon told him.

"What the hell does that mean?"

"We found somebody at the rental car company who was willing to give us the GPS location of the car Quarrels was driving. For a price, of course."

"Everything and everyone has a price," Miguel replied. "Have you found the man?"

"Not yet. But as I said, we are making progress."

"Has he abandoned the car somewhere?"

"I don't know, Miguel. We went to the place where it was supposed to be, but it was not there."

"So then you have nothing?"

"No, not yet," Ramon admitted.

"Where is this place?"

"A small town called Somerton, up in the north part of the state. The GPS location was a house a short distance outside of town. When we got there last night there was a man, but it was not the man we are looking for. He said there had been no car there, but I know he was lying. And he had a gun. Who has a gun if they have nothing to hide?"

"Everybody has a gun in this state, you idiot," Miguel said. "Who is this man?"

"That is the thing, his name is John Lee Quarrels. The same last name as the man we are looking for."

"How did you find his name?"

"It was easy, Miguel. We went back today when he was not home and I looked at the letters in his mailbox."

"Of course it was easy," Miguel snarled. "If it was harder than tying your shoelaces you could not have done it without help.

Find out everything you can about this John Lee Quarrels. He knows where my money is. Why else would the man go there?"

"I will do that and report back to you."

"The next time you call me, the only report I want to hear is that you have my money."

"Yes, Miguel. May I ask, how is Gabriella?"

"How is she? I will tell you how she is. She is wet and tight. But don't worry, every day I make her a little bit more loose. In fact, your phone call has disturbed me so much that I need to go to her and work off some of my anger."

"No! Please Miguel, I am begging you..."

But Miguel couldn't hear him. He had already ended the call.

Miguel slammed his hand down on his desk and cursed. He needed to find the money and he needed to find it fast. He had already stalled Esteban once, but he knew he could not do it a second time. Why had he ever trusted Ramon to handle something so important in the first place? He had planned to simply have Laurencio cut the worthless dog's throat once they had found Quarrels and brought the money back, but not now. Now he wanted to be there when Ramon died. He wanted to see it, and he wanted it to take a long time.

Miguel pushed his chair back from his desk and walked out of his office and down the hall, Jorge following behind him. When he got to the door of the bedroom where he was keeping the woman, he unlocked it and told the bodyguard to wait there for him.

Gabriella was curled up on her side on the bed, but quickly sat up when she heard the lock being turned in the door. She looked at him fearfully, visibly trembling though she tried to remain calm.

"Has Ramon returned?"

"No, he has not," Miguel told her. "He has greatly disappointed me. If he were here I would cut his heart out and show it to you. But he is not. So that leaves you and me. Take off the dress."

"Please, not again," she begged.

In response he grabbed her by the throat and pulled her to her feet. She started to raise her hands to pry his fingers loose, but he punched her in the stomach with his left fist, feeling her body sag.

"I told you to never disobey me!"

"Please, señor. Please don't do this," she said, gasping for breath.

He punched her in the stomach again, then grabbed the front of the dress and ripped it open. He threw her back onto the bed, and ignoring her weeping, he unbuckled his pants and crawled onto the bed on top of her.

***

Ramon Sainz was terrified, and he had good reason to be. Not just for the punishment that he knew his uncle was doling out to Gabriella at that very moment, but for the punishment he knew he himself would receive once they found Quarrels and the money. When the problem first began, he had hoped for no more than a verbal berating and a loss of face, but things had gone too far now. Much too far. Miguel Torres was not someone to anger, and Ramon knew his uncle was in a rage. And rightly so, he must admit.

Ramon had failed. He had failed terribly. He thought he could trust Quarrels, and at first it had gone smoothly. But when the man's deceit was discovered, instead of acting on it immediately, Ramon had tried to work things out on his own. And when that didn't work and he had to go to Miguel and confess his failure, he had grown squeamish and left the dirty business to the two soldiers his uncle had sent with him, while he waited at a restaurant two blocks away. When they had not come to meet him as planned and did not answer their phones, he went to the little house where they had taken Quarrels. When he saw what had happened there he had lost his lunch. So much blood. It looked like someone had painted the walls with it. And now two men were dead and he still did not have his uncle's money, or Quarrels. Ramon knew that if he didn't find both the man and the money soon, he too would be dead. And even if he did succeed, his uncle might still kill him as an example to others of what could happen if they, too, failed to do as ordered.

But maybe there was another way. Why take that risk? If they did recover the money, maybe it would be better to just take it and disappear. Go someplace far away where no one knew him and where Miguel could never find him. Of course, he would have to kill Quarrels and Laurencio. Ramon had never killed anybody before, but he thought the accountant would be easy enough. Then again, look what he had done to the two men who were supposed to get the money from him. Maybe not so easy after all. But he would do it.

Dealing with Laurencio was another matter. Just thinking about it was enough to make him feel he might lose control of his bowels. Laurencio was a professional killer, as cold and deadly as a water moccasin. Ramon shivered when he remembered what had happened to a pimp named Sweet Ronnie who had put two of his whores on the same street where one of Miguel's brothels was located. His uncle did not appreciate anybody trespassing on his turf, especially whores on the stroll, and had sent someone to tell the pimp to take his women and not come back.

Sweet Ronnie was a big man in some circles. He had diamonds implanted in his three gold front teeth and every finger of his hands was adorned with oversized diamond rings. He drove a customized Mercedes and carried a gold plated Beretta 9 mm pistol everywhere he went. Every pimp and prostitute in Orlando feared him because he never hesitated to use violence when it suited him. Sweet Ronnie had smashed his uncle's messenger in the mouth with a steel pipe and warned him to back off if he wanted to live.

But while the pimp may have been feared by many, he was a mere child used to ruling a playground sandbox compared to Miguel Torres. Miguel could not let such an insult go unanswered.

Hours later a crew of men dragged Sweet Ronnie from the bed where he was being entertained by two of his young hookers and brought him to Miguel. Jorge and Lorenzo had used their knives on the man for hours, never cutting deep enough to kill him, but enough to cause him excruciating pain as his flesh was slowly stripped away. Through all of the bloody work, Jorge wore an evil grin, relishing in the torture he was giving their victim. That was bad enough to see, but watching Laurencio was even more terrifying because he had remained impassive to the pimp's screams of agony. He could have just as easily been butchering a chicken as a human being.

When Sweet Ronnie finally died of shock, his mutilated body was dumped in front of a bar called the Wet Kitten, where many of Orlando's pimps hung out to show off their latest acquired bling, talk about business, and relax away from the pressures of running a stable of working girls.

No, there was no way Ramon could win in a battle with the big bodyguard his uncle had sent to keep an eye on him. For a moment he toyed with the idea of offering to split the money with Laurencio, but then realized that one of two things would happen. Out of loyalty to his uncle, the bodyguard would deliver him to Miguel and expose his planned betrayal, or else Laurencio would decide to keep all the money and kill Ramon instead. His only chance was to shoot Laurencio in the back of the head the first chance he got.

Or at least the first chance he got after they had recovered the money. He thought briefly about going back to rescue Gabriella once he had the money, but he knew that was impossible. He loved his wife, but he could not take that risk. No, it was better to leave her to her fate and just disappear. But first they had to find Quarrels and the money.

John Lee Quarrels Series

Chapter 17

ON THE DAY HIS FATHER had shown up, John Lee had left his patrol car, a powerful Dodge Charger, with the Sheriff's Department's mechanic for an oil change, expecting to pick it up when he went on duty the next morning. Knowing how much Flag had resented D.W. assigning the Department's newest car to him, when he left his grandparents' house he swung by the garage to check on it.

"Yep, she's ready to roll," Buster Gibbs said. "I changed the oil, topped off the windshield wiper reservoir, and rotated the tires. You're good to go for another 3,000 miles, as long as you don't shit your pants and ruin the seat while you're doing it."

John Lee was tempted to go into the dispatch office and strangle Sheila, but instead he just thanked Buster and asked, "Can you drop it off at my place on your way home?"

"Not a problem," the mechanic told him. "I'll have my old lady follow me when she gets off work, and if you're not there I'll leave the key on top of the right rear tire."

"Thanks. I should be there." He handed Buster a five dollar bill and said, "Get yourself a six pack on me for your trouble."

The mechanic waved it away with his hand. "No trouble, John Lee. Happy to do it. Besides, I like driving this sumbitch. It hauls ass."

"Well, just don't wreck it, okay? That would really piss Flag off."

"Hey, better be pissed off than pissed on," Buster said. "I'll see you after work."

He was getting back in his truck when he saw Maddy pulling into the parking lot in her patrol car. He walked over as she was getting out and said, "We need to talk."

"Well, hello to you, too, John Lee! Are you breaking up with me?"

He ignored her phony pout and said, "I had visitors last night."

"The way I hear it, you have visitors just about every night. And yet I never get invited."

"No, seriously, Maddy, these weren't the fun kind of visitors."

Her face instantly grew serious and she asked, "What happened?"

John Lee looked around to make sure no one was within earshot, then told her about the two strangers who had shown up at his place late at night, claiming to be repo men.

"Damn, what has your father gotten himself into?"

"I don't know, but it's big." He told her about his calls to Ohio, about Herb's disappearing act, and about the extra $5 million that his father's boss had discovered in his company's bank accounts.

"This is getting big, John Lee. I think we need to talk to somebody about all of this."

"Yeah, but who? You and I both know that as good a guy as D.W. is, this is way over his head. The only thing he'd know how to do is call a news conference. And Fig would use this as an excuse to stick it to both of us."

As if on cue, the chief deputy walked out of the back of the Sheriff's Office and saw them talking. He walked towards them like a man with a purpose, and John Lee knew that purpose would not be good.

"I thought you were off sick?"

"I'm better now," John Lee told him. "I'm due to go back to work in the morning."

"What about you, Maddy? Why are you standin' around here talkin' instead of bein' out on the road? That's what the taxpayers pay you to do."

"I don't go on duty for another hour," Maddy said. "I need to pick up a couple more ticket books before I do."

"Well then, do it. I don't want to see you two standin' around here lollygaggin' when there's work to be done."

"Like I said, I'm still off duty," Maddy told him.

"Don't you sass me, girl! You may get away with a lot of shit by wigglin' your pretty little butt with other people, but that don't fly with me."

"Back off, Fig."

The big man turned to John Lee and snapped, "I wasn't talkin' to you."

"Yeah, well I'm talking to you."

"You watch yourself, boy. You're 'bout to step over the line with me."

"You keep telling about this line I'm about to step over, but where exactly is that line, Fig? Because every time you tell me the same thing you seem to back up and take that line with you." John Lee moved forward until they were almost touching. "Is this close enough? Have I crossed that line yet?"

"Last chance, Deputy. Back up or I'm takin' you out."

"Okay, let's do this," John Lee said with menace in his voice. "Take your best shot."

"Come on guys, both of you step back," Maddy said.

John Lee could actually taste Flag's bad breath, but they had come too far and there was no way he was going to drop it. The showdown between the two of them was long overdue. He kept his eyes locked on Flag's. He had been in enough brawls and broken up enough bar fights to know that the eyes would telegraph the movement before the other man ever started to swing. But it never happened.

"Unless you two are plannin' to kiss, I'd suggest you both move back a foot or two," Sheriff D.W. Swindle said, walking toward them faster than one might think a man his size could move. "I'm all for diversity and all that nonsense they keep sayin' we need to embrace, but not in public. So whatever you two are goin' to do, don't do it here where the citizens can walk by and see it."

"You need to tell your pet monkey here to learn some manners," Flag said, not budging.

"And while you're at it, you might tell this baboon that they invented this thing called a toothbrush a long time ago. Apparently he never got the memo about that," John Lee added, just as unwilling to back off.

The sheriff put his arms on both men's shoulders and pushed them apart like a referee in a boxing match, though neither moved easily. "Whatever it is that's got you two started this time, I said not here."

"You and me, it's gonna happen," Flag said pointing his finger at John Lee.

"You keep telling yourself that if it makes you feel all big and important, Fig."

"That's enough," D.W. ordered. "John Lee, you're off duty. No reason for you to be here. And Flag, if all you got to do with your time is act like a schoolyard bully, how 'bout I send you down to the grade school with a stop sign and you can play crossing guard until you decide to grow up?"

The look of pure hatred the chief deputy gave to the sheriff was so real that John Lee could feel it in the air. If there was anybody Flag despised more than John Lee, it was his brother-in-law. Sooner or later he was going to make his move, and when he did it was going to be ugly. There was no question about that. But this wasn't the day. The big man turned on his heel and stalked away.

The sheriff and his two deputies watched until he went back into the building, then D.W. turned to them. "You two watch yourselves. That there is a snake, and first chance he gets, he's goin' to strike."

"I wish he would," John Lee said.

"Be careful what ya'll wish for, John Lee. I know Flag's a blowhard and all that, but don't fool yourself. He's a dangerous man and a vindictive one. He don't believe in fight'n fair and he'd just as soon shoot you in the back as anything else."

John Lee knew that D.W. was right, and that sooner or later things were going to explode with Flag. But right now he had other things to worry about. He knew he had not seen the last of his visitors from the night before. He needed to find out what was going on, where Herb had disappeared to, and how to distance himself from whatever kind of mess his father was involved in. But he had a feeling that it might already be too late for that.

John Lee Quarrels Series

The Gecko In The Corner
Chapter 18

EVERY TIME HE HEARD A car pull up in one of the parking spaces near his motel room Herb Quarrels panicked. Too afraid to peek out the heavy drapes he kept pulled tightly over the room's one window, he sat on the bed watching the doorknob, fearing it would turn and more of Torres' men would burst inside.

Sometimes he wished he had kept the gun he had snatched from one of his torturers' belts, but he was just as glad he had thrown it out the window of the rental car when he made his getaway. Though he had shot both of the men in that room, Herb was not a killer and knew he had gotten incredibly lucky the first time around. He also knew that when they came for him again, and there was no question that they *would* find him and come for him again, he didn't stand a chance.

Why had he ever allowed himself to become involved in this mess? He should have figured out another way to help Jason. There had to have been a better way. What was that they said about hindsight being 20/20?

He heard a car pulling up out front and doors slamming. His heart stopped beating and he began to shake all over, then he heard the voices of children asking if they could go to the swimming pool. It was just another family ending a long day on the road and happy to have a place to rest for the night. Herb started to relax, but he knew it was only a matter of time before the doors slamming were not weary travelers, but grim faced men coming to take him away.

***

"We need to put an end to this and get Miguel's money back now," Ramon said. "So what if this man has a gun? We have guns, too. And this time we will be prepared and ours will be in our hands before he has the chance to reach for his."

Laurencio didn't reply. The man almost never spoke, which Ramon found unnerving. He would have preferred to have somebody with him who would communicate, who would help him form a plan to find Herb Quarrels and Miguel's money. Or at least somebody who would nod and say something, *anything*, in response when Ramon talked. But Laurencio could have been a mannequin sitting beside him. That is, if mannequins were capable of flaying the flesh off of a man, or slashing a throat, or cutting a tongue out, all of which he knew Laurencio had done on more than one occasion.

"So this is the plan," Ramon said. "We drive by to make sure he is home, and then we park in the driveway to the empty house past his so he does not know we are coming. The first thing we do is shoot the dog. If the man tries to reach for his gun, we shoot him, too. But try not to kill him if you can. At least not for now. We need him to tell us where the money is so we don't have to spend a lot of time searching for it. Understood?"

There was no response from Laurencio, and he didn't expect one. That was fine. Let the big man keep silent. He was probably too stupid to have anything worthwhile to say, anyway. Just as well. One did not require intelligence to be a killer. And when the time came, Ramon would silence him forever. But first they had to find the money.

They drove down the road slowly, both looking to see if the pickup truck was in the driveway. It was, but when they saw the second vehicle Ramon almost slammed on the brakes. This was a complication that he did not anticipate and did not need. He cursed under his breath.

***

"I know the man is a cop," Miguel told him. "I knew that five minutes after you told me his name. I also know that he is the son of the man we are looking for. If you were doing your job, you would have known these things, too."

"I am not sure what to do now," Ramon admitted with great reluctance, knowing that no matter how quickly he managed to recover his uncle's money, his own fate was now sealed. His only chance to live was to get the money and disappear.

"You never knew what to do from the start," Miguel said.

"I am sorry, Miguel."

"We will deal with that later. The sooner you find the man and get my money, the better it will be for all of us."

"How should I proceed?"

"What was your plan? Surely you had some sort of plan, Ramon."

"I planned to take the man, the son, and make him tell us where the money is. But him being a cop changes everything, doesn't it?"

"Why would it change anything? So what if he is a cop? He is still a man. He still bleeds like any other man."

"But maybe he doesn't know where the money is."

"Why? Because he is a cop? Do you think I don't have cops who do what I want for a price? Do you think cops don't come to my whorehouses? Cops are men, Ramon. No more and no less. They have the same greed and lust and weaknesses as any other man. He knows where the money is. And if he doesn't know, he is still the bait we need to draw his father out from wherever he is hiding."

"But what if..."

"No more questions. No more delays. Just do it! And Ramon, I warn you, do not fail me again."

Before Ramon could reply, Miguel punched the button to end the call. His blood was boiling and he wanted to go back and have Gabriella again, but before he could push his chair away from his desk his phone rang. Now what did Ramon want? His excuses were wearing thin and it took every bit of restraint Miguel had not to text Laurencio and tell him to just kill the worthless pup and have it done with. But no, for now he needed Ramon to get his money back. And then he would do the killing himself. It had been a long time since Miguel had dirtied his hands in such a way, but he was still fully capable of it, and in Ramon's case, he knew he would find it enjoyable.

"Now what?" he demanded when he pushed the button to answer the call.

"That is the way you greet me when I call?"

A cold chill passed through Miguel's body when he recognized the voice. Why had he not looked at the caller ID before answering?

"I am so sorry, Esteban. I thought it was one of my workers."

"A problem?"

"No, just an irritation."

"They say good help is hard to find. But irritations are not hard to dispose of," Esteban said.

"It will not come to that," Miguel assured him.

"You sound like you are over your sickness."

"My sickness? Oh yes, I think I am almost better now."

Miguel had managed to delay meeting with Esteban five days earlier by claiming he had come down with some sort of bug and did not want to pass it on to the other man. Esteban was old and frail, and had a fear of illness. But that did not make him any less dangerous. Miguel's patrón was the only man he feared. Esteban ruled the drug trade along Interstate 4 from Tampa to Orlando and on to Daytona Beach with a heavy hand, and though he was nearing his 80th birthday he was still as mentally sharp and as vicious as he had been when he left the barrios of Bogotá to begin his rise to power.

He had surrounded himself with an army of hired guns who suppressed any resistance to his methodical takeover of the territory once owned by weaker drug dealers. Some, realizing that change was inevitable, had allied themselves with Esteban and were allowed to continue doing business as before, giving a healthy percentage of their profits to him in return. In other places, those who tried to stand up to him simply disappeared. Esteban was a subtle man who did not believe in car bombs or other actions that would attract publicity. He didn't have to. The word spread quickly enough.

In places where a change was necessary, he had appointed different men to oversee operations, and in every city and town within his realm, they all answered to one trusted member of his organization who served as an overlord. Esteban gave these men wide latitude to operate, caring little for anything but the end result. Orlando was the crown jewel and Miguel had worked long and hard to win the position as top man there. Now that position, and his very existence, were in jeopardy.

"Almost better? What does that mean?"

"I still have some symptoms," Miguel replied, then coughed loudly, hoping it sounded real. "But I'm feeling much better. I think a day or two and I will be back to normal."

"That is good. I missed our meeting last week."

"I did, too," Miguel told him. "I could come tomorrow, if you wish."

He coughed again and Esteban said, "No, I don't want to catch whatever it is that made you sick."

"Perhaps I could send my nephew Ramon, with something for you," Miguel suggested.

"No. I can wait two more days. But make sure you are well before you come to see me."

"Whatever you think is best, Esteban."

"Two days. By then I hope you are feeling better. If not, I can send somebody over to fill in for you while you take a long rest."

"That is not necessary," Miguel assured him. "I will see you in two days."

Miguel said his goodbyes and ended the call, hoping that Esteban had bought his story. He knew that since he had his heart transplant nearly ten years ago the old man had developed a phobia about germs of any kind. He seldom ventured out of his gated estate and always wore a cloth mask over his mouth and nose, and required anyone who approached him to do the same. And the ruse of offering to send Ramon in his place had been brilliant. Esteban had grown paranoid over the years, and only a chosen few were allowed into his inner sanctum. Miguel knew that there was no way Esteban would have agreed to meet with Ramon, but by offering to send him, he hoped it showed he had nothing to hide and it truly was only sickness that had kept Miguel away from their regular meeting.

Two days. That wasn't much time. He needed to take action himself and not wait while that fool, Ramon, stumbled around trying to figure out what to do. Someone should have bashed his head in when he was born. Why had he even listened to his sister when she told him that Ramon needed an opportunity and begged him to take him on to spare him a life of labor in a brick yard back at home? But he had, and this is what it brought him. He picked up the heavy glass tumbler from his desk, drained the last of the whiskey from it, then threw it across the room where it shattered against the wall.

He pushed his chair back and shoved his bodyguard out of the way without a word, stomping down the hall to the woman's room, his fists clenched in anger.

Chapter 19

ESTEBAN MUÑOZ LOOKED AT THE phone a long time after his call with Miguel ended. He considered himself a patient man, and a benevolent one. Once their loyalty was proven to him he offered opportunities to men who would otherwise have had few choices in life, and he allowed them a lot of freedom to do things as they thought best. While Esteban himself found prostitution repellent and wanted nothing to do with it in his own business, he had said nothing and permitted Miguel to operate his whorehouses. To him it was like allowing a child to have a hobby. If Miguel got some thrill out of it, as long as it did not interfere with their business, he would turn a blind eye to it, although it made no sense to him. They dealt with millions of dollars and Miguel was well compensated. Whatever little money the whores made was insignificant. But he knew his underling well enough to know that it wasn't about the money. It was about the power he had over the women. That was worth much more than any amount of money they might bring in.

So why was Miguel lying to him?

***

They had hardly set foot on the property when they heard the big German Shepherd barking.

"Damn! Get down!"

But Laurencio did not need any instructions. He had already fallen back two steps and crouched down behind a tree. The dog barked again and the porch light of the darkened house came on. They saw the man look outside, then he said something to the dog and it came up onto the deck and he allowed it inside. The door shut again and the porch light was extinguished. They waited in silence for what seemed a long time.

"Maybe he thought the dog was barking at a raccoon or something," Ramon said.

Laurencio did not respond. He seemed not to feel the bites of the mosquitoes that had swarmed around them. The man was like a robot.

"Let's give it five more minutes, then we'll go in."

***

John Lee checked to make sure both the front and back doors were locked, then stood with his shotgun cradled in his arms, waiting. He knew by the tone of the dog's barking that whatever had alerted Magic was more than some creature of the night. What was the best way to play this? If he thought it was just some prowler, he would have called Dispatch for backup, but that wasn't an option in this case. He needed to keep things as low-key as possible.

As he saw it, he had two choices. He could wait for the men to come to him, or he could go to them. Which was better, tactically? The house provided shelter and cover, and nobody was going to get in without him knowing it and facing his shotgun. But at the same time, it could also trap him. It would be easy to throw a firebomb through a window and force him out. A lot depended on what they wanted from him. He was sure that whatever it was, it had to do with his father. Did they think John Lee knew where he was? If so, they wanted him alive until he told them. But maybe they wanted to send a message to Herb and planned to do so by hurting or killing John Lee.

No, he decided, staying in the house and being a sitting duck wasn't the best way to handle this. As a deputy, he had learned a long time ago that assertiveness and taking charge of a situation was always the thing to do, rather than waiting to see what would happen and then reacting to it.

John Lee wasn't a hunter, but he had spent a lot of time roaming the woods and swamps of Somerton County as a boy and he was sure he was more familiar with the outdoors than the city men out there. He would take the fight to them. He checked his pistol to be sure that it was fully loaded, slipped it behind his belt, draped the strap to his night vision binoculars around his neck, and was heading for the back door when his phone rang. If it was a regular call he would have ignored it, but it was the special alert ring tone from the Dispatcher's office. They only called out on that line when it was very important. He answered the call and said, "John Lee here."

"John Lee, we need everybody out on County Road 37 by Bradley's Fish Camp. Officer down and suspect at large!"

"I'm on my way."

He ended the call and cursed. Whoever was out there waiting for him was going to have to wait a while longer. When a call went out for an officer down, nothing else mattered. Whether you were sleeping, or in the middle of a family birthday party, or watching your favorite football team on television, you stopped what you were doing and went to help a brother officer in need. Now he just had to figure out how to make it to his patrol car alive to answer the call!

He pulled his ballistic vest over his shirt, grabbed his handheld radio and tactical flashlight from their chargers, and slung his shotgun over his shoulder by its strap. He hooked a long lead to Magic's collar and commanded "Car" as he went out the door. Once he was off the deck it was only a dozen or so steps to the Charger and he bent low and crossed the distance quickly. When he got to the rear passenger door he hit the button on his key fob to activate the car's red and blue roof lights and siren, then yanked the door open so Magic could jump inside, grateful that the button in the car's doors that automatically turned on the dome light was deactivated, as it was with all Sheriff's Department vehicles.

As most deputies did, John Lee always parked his car facing out so if he had to leave in a hurry no time would be wasted turning around.

Keeping low, his pistol in his hand, John Lee pulled open the drivers door, expecting a bullet at any moment. But apparently his plan had worked and the sudden burst of noise and light had distracted whoever was out there enough that he could get into the car. Keeping as low as he could, he stuck the key in the ignition and started the Dodge, then pulled the gearshift lever into Drive and floored the accelerator, shooting out of the driveway as fast as he could. When he hit the road he spun the wheel, straightened up, and was gone in a cloud of gravel and dust.

Behind him, Ramon and Laurencio remained crouched down, not knowing if the man would be returning with reinforcements in a moment or what to expect. When he didn't come back after a few moments, Ramon turned to his companion and asked, "Now what do we do?"

But Laurencio did not reply. He never had anything to say. Why should Ramon expect any advice from him now?

The Gecko In The Corner
Chapter 20

GREG CARSON LOOKED MORE LIKE a high school kid than a sheriff's deputy. That was probably because he was only two years out of high school when he joined the Department. Red haired and borderline chubby, the young deputy had peach fuzz on his upper lip and teenage acne that caused many people to underestimate him at first glance. Like all rookies, he had been the butt of jokes when he first came on the job, and he had taken the razzing good-naturedly. But Greg was a hard worker, dedicated, and a quick learner. It didn't take long for the other deputies to accept him as an equal.

At least all of them except for Flag. He seemed to have taken an immediate dislike to Greg and never missed an opportunity to criticize him or put him down in front of his coworkers. John Lee wasn't sure if that was because he and Greg seemed to click from the start, or maybe they had come together because they were both frequent targets of the chief deputy. It was sort of a which came first, the chicken or the egg kind of thing. So when he called Dispatch from his car's radio to say he was headed toward the scene and asked for an update, he was even more concerned to hear that Greg was the officer involved.

The dispatcher told him that Greg had called in to report he was stopping to assist a stranded motorist and gave the license plate number of a 2003 Chevrolet Cavalier, and then there had been nothing else from him. The computers were running slow that night, but when Dwight Potter, the dispatcher working the night shift, did not hear back from Greg in a reasonable time, he called him on the radio and got no response. When he called a second time and Greg failed to answer, Dwight's instincts kicked in. A retired cop from Indiana, the next thing he did was call Greg's cell phone. After six rings it went to voice mail.

Somerton County had a small Sheriff's Department and only three deputies were on duty that night. The closest was Maddy, but she was in the middle of settling a domestic dispute between a mother and her fifteen year old son, an incorrigible boy who was well known to the deputies and school authorities as someone whom everyone was sure would eventually do time behind bars. Maddy was explaining to the young man that no matter how cool he thought he was, stealing beer from the local convenience store and coming home smelling of alcohol and tobacco was not acceptable, and that yes, his mother had every right to ground him.

With Maddy tied up, Dwight had called the other on-duty deputy, Andy Stringer. An easy-going man with a big belly and hands the size of catcher's mitts. Andy tried to call Greg on his radio, but there was no answer. Just as Andy hung up his microphone the dispatcher came back on the air to say that the computer had finally returned a hit on the Cavalier as stolen from Jacksonville the day before. Andy was twelve miles away and sped toward the scene Code 3, lights flashing and siren screaming through the night.

Hearing the report on her portable radio, Maddy had warned the teenage boy that if she had to come back again he was going to spend a night in jail, then ran to her patrol car and headed for County Road 37. It was a narrow, winding road that followed the shore of Baxter Lake, popular with fishermen and teenagers looking for a place to party. Coming around a sharp curve, she had to hit her brakes to avoid colliding with a deer that jumped onto the pavement in front of her. Feeling the rear end of her car start to slide, Maddy turned the steering wheel in the direction of the skid, punched the accelerator, and felt the car respond and straighten up. On any other night she might have whooped out loud and given the air a high five for her driving skills, but there was no time for that now. She had to get to Greg.

There was still a cloud of dust in the air from Andy's car sliding to a stop when Maddy arrived on the scene. Greg's patrol car was parked on the shoulder of the road, the driver's door open.

The Gecko In The Corner

A white sedan was a short distance in front of it, the trunk open and the spare tire leaning against the bumper.

"Do you see him?" Maddy called as she got out of her unit.

Andy was sweeping the Cavalier with his flashlight. "No. I just got here. Back me up, let's check out this car."

They approached the sedan, pistols drawn. Andy took the driver's side and Maddy the passenger's. The car was empty.

"Unless there was a third car, Greg and whoever was in this one have to be around here pretty close," Andy said, then called, "Greg. Where are you?"

Nothing.

They heard sirens coming from a distance. "You take this side of the road, I'll take the other," Andy said. "Work your way from the suspect vehicle back towards his car a ways."

More sirens were coming closer, and soon two more cars arrived. Donny Ray Mayhew, one of the few college graduates on the Department, closely followed by Bob Patterson.

"Anything?"

"Not yet," Andy said, then called Greg's name again. As first officer on the scene, he was in charge until a supervisor arrived. "You guys check up in front of the Cavalier, Maddy and I will keep looking back here."

They resumed their search, and a moment later heard Donny Ray shouting "over here," from a few feet in front of the Cavalier. "I found something."

A short, barrel chested man who wore his black hair close cropped, with a mustache and goatee, Donny Ray had been off duty and was wearing cargo shorts and a T-shirt. He pointed to a broken pair of glasses on the shoulder of the road. "Aren't those Greg's?"

"I think so," Maddy said.

"The weeds look trampled over there," Bob Patterson said, shining his light across the road. More cars were arriving and John Lee joined them, quickly followed by Flag and Jack Fausto.

"What we got?" Flag was in full uniform even though it was after 10 PM. John Lee wondered if he ever took it off, even to sleep.

"Not sure at this point," Andy replied. "Dispatch said..."

"I know what the hell Dispatch said," Flag snapped. "I've got ears. Have y'all found anything here."

"We think those are Carson's glasses," Donny Ray told him, shining his light on them.

"You think? That the best you can do is think?"

"Well hell, Flag, we haven't had time to run a DNA test yet," Andy replied sarcastically, smarting from the chief deputy's sharp comments.

Before Flag could reply, Bob said, "I think someone went off through the weeds over there where they're smashed down."

"Then why the hell are y'all standing around here with your thumbs up your asses? Go check it out!"

Donny Ray and Bob started forward, but John Lee stopped them. "Let me go in there, Donny Ray. With your bare legs you're liable to get eaten up by something."

"Screw it," Donny Ray said looking back toward the chief deputy, who had walked back to the Cavalier and was looking inside it. "If I stay out here much longer I may wind up kicking Flag's ass. Besides, if Greg's out there we need to find him."

Never one to stay back and avoid the dirty work, Maddy joined them and the four deputies spread out, walking through the waist high brush.

The Gecko In The Corner
Chapter 21

MIGUEL STARED AT THE BROKEN, naked body of Gabriella Sainz and shook his head. Such a waste. Why would a woman with such a fine body and beautiful face be so unwilling to accept things the way they were? Miguel had tried with her. He had shown her more patience than he would any other puta. At first she had tried to fight him off, but that hadn't lasted long. One or two good beatings and all the fight left her. After that she would just turn her face away and silently submit.

But what good was that? A man wanted some kind of response from a woman when he was taking her. At least the whores would moan and call his name and scream in false ecstasy, making it worth his effort. But not this one. There was nothing. Yes, if he twisted her nipples hard enough she might grimace for a second, but she soon learned to stifle even that. The harder he used her, the more he abused her, the further she retreated into herself. Except for the warmth of her flesh she was no more than one of those plastic sex dolls the perverts who could not afford a real woman used.

Miguel had such hopes for her. A beauty like that could have given him many hours of pleasure. Not to mention the many thousands of dollars she could have earned for him. But no, she was just as useless as her husband. Thinking of Ramon and the situation he had placed him in, Miguel felt his anger rising again. It was because of Ramon that Gabriella was dead and he himself was in peril. It was Ramon's failure that had started this whole process. Why would such a woman, with so much promise, become involved with a useless dog like Ramon. Damn you, Ramon! Damn you and your cold fish of a wife! Once, twice, three times he punched Gabriella's face. Of course there was no response. There had been nothing when she was alive, why should he expect something different with her dead?

He went into the bathroom attached to her bedroom and washed the blood away, then pulled his clothes on. He went out into the hallway, where his bodyguard set on a chair. "Take that piece of garbage out and get rid of it," he said, then walked back to his office alone.

***

They waited for fifteen minutes after John Lee left before Ramon decided that whatever had called him out in such a hurry was probably going to take a while. With a last look around, he said, "Come on. Let's look inside." Silently, Laurencio rose and followed him across the yard.

Ramon was glad the deputy had taken the dog with him. Big aggressive dogs frightened him. Once, when he was a boy, he and his friend Pablo had watched the owner leave and then climbed over the wall of a villa, looking for something to steal. They had watched the place for days and knew the owner's patterns. He woke up early in the morning, spent some time sitting under his veranda drinking coffee and reading the newspaper, then he went inside and never came back out until just after noon. When he did, he always walked five blocks to the little business district, where he went into a cantina and drank and chatted with his amigos until late in the afternoon. Then he would stop at one of the little restaurants and eat, and sometimes take a stroll around the business district before returning to the cantina for another hour or two before he staggered home.

The only time the pattern changed was on Tuesdays and Fridays. On those days, after lunch he stopped to see a woman named Blanca Pérez and stayed with her for at least two hours, sometimes longer. Blanca's husband Roberto had traveled north all the way to America, where he found work as a laborer on a construction project. For the first year he sent money home faithfully every week to support his pretty wife and two young children. Then the money orders became less frequent, sometimes only one or two a month would arrive, and eventually they stopped coming at all.

Some said Roberto had found a new woman up there and forgotten about his family back home. Others said he had gotten into a drunken fight and been killed in Arizona. A third rumor had him doing time in prison somewhere in California. Nobody really knew. What Blanca *did* know was that she had to find a way to support herself and her two little ones. She was serving beer in the cantina when she met Señor Fernandez, and he had quickly taken a shine to her. So what if he was old enough to be her father, and fat and bald? He was a generous man and he always treated her with respect. And surprisingly, he was a gentle and capable lover who always made sure her needs were met before his own. Blanca knew that many people looked down on her for what she was doing, and she heard the whispers when she went to the market, but she ignored them. Who else was going to make sure her babies were fed and had a roof over their heads?

On that bright and sunny Tuesday, Roberto and Pablo had followed the man at a distance just to make sure his schedule would not change, though there was no reason for it to do so. Once he was in the cantina they waited another thirty minutes, just to be sure. Then they had returned to his villa and crawled over the back wall. The house was not grand, nothing was in their small village, but it seemed like a palace to the two poor boys.

"Look," Pablo had said, laughing, "he does not even close the door to the veranda. It is like he welcomes us to come and take what we want."

Two heartbeats later they knew why the man felt no need to lock his door. A pair of large pit bulls, one black and white and the other a brindle, rushed at them from inside the house growling fiercely. Terrified, the two intruders raced for the back wall of the villa. Ramon was almost over the top when he heard his friend scream. He looked back to the terrible sight of one of the dogs hanging onto Pablo's bare leg, bright red blood gushing from its mouth. Pablo grappled for the wall, screaming "help me, Ramon!" But all Ramon could do was stare in horror. Pablo tried to kick the dog away with his other foot, but when he did the brindle grabbed that ankle and they took him down. After that Ramon had never cared to watch any kind of horror movie with all the blood and guts that so many young people enjoyed. He had seen it in real life, and he would be haunted by nightmares ever after.

There was an investigation, of course, and the police had come to the little shack Ramon shared with his parents and five siblings. Yes, Pablo Lambis was his friend. No, he had not seen him in a week. Pablo had said something about going to visit his abuelo in the next village. His grandparents were old and frail and sometimes he went to help them with chores. No, he had no knowledge of the burglary. No, he knew nothing about Pablo being killed by any dogs. How can that happen? It was impossible. Pablo was a good boy who never got in trouble. The officers, one short and fat who sweated a lot and the other tall and skinny who looked to be not much older than Ramon himself, did not believe him. But what did it matter? Sooner or later they would catch him at something. In the meantime, the word would spread and maybe burglaries would stop for a while. Who knew how many other dogs were guarding the villas around town? Two days later his mother had written to her brother in Florida, saying the only opportunities for a boy in their village was to work in a brick yard with no future and begging him to allow Ramon to come north and work for him.

Even though he knew the dog was gone, Ramon still felt the fear as he had circled the house, using a small flashlight to look for any evidence of an alarm system. Finding none, they stepped up onto the back deck and knocked on the door, just to be sure there wasn't another dog inside. Hearing nothing, Ramon took a deep breath and nodded to Laurencio. The big man drew back his foot and sent a powerful kick into the door just below the knob. There was the sound of wood splintering, but the door held fast. It took two more kicks before the door crashed inward and they entered John Lee's house, pistols in their hands.

Chapter 22

THEY FOUND GREG CARTER LYING on his back a few yards in from the road. His face was bloodied and swollen and his uniform shirt had been ripped open. The ghastly sight of their fellow deputy was made worse by the swarms of mosquitoes and flies feasting on his flesh.

"Oh my God," Maddy said, dropping down beside him and feeling his neck for a pulse. It was there and she heaved a sigh of relief.

Donny Ray keyed the microphone button on his portable radio and said they had found Greg and needed an ambulance.

"Trail keeps going that direction," Bob Patterson said. He was a skilled hunter who knew how to track everything from deer to wild boar to men through the rough country of Somerton County. "Let's go find the son of a bitch!"

"I think we should grab some more firepower first," John Lee said. "We don't know if he's armed."

"Greg's weapon is still in its holster," Maddy said.

"Doesn't mean he doesn't have something else on him," John Lee replied. "Just see to Greg and hang tight a minute, guys."

He returned to the road and retrieved his shotgun from the Charger and let Magic out of the car. He grabbed another shotgun from Maddy's unit and was headed back into the brush when Flag stopped him.

"Don't take that dog in there!"

"Why not? He can see and smell a hundred times better than any of us can."

"I don't care, he's not certified for K-9 work."

"We don't have a K-9. Certified or not, he knows what he's doing," John Lee said.

"I told you no! You put that mutt back in your car or else."

"Or else what, Fig? What you gonna do about it?"

"I'm givin' you a direct order, Deputy."

"Stick your direct order up your fat ass," John Lee said hotly. "I don't have time for your bullshit. We've got a deputy hurt and whoever did it to him is out there. You can stand here on the road and flap your lips all night playing God if you want to, but the rest of us have a fugitive to find."

"I'm warnin' you, John Lee, you lock that dog in the..."

But John Lee had already gone back down the trail to join the other deputies. He handed Maddy's shotgun to Bob and said, "Let's do this."

As it turned out, they didn't need Magic after all. Three hundred yards down the trail they heard someone calling for help. Moving forward cautiously, weapons at the ready, they came across a shirtless man mired in the brackish waist deep water of the swamp.

"Get your hands up where I can see them," Bob ordered. "Do it now!"

"Help me, there's gators in here!"

"You got a lot more to worry about than alligators," Bob told him. "Now get your hands up in the air like I told you, because if you don't I'm gonna blow you in half."

The man held his hands high over his head and pleaded with them to save him.

"Do you have any weapons on you?"

"No."

"Turn around in a circle slowly," Bob ordered. "And I'm tellin' you right now, if you drop your hands for even a second we're goin' to think you're reaching for a weapon and we're goin' to kill you. Do you understand me?"

"Yes, sir. But I can't move. I'm stuck in this here mud and I'm afraid if I do that gator will get me."

"He might," Andy agreed, "but if you don't, I'm gonna shoot you. You take your choice. I'm not screwin' around with you, asshole. You've already hurt one of our deputies and we're not give'n you a chance to hurt another one. It's just as easy to kill you where you stand. Now last chance, turn around like I told you or you're a dead man."

The suspect turned slowly, all the while watching the dark water around him.

"Okay, I turned around. Now somebody please help me get out'a here."

"You got yourself in there," John Lee told him. "Now get yourself out. Keep your hands up and walk toward us."

"I can't! I told you I saw a gator. I'm afraid if I move it'll get me!"

"Screw this bullshit," Donny Ray said. He looked around and found a large branch and picked it up, breaking off a few smaller branches from it.

"That's not long enough to reach him," John Lee said.

"No, but it's enough to get his attention."

It had been a few years since Donny Ray had thrown a javelin at the University of Florida in Gainesville, but he still did a pretty good job of it, launching the branch into the air. It hit the water with a loud splash four feet from where the suspect stood. He screamed and rushed forward, splashing water high in the air and launching himself onto solid ground.

The deputies were immediately on top of him pinning him down and handcuffing his hands behind him. Then they jerked him to his feet. He was wild eyed, his skin sunken around his face, and when he spoke the few teeth he had left were no more than broken stumps.

"Where's your other shoe?"

"What?"

"Your other shoe," Andy said. "Where is it?"

The prisoner looked down at his feet and shook his head. "I don't know, man. I guess it's still back there in the swamp. Are you gonna make me walk back to the road with just one shoe on?"

"You're welcome to go back and look for it if you want to," Andy told him.

The thought of going back into the black water where the alligators and moccasins waited for him brought a shiver to the man. He shook his head.

"That's what I thought," the deputy said and they led him back the way they had come.

"Son of a bitch smells like shit," Donny Ray said.

With all the muck and slime dripping from his body it was hard to say what else there might be, but John Lee replied, "If I was out there and you threw that damn branch at me, trust me, I'd a shit so hard even the gators would've been running out of that swamp!"

"Way I heard it, you already been doin' a lot of shittin' lately," Bob Patterson quipped.

An ambulance was on the scene and they were loading Greg into the back of it by the time they returned to the road with their prisoner.

"How is he?"

Maddy, who had stayed with the injured deputy while the others went after his attacker, shook her head and said, "He's beat to hell, that's how he is. Looks like the bastard took off running and when Greg went after him in the brush he jumped him and hit him over the head with the jack handle. I found it in the weeds near Greg. Paramedics say there's a good chance he's got a concussion. But at least he's awake now."

John Lee put Magic in the back of his car, then crawled into the ambulance and knelt beside the stretcher.

"How you doing, buddy?"

"I screwed up, John Lee. I know I should've waited for backup when he took off running, but I just wasn't thinking. I'm sorry."

"Nothing to be sorry for," John Lee assured him. "I'd have probably done the same thing if I was in your place."

"Did you get him?"

"Yeah, we got him. Looks like he's some kind of meth head."

"We need to get rolling, Deputy," one of the paramedics said. "Are you coming with us?"

"No, I need to stay here and help wrap things up," John Lee said, then turned back to Greg.

"Don't you worry about a thing, okay? These guys are going to take good care of you and we'll have people there at the hospital. As soon as I can, I'll be there, too."

He climbed out of the ambulance, closed the back doors and slapped the side, signaling the driver it was okay to leave. He watched as it drove off, lights and siren on, escorted front and back by Sheriff's Department cruisers.

D.W. had arrived sometime during their pursuit of Greg's attacker and was standing by while two deputies searched the suspect's car.

"Steering column's been punched," said Joey McKenzie. "And we found this," holding up a large Ziploc bag full of a powdery substance and confirming everybody's suspicions that the man who had attacked Greg was a meth user, and apparently a low-level dealer.

"Any idea what happened out here?"

"Looking at Greg's dashboard camera, seems like he came across this car and the guy was changing the tire," Deputy Samuel Gerrison said. "Greg stopped to see if he needed any help and when he leaned down to look at the tire the guy took off running with the jack handle in his hand. Next thing it showed was Greg going after him, then he ran out of the picture. After that there isn't anything until Andy and Maddy showed up."

Flag pushed aside a deputy who was in his way and interrupted Samuel to say, "You need to know that I'm writin' Deputy Quarrels up for insubordination, D.W., and I'm not back'in down this time just 'cause you two are related."

"Good evening to you, too, Flag. Whatever's got your drawers in a twist can wait 'til later. Samuel here was just giving me an update on the incident."

"There wouldn't be an incident if that dumb ass rookie had half a brain. Who goes runnin' off into the brush chasin' somebody by themselves at night?"

"That's enough of that," D.W. said sternly. "We're not goin' to stand out here and discuss procedure and badmouth one of our men. Whatever happened, right or wrong, and whatever mistakes may have been made, we got a deputy injured bad and an investigation goin' on. That's the priority here. Anything else we can talk about later."

"You're damn straight we're gonna talk about it," Flag told him. "Maybe if we had a real sheriff wear'n that badge of yours things like this wouldn't be happenin'."

D.W. stepped closer to the chief deputy and looked the other man in the eye. "I said that's enough! You keep thinkin' you want to be sheriff someday, but let me tell you somethin' right now, Flag. Standin' out here talkin' like you're doin' in front of half the deputies we got and runnin' down Carson and complain'n about John Lee instead of taking care of business shows me and everybody else that you're not the man for the job. This is a time we need to be standin' behind our men and puttin' up a united front. Now, if you're not here to help this investigation, you can just go back to the office and start cleaning out your desk."

The sheriff's words were low enough that the deputies could not hear what was being said, but the look of hatred on Flag's face as he turned and walked away was enough to tell them all they needed to know.

"Okay boys, keep doin' what you're doin'. Looks like we've 'bout got it wrapped up out here. I'm goin' to head to the hospital to check on Deputy Carson. Ya'll did good out here tonight. I'm proud of you."

Chapter 23

"It could have been a lot worse," the doctor at the hospital in Perry told them. "He's beat up pretty bad and has a broken nose, and I had to put some stitches in his skull, but the x-ray shows there's no fracture, so I think we can rule out a concussion. We're going to keep him overnight for observation, but he'll be able to go home tomorrow."

"Well, thank heavens for that boy's hard head," D.W. said. "Can we see him?"

"Sure thing. He's right down the hall, Room 217, on the right. His parents are in there with him now. He's on pain meds, and we gave him some Benadryl because of all the insect bites, so he may be pretty groggy."

"Thank you, Doctor," D.W. said, and he and John Lee went to Greg's room and knocked lightly before opening the door. His mother and father and younger sister Darcy were all in the room, and D.W. nodded politely at them. "Jesse, Sandra, I'm so sorry this happened to your boy. How you folks holdin' up?"

"Best we can," Jesse Carson replied. "Did you get the man who did this to him?"

"Yes, we did. Deputy Quarrels here and some of the other deputies caught him standin' in the swamp screaming' his head off because he thought he saw an alligator."

"I wish you'd have let the gators eat him alive," said Darcy. "That would'a fixed him!"

"That's no way to talk, Darcy," Sandra told her daughter. "Vengeance is mine sayeth the Lord."

"Well, I wish the Lord would've let the gators eat him."

"I know how you feel, Darcy," the sheriff said. "But don't you worry about it, that old boy that did this is goin' to go to jail for a long, long time."

"That's not good enough after what he did to my brother."

"Calm down, Darcy," her father said. "We'll let the law handle that, our job is to take care of your brother."

"The good news is the doctor says he'll be able to go home tomorrow," D.W. said. "Folks, I want you to know that the whole Department's behind Greg here. He's a fine young man and a fine deputy. He got hurt tryin' to help somebody who turned out to be a bad man. But that don't take away from Greg. That's why he became a deputy, to help people. This job ain't all about writin' tickets and lookin' for thieves and such. A lot of it is just doin' what Greg was doin' tonight. Look'in out for folks in trouble and tryin' to help them. Ya'll should be proud of him. I know I am."

From his bed, Greg mumbled, "That you, Sheriff?"

D.W. went to his side and said, "It's me, Greg. And I've got John Lee here with me. And a bunch of other deputies are out there in the waitin' room."

"I'm sorry, Sheriff. I messed up pretty bad, huh?"

"No, sir! No, sir, you done just fine. If I was in your shoes, I imagine I'd a done the same thing. Ain't your fault that fella was waitin' to waylay you. You just chalk this up to a learnin' experience, Deputy. Now you get yourself some rest and we'll talk tomorrow, okay?"

"Yes, sir."

John Lee took one of Greg's swollen hands and squeezed it gently. "You get some rest, buddy, and get well. We need you back out there on the road with us when you're up to it."

"Okay."

Looking at his friend, his head wrapped in a gauze bandage, his nose taped, his face covered in bruises from the assault and welts from the insect bites, John Lee had to wonder if Darcy might not have been right. Maybe they should have left the man who did this to Greg standing there in the swamp and let the alligators handle it.

There was no hospital in Somerton County, just a small medical clinic, so anything more pressing than a minor injury was handled in Taylor County, at the hospital in Perry. A small crowd of deputies and a couple of reporters were waiting for news about

Greg's condition. The sheriff give them a quick rundown, then said he needed to get back to work and would have more details later. "Ain't no reason for the rest of you guys to stay here. Deputy Carson's in good hands, and his family's here with him. Get yourself some rest, I need you all fresh and alert when you hit the road for your next shift."

As they walked out into the parking lot, John Lee asked the sheriff if he wanted him to follow him to the office to help interview the man who had assaulted Greg.

"No need for that," D.W. said. "It's after midnight and you're scheduled to go on duty at 8 A.M., so why don't you go home and get some rest."

John Lee was too wired to sleep, but at the same time, there was also the problem of the men he suspected had been casing his place, assuming that *was* what Magic was barking at just before the call came in about Greg. Were they still there waiting to ambush him? Screw them, he decided, they could wait. he wasn't going to spend his life looking over his shoulder. If they were there, it was time to put an end to whatever nonsense his father had gotten him into.

***

The prisoner's name was Jamie Bowers and he had a long rap sheet that included arrests for burglary, grand theft auto, possession of narcotics, and possession for sale. He was currently on parole and there was an arrest warrant out for him for failure to report in for his required monthly meetings with his parole officer. And now that he was safely out of the swamp and away from the alligators he had developed an attitude.

"I want to file charges against those cops that arrested me," he said the moment D.W. introduced himself as the sheriff. "They abused me!"

"Is that so? And just how did they do that?"

"Instead of saving me from those gators they stood there and made fun of me. I could'a been eaten alive! And then when I got out and they handcuffed me, one of them called me a son of a bitch and said I smelled. That there's verbal abuse, right there. And then made me walk back to the road with just one shoe. I could'a been bit by a snake or somethin'!"

"You're just damn lucky somebody didn't shoot your ass," Flag said.

"I don't have to take that shit from you!"

"Okay, that's enough of that," D.W. said. "You got yourself in a lot of trouble, boy. Best thing you can do is tone down that attitude of yours."

"I'm in trouble? You all are the ones in trouble, not me. All I was doin' was changin' a flat tire when that deputy showed up and started abusing me. That's why I run off. He was threatenin' to kill me!"

"That's not what his dashboard camera shows," D.W. said. "And that car you are drivin'? The one with the flat tire? That's a stolen car. And we found a whole bunch of dope in it. What do ya'll have to say about that?"

"No way, man! If there was dope in that car, you guys planted it."

"And I suppose whoever reported that car you were in as stolen just forgot that they loaned it to you? Is that what happened?"

"Man, I ain't sayin' nothin' more. You guys are tryin' to railroad me. I want an attorney before I say another word. And I want a shower and some clean clothes and somethin' to eat. I know my rights!"

"Well now, I'll tell you what. First chance I get, I'll have somebody take you for a shower, and we got a nice orange jumpsuit you can put on. I might even be able to find you a baloney and cheese sandwich someplace. But since you don't want to talk to me, first thing I'm goin' to do is call your parole officer over there in Jacksonville and tell him I've got you. I don't suspect he's gonna be in a good mood with me callin' him this time of night. Meantime, you just sit tight there."

"I want to talk to an attorney, too!"

"Yeah, yeah, you sure do want a lot."

They left him in his cell and walked back to D.W.'s office. Once they were inside and the door closed, D.W. sat down behind his desk and picked up the incident report Flag had written about John Lee disobeying his order to keep Magic in his patrol car.

"What do you expect me to do about this?"

"I'll tell you what you're goin' to do. You're goin' to suspend that deputy for insubordination. That's what you're goin' to do!"

"So would you rather have had a deputy get shot out there if that fella would've had a gun, Flag? That dog could've saved somebody's life."

"But he didn't, did he? The perp didn't have a gun and the dog didn't do shit. But that ain't the point, D.W. and you know it. When I give an order, I expect it to be obeyed!"

"Maybe you should spend more time workin' *with* our deputies and less time orderin' them around. They know how to do their jobs."

"I'm not here to be their buddy, I'm here to see that things get taken care of the way they should be."

"And who decides how things should be done, Flag?"

"I do if I'm the highest ranking officer on the scene. I did notice you didn't show up until things were all over with."

D.W. ignored the barbed jab and said. "So what you're tellin' me is that no matter how much experience any deputy out there has, they don't know nothin' compared to you. Is that right?"

"I'm sayin' somebody has to be in charge of the situation. And I was in charge out there and John Lee disobeyed a direct order to keep that mutt of his inside the car."

"John Lee tells me that dog can do anything a K-9 can, he's just not certified."

"And that's the point," Flag said. "It's not certified. If it mauled somebody out there the county could get sued. That's why I ordered him to put the dog back in the car."

"Well, here's an idea. Maybe we should look into gettin' him certified. That would take care of that problem, wouldn't it?"

"So you're just goin' to let this whole thing go? You're goin' to let John Lee get away with disobeyin' an order like it never happened?"

"I don't believe it was a wise order," the sheriff said. "No deputy is required to obey an unlawful order or one that puts himself or anybody else at risk. John Lee said he thought the dog could help catch the perp. I've seen him put Magic through his paces, and I agree. End of that story."

"So now every deputy we have thinks he can just ignore me when I give an order. If you had any sense at all, you'd know that can't happen. I won't have it, D.W.! If I don't have respect from the deputies I can't do my job."

The sheriff leaned forward and put his hands on his desk. "I've been real patient with you only because you're my wife's brother. But I'm about at the end of my rope with you, Flag. You talk about respect, but what you did out there tonight, talkin' to me the way you did in front of the deputies, that's not goin' to happen again. If you and me have got problems, we deal with them behind closed doors. I know you think I'm not much of a sheriff, and that's just fine. Personally, I don't think you're much of a human bein'. But I have never put you down in front of the deputies or anybody else. I expect the same from you. So either you take off that badge right now and you set it on my desk and you get out of here and don't come back, or you understand that I'm in charge around here, like it or not. If you want to run for Sheriff next election, you do it, and more power to you. But as long as I'm sittin' behind this desk, I'm the boss and you work for me. Got it?"

Flag's jaw was clenched and his face was red with anger, but all he did was nod and say, "Got it."

"Good. Now get out of my sight. I need to call that prisoner's parole officer."

Flag left the office, slamming the door, and the sheriff sat there for several minutes wondering what would happen next. He knew Flag wasn't done, and sooner or later things were going to come to a head. Maybe he should have fired him and got it over with, even if there would be hell to pay at home. He opened his desk drawer, took out a bottle of Rolaids, and popped three into his mouth, chewing them as he reached for the telephone to call Jamie Bowers' parole officer.

John Lee Quarrels Series

Chapter 24

Ramon cursed when his telephone rang. They had searched the man's house from top to bottom and found nothing. What was he going to tell Miguel? He was tempted to ignore the phone, but knew he must answer it.

"Hello?"

"Tell me something good for a change."

"I don't know what to say, Miguel. We have spent hours searching the man's house. There is nothing here. No money, no letters, nothing that helps us."

"Do you have the man?"

"No, Miguel. He left in his police car with his siren and red lights on before we got to the house. And he has not returned."

There was silence on the other end of the line. If there was one thing Ramon feared more than his uncle's rage, it was the man's silences. Nothing good ever came from them.

"What should I do now, Miguel?"

"Come back here."

"Please, give me just a little more time. I'm sure I can find some way to..."

"Enough," Miguel said. "All you have done is waste my time and cause me to lose my money. Come back here now. I will find somebody else who can do what needs to be done."

"I beg of you, Miguel....."

But the line was dead and there was no response.

"He wants us to go back to Orlando," Ramon said.

Laurencio did not reply. He never replied.

Ramon looked around the living room of John Lee's apartment, wondering if there was anything they had missed. He didn't know what it could be. They had searched everywhere, emptied every closet and all of the drawers, and the refrigerator, too. They looked everywhere in the kitchen, cut open the mattresses and the furniture, pulled the carpets away from the floor, all for nothing. He looked once more at the big gun safe, the one they had spent hours pounding on, trying to open with no success. Maybe what they sought what was in there. But it was bolted to the floor and impossible to move. The only way to know that was to wait for the man to come home and force him to open it. He was tempted to do that, but then he heard Laurencio's cell phone vibrate and saw the big man look at the text message he had received. Ramon felt himself trembling, wondering what the words on the screen said. Was it a message to kill him? Or was his uncle going to wait until he was there to witness it? Knowing Miguel, Ramon was sure that was what was going to happen.

For the first time, Laurencio spoke. "He wants us there now."

***

They went out the way they came, through the kitchen door and onto the back deck. Ramon could feel the weight of the pistol in his belt and thought about his choices. He knew that going back to Orlando was a death sentence. Could he try to reason with Laurencio? Offer to split the money with him once they found it? No, he had already decided that would not work. The bodyguard's loyalty to his uncle was unquestioned.

His only chance now was to kill Laurencio and make a run for it. Forget the money, forget Gabriella, forget everything and get as far away as he could, as fast as he could. Maybe California, or New York. He had a few hundred dollars on him, and credit cards. They would take him a distance. But he knew Miguel had ways to track the credit cards. Maybe he should start going in one direction using the cards to create a false trail, then turn around and go in another direction using cash only. Let them look for him in New York while he was making his way to California. From there maybe he could go south into Mexico and eventually make his way south and get back home. No, that was foolish. Miguel could easily find him there. He had to go somewhere where no one had ever known him.

Yes, that's what he would do. There were three steps down to the ground. At the bottom he would pull the pistol and turn quickly and shoot Laurencio. Ramon was not a good shot, but at that distance he didn't think he would miss. He would shoot the big man until he fell, and then he would begin his run. It was the only way. He stepped onto the first step and casually moved his hand to his right side, where the pistol was. Two more steps, and then he would do it.

Suddenly a bright light was shining in his face and he heard a shotgun racking a shell into the chamber.

"Freeze right there! Both of you put your hands up in the air and keep them there. If you make a move you're dead!"

***

John Lee had driven slowly down his road, looking for anything out of the ordinary. He found the black SUV where Ramon and Laurencio had left it and parked behind it. He called Dispatch and ran the license plate, and it came back registered to a company called Zelina Acquisition Services LLC, with a post office box address in Winter Park, a city on the north side of the sprawling Orlando metropolitan area.

"How do you want to handle this?" Maddy asked. Even though her shift ended at midnight, when John Lee told her about his suspicions of the two mysterious men returning she had insisted on following him home in case he needed back up.

"Let's leave our cars here blocking their vehicle and go in on foot. Bring your shotgun."

Giving Magic a signal to be quiet, they approached his house carefully. Though the lights were turned off, they saw flashlights moving inside. Circling the house, they came to the back deck and discovered the smashed in door. They moved into position with Maddy on the deck a few feet to the side of the door and John Lee on the ground and waited for the intruders to come out. It didn't take long.

They were coming down the steps when John Lee put his flashlight on them and ordered them to freeze. The smaller of the two, the man in front, immediately did as he was ordered. The taller one hesitated for a second, looking around as if seeking an escape route, but when Maddy's flashlight came on and he saw her shotgun, he followed suit.

John Lee ordered both men down onto their knees and then face down on the ground, and said, "Keep your hands up where I can see them at all times. I'm gonna handcuff you, and if either one of you so much as blinks an eye, this other deputy is going to shoot you. And then my dog is gonna eat whatever's left of you? Understood?"

Both men nodded their heads. Once they were handcuffed, Maddy went onto the deck and turned on the floodlights that illuminated the backyard. John Lee searched the shorter of the two first and found a Beretta 9 mm pistol in his belt, along with a cell phone, car keys, and a wallet containing a little over $800 in cash. The taller one carried his Beretta inside his belt in the small of his back. He also had a wicked looking switchblade in his right front pocket. He did not have a wallet or any kind of identification. Besides his weapons, the only things on him were $490 in cash and a cell phone. When the men were disarmed, John Lee had them roll onto their backs and then sit up.

"Okay, I know you're not repo men, so who the hell are you guys and what you want from me?"

Neither said anything.

John Lee looked through the wallet the shorter of the men had been carrying and took out the drivers license. He compared the picture on it with the man's face, and said "Ramon Sainz. You want to tell me what's going on, Ramon?"

No reply.

"How about you? Do you have anything to say for yourself?"

The Gecko In The Corner

The man looked to be some kind of Indian, with his long hair and high cheekbones. John Lee wondered if you might have some Aztec or Incan ancestry. He ignored the deputy's questions.

"Okay guys, it's late and I've had a long day. So somebody better start talking to me."

Maddy had gone inside to clear the house, and when she came out she said, "You'd better take a look in there, John Lee. They really trashed the place."

While she guarded the prisoners he made a quick pass through the house, seeing all of the destruction. When he came back outside he said, "You know, I'm about half tempted to shoot both of you. Florida has a Stand Your Ground law and I'd be well within my rights. What do you think, Deputy Westfall? Shoot them both, take off the handcuffs once they're dead, and then called it in and say we came home and found them and I had to kill them defending ourselves?"

"However you want to do it is fine by me. I've got your back."

"The problem is, whoever sent these apes would just send somebody else. No, I need to figure out who sent them and what it is they want. And I think I know how to do it."

There were no calls made from the big man's phone, just three text messages, two of them sent the day before to the same number, which simply said "Nothing" and one received thirty minutes ago that said "Bring him to me."

He pushed the telephone icon on Ramon's phone and looked at the numbers for calls placed and received. There were thirteen calls made and received, all to or from the same number, identified only with the letter M. The last one was made just over thirty minutes earlier. John Lee pushed the dial button and waited. The phone rang six times and was answered on the seventh ring.

"What do you want now, Ramon?"

"This isn't Ramon," John Lee told him. "This is Deputy John Lee Quarrels from Somerton County and I've got your buddy Ramon and another fellow here in handcuffs. I've got a feeling you know more about what's going on here than I do. Care to clue me in?"

There was silence for a long moment and then John Lee heard a small beep and the call was ended.

"Well that's interesting," he said. "Whoever this "M" is hung up on me. That's kinda rude, isn't it?"

He nodded to Maddy and they walked a short distance away, keeping their eyes on the prisoners.

"What do you want to do, John Lee?"

"I was only bullshitting about shooting them, but I've got to tell you, the way they tore my place up, I'm half tempted."

"I meant what I said," Maddy told him. "Whatever you want to do, I've got your back."

He knew what she said was true. They had always been there for each other, and he had no doubt that Maddy would put her career and her very life in jeopardy for him if that's what it took. And he knew that he would do the same for her.

John Lee shook his head. "No, that would just make things worse. Like I said, whoever sent these goons is who we need to be talking to. Unless we can make them talk."

"What do you mean?"

"I've got an idea."

They went back to the prisoners and John Lee jerked Ramon to his feet.

"Keep an eye on this other one here," he said and led Ramon for enough away that they could talk and not be overheard.

"Okay, let's cut to the chase. Whoever you are, I know you're just hired help. Your buddy over there, I can tell by looking at him that he's a hard case and I'm not going to get anything out of him. So I'm going to offer you a deal, and it's a one-time offer, take it or leave it. You tell me what's going on and I'll figure out some way to get you into witness protection or whatever it takes. Otherwise, I'm going to arrest both of you for burglary and let your boss figure out how he wants to handle things."

Ramon was tempted, John Lee could see it in his eyes. For a moment he thought the man would talk, but he was wrong. Ramon just looked away.

"Before you decide, you might want to look at this," John Lee said, showing him the message on the other man's phone. "I assume that when the man who sent this said 'bring him to me' he was talking about you, seeing as you had a call from that same number just before that. I've got a feeling that you've managed to step on your dick and got your boss pissed off some way or another. I think you're better off talking to me than dealing with him. What do you say?"

He could smell the fear coming off of Ramon, but still the man said nothing.

"Okay, you had your chance."

He walked Ramon back over and sat them down beside the other man, then pulled his cell phone out of his pocket and called Dispatch.

"This is John Lee," he said, "myself and Deputy Westfall just caught two armed burglars coming out of my house. We've got them secured, but we're going to need some help out here."

John Lee Quarrels Series

The Gecko In The Corner
Chapter 25

"Jesus H. Christ, could you pick a worse night to pull this shit? It's not enough that dumb ass Carson went and got himself ambushed and all banged up, now we got to deal with this, too?"

"I'm sorry Fig. The next time somebody wants to break into my place, I'll check with you first and see if there's a more convenient time for them to do it."

"Don't you sass me, John Lee!" He turned to Maddy and asked, "And just what the hell were you doin' here, anyway?"

"I don't know that that's any of your business. We're both off duty."

"Hey, if you two want to play stink finger on your own time, that's fine with me," Flag said. "I just think it's kind of convenient that you were both here the one night these two guys decided to break in."

"That's twice in less than 24 hours you've made a sexist remark to me," Maddy said. "I don't care if you are Chief Deputy, I'm telling you right now, if it happens again I'm going to file a sexual harassment complaint against you."

"Oh come on, Maddy, I didn't mean nothin' by it. Don't get your panties in... don't get all upset, okay?"

Samuel Gerrison walked out of the house and joined them on the deck. "Man, they about tore your place to pieces, John Lee. If I'd have been in your shoes I might have popped a cap on both of them." Samuel was a tall, broad shouldered African-American deputy with a bullet-shaped shaved head who had played college football and looked like he was on a path to one of the big professional teams until a knee injury while serving with the National Guard during the summer before his senior year put him out of action and ended that dream.

"I won't say I wasn't tempted," John Lee told him.

"Okay, so run this down for me again," Flag said. "I'd like to get at least a couple of hours sleep tonight if that's all right with you."

"Like I told you, I was on my way home and I noticed that SUV pulled off the road down there. I know nobody lives there, so I pulled in to check it out. It was empty and I ran the plate number. Then Maddy and I came and checked out my house. We got to the back door just as those two were coming out. Once we had them cuffed and searched, I called it in."

"Why didn't you call it in before you came to the house?"

"Call what in? I'd already called in the license number of the vehicle. At that point all we knew was that there was a suspicious vehicle out here."

"If y'all thought there was somethin' going on at your house, why didn't you call for backup?"

"Because I knew half our people were already worn out dealing with Greg's case. Besides, if I had to answer a prowler call someplace while I was on duty and called for backup, they'd send one more deputy. There were already two of us here."

Flag started to say something about the two of them being together off duty so late at night, but one look at Maddy and he changed his mind. He had enough trouble as it was without that split-tail bitch giving him a bunch of grief and starting some kind of sexual harassment bullshit. She'd get hers when the time was right. He'd see to that.

Andy Stringer joined them on the porch and said, "I can't get a word out of the big Indian lookin' fella. The other guy ain't talkin' either, but I ran his name and he's got a record. Did eighteen months for possession of narcotics six years ago. You want me to go ahead and transport them to the jail?"

"No, you go home and get some rest. You were off duty hours ago," Flag said. "We'll take care of 'em."

Andy put his hand on John Lee's shoulder and said, "I'm really sorry about this, bud. If you need some help cleaning up I'll be happy to hang around."

The Gecko In The Corner

"I appreciate it, but there's no need for that," John Lee said. "You get yourself some rest, Andy. I'll catch you later."

His friend nodded and said, "I'll tell you what. You're a better man than I am, John Lee. See'n what they did to your place, if it was me, I'd a blown them both away." That seemed to be the general consensus, and John Lee nodded in agreement.

***

It was almost daylight by the time the preliminary investigation was done and everyone had left. Maddy looked at the wreck the intruders had made of John Lee's home and asked, "You want me to help clean this place up, or what do you need?"

He looked at his watch and said, "I'm supposed to be on duty in just over an hour, and you've been up all night, too. Go home and get some sleep before you have to go back on."

"It's my day off and then I transition to day shift," she said. "I don't mind staying and cleaning up a little bit."

"Really, there's no need for that. I'll deal with it when I get off duty. Right now I need to take a shower and drink about ten gallons of coffee so I can keep my eyes open."

"You go ahead and take your shower, I'll make the coffee."

"You don't have to do that."

"I don't have to do anything, John Lee. I *want* to. Go take that shower. You smell like swamp and sweat."

He sniffed the air and said, "That's not exactly Evening In Paris you're wearing, is it?"

"Bite me, you sweet talking devil, you," she said, slapping him on the rear end as she headed for the kitchen. "Now go take that shower."

Maddy rummaged through the mess in the kitchen and found the coffeemaker and a can of coffee. While it was brewing she started putting the kitchen back in order. She could hear the shower running and was tempted to strip down and join John Lee. After all, as he had pointed out, he wasn't the only one who smelled like swamp and sweat. She went into his bedroom and stood outside the bathroom door for a moment. What would he do if she did climb in there with him? No, it was a bad idea. They had never crossed that line before. And besides, the timing was bad in so many ways.

"Someday, John Lee, someday," she said and went back to the kitchen.

Once John Lee had soaped himself down and rubbed shampoo into his hair he rinsed off, he turned the water to cold, hoping it would help keep him awake and also drive away thought's he had had about Maddy. Sometimes he wondered what would happen if... *No, don't even go there*, he told himself. *You've got enough complications in your life as it is.*

After he dried off and shaved, John Lee dressed in a uniform and went back to the kitchen, where the aroma of Maddy's strong coffee seemed like the sweetest smell on earth. She poured each of them a cup, then set a plate of microwaved breakfast sandwiches on the table.

"Damn, girl, you didn't need to do all this," he said, looking around at the order she had brought out of the chaos the burglars had left

"No big deal," she replied. "I'm going to go home and shower and change clothes, then I'll come back and clean up some more."

"You know I appreciate it," John Lee told her, "but you really don't have to. I can take care of it when I get home."

"What's the matter, afraid I'm going to find your girlie magazine stuffed under the mattress?" She fluttered her eyelashes as she teased him.

"Oh yeah, what do you keep under *your* mattress?"

"That reminds me, I need to stop at the store and get batteries," Maddy said, then looked at him and asked. "What? I was talking about batteries for my flashlight. Get your mind out of the gutter."

"Uh huh, if you say so."

"Yeah, I say so. Now eat up, you need to check in within the next fifteen minutes or Flag is going to be trying to dock you for being late going on duty."

He had not realized how hungry he was, but he quickly wolfed down three of the sausage and egg biscuits. Maddy had washed the thermos he kept in his patrol car and filled it with coffee. He grabbed it on his way out the door, ruffled Magic's fur, told Maddy one more time that she did not have to stay and clean his house, and then was gone. Maddy stood on the front deck and watched the Charger drive out of sight. She felt Magic bump his head against her knee, seeking attention. She bent down and hugged the dog and said, "I know, boy. I feel the same way every time I see him leave."

John Lee Quarrels Series

The Gecko In The Corner
Chapter 26

JOHN LEE'S CELL PHONE RANG five minutes after he called Dispatch to say he was on duty.

"You could'a taken a personal day," D.W. said. "I know you was up all night."

"More than half the people we have were up all night," John Lee replied. "Any news on Greg?"

"Yeah, I just talked to his old man on the telephone. He's sore and stiff, but he sittin' up in bed and rarin' to get out of that there hospital. The doctor was in about 7:30 and said everything looks good. I imagine they'll be sendin' him home anytime now."

"Glad to hear it," John Lee said. "I'll try to swing by his place later on and check up on him."

"You got anything to add to what you put in the report about these two guys that broke into your place?"

"Everything I know, I put in the report," John Lee said. That wasn't exactly true, but he still wasn't ready to reveal information about his father's visit or his encounter with the two suspects when they came to his home pretending to be repo men. He also had not mentioned the two cell phones he had taken from them and put away in the trunk of the Charger in his report.

"Hell of a note when even a deputy's home ain't safe while he's out workin' these days," D.W. said. "I'm glad you caught those guys. I was down to the cellblock talkin' to them, or at least tryin' to, but I couldn't get a word out of either one."

"What about the guy that attacked Greg? Anything new on that front?"

"I talked to his PO last night. Far as he's concerned, we can keep him. County Attorney's goin' to ask for a no bail hold for attempted murderer on a police officer, along with a stolen car and the drug charges. He's not goin' nowhere."

"Sounds good," John Lee replied, then took a radio call from the dispatcher requesting an officer at an intersection outside of town where an elderly driver had failed to stop and broadsided a pickup truck. The dispatcher said there were no injuries and John Lee replied he was on his way.

"Got to go, D.W.," he said on the cell phone, "talk to you later."

Some days were busy and he was kept hopping from call to call, while others are pretty slow. John Lee normally preferred the busy days and was glad this was one of them. Otherwise he might have fallen asleep parked somewhere waiting for a call.

After he cleared the accident, he took a call about a mailbox that some passerby had smashed, and found three more along the same road that had been vandalized the same way. He knew it was a common occurrence and guiltily remembered swinging a baseball bat at mailboxes himself a time or two when he was a teenager. He took photos of the damaged mailboxes to include with his report.

That done, he drove to Rafe Peterson's place and took a report about a stolen riding lawnmower.

"What the hell do we pay you guys for, anyway, when a man can't even leave a piece of equipment in his yard without some asshole stealin' it?"

"I know how you feel," John Lee told him.

"How the hell do you know how I feel? You ain't the one missin' a lawnmower that ain't even paid off yet!"

Rafe was a volatile man under the best of circumstances, given to explosions of temper whenever something went wrong.

"Calm down, Rafe," John Lee said. "I know you're pissed off, and I don't blame you. I'm feeling the same way right now. Last night I came home and caught two guys coming out of my house."

"No shit?"

"Nope, caught them red-handed."

"Man, that sucks. I'm glad it was you and not me. I'd a shot the sons of bitches!"

"You're not the first person to say that," John Lee told him. "And trust me, once I saw how they tore my house to hell, I kinda wish I would have."

"Do you think they could be the same ones that took my lawnmower?" Rafe asked hopefully.

"Hard to say," John Lee said, though he knew the two men he and Maddy had caught were not common thieves. "If they are, I'll damn sure find out about it."

Rafe spit tobacco juice off to the side and nodded his head. "I sure hope you do. Still got eight payments left on that damn Toro."

John Lee said that he would do all he could do, shook the man's hand, and went back on patrol.

He was a mile from Rafe's place when he had to slam on the brakes to keep from hitting a motorcycle that pulled out in front of him. The kid riding it almost dropped the bike, but he managed to keep it up, and when he saw the police car he roared away in a cloud of dust.

"Oh, I don't think so," John Lee said, flipping on his lights and siren and going after the motorcycle.

It was a short chase and the rider went exactly where John Lee expected him to go. When the motorcycle roared into the driveway John Lee was right behind it, and jumped out as the boy dropped the bike and started running toward the house.

"Sheriff's Deputy. You freeze right there!"

The boy looked over his shoulder, back toward the house as if it might offer some sanctuary, and then his shoulders slumped and he stopped.

"That's about the smartest thing you've done all day," John Lee said as he turned the boy around and handcuffed him. Which one are you, Bill Junior or Leonard?"

"I'm Leonard," the boy said, his head downcast.

"Where's your partner in crime?"

"Who?"

"Your brother. Where is he?"

"Don't know."

"Sure you know," John Lee said. "You two are damn near joined at the hip. I've never seen one of you when the other wasn't far away."

"I don't know where he is."

"No problem, I'm sure he's here somewhere."

"Look, if I promise not to ride the bike anymore, can you give me a break and let me go?"

"Really? First you ride out in front of me and almost get yourself run over, then you take off trying to get away from me and I had to chase you down, then we get to your house and you start running away on foot, and to top it all off, you lie about where your brother is! And you expect me to give you a break?"

The boy was about fifteen or sixteen, with unruly brown hair and a wisp of mustache on his upper lip. "I'm sorry man, I really am. That's the first time I ever rode that motorcycle. And I swear, if you let me go I won't never get in trouble again."

"Now there you go lying to me again," John Lee told him. "I've had reports about you and your brother riding that motorcycle around making all kinds of noise and raising hell."

"No, we haven't. I swear!"

"Does your daddy still work for the dairy?"

"Yes, sir. But please don't call him."

"Sorry, you had your chance to come clean and be honest with me and you blew it," John Lee said. He called dispatch to get the number of the Florida Sun Dairy, then called it on his cell phone and asked for Bill McCoy. It took a few minutes for the man to come on the line, and when he did John Lee identified himself and said, "Bill, I'm sorry have to have to tell you this, but I've got one your sons here in handcuffs. Is there any way you can come home?"

When John Lee ended the call he looked at the boy and said, "I've got a feeling you're going to wish you never woke up this morning."

The Gecko In The Corner
Chapter 27

BILL MCCOY WAS A SLENDER man with a large bald spot on top of his head and hands that were rough and coarse from years of hard labor as a mechanic for the dairy. John Lee had known him since high school, where McCoy was a year or two ahead of him, and always respected the man, who was now a single father trying to do his best. When he arrived home and got out of his pickup truck, John Lee met him and they shook hands.

"Sorry to bother you at work, Bill, but your boy has gotten himself into some trouble."

"What's going on?"

"Well, for starters, he rode that motorcycle there off some trail and right out in front of me. I damn near hit him. Then he took off like a bat out of hell and I had to chase him all the way home. And when we got here he dropped the bike and took off running."

McCoy looked at the motorcycle and then at his son, and asked, "Where the hell did you get that thing, and what's wrong with you, acting like that?"

"I'm sorry, Daddy," the boy whined.

"Yeah, you're damn sure sorry. Now answer my question. Where'd that motorcycle come from?"

"I found it."

"Where did you find it?"

"Over in the woods 'bout a mile from here."

"When?"

"I don't know, an hour or so ago, I guess."

"So you just find something and you take it, even if it doesn't belong to you?"

The boy didn't answer, just kept his head down and shuffled his feet.

"Where's your brother at?"

"I don't know."

McCoy grabbed the boy's chin in his strong hands and jerked his head up. "You look at me when you're talkin' to me, boy. Now I asked you where your brother is."

"I don't know, Daddy I swear I don't."

John Lee wondered if the man might smack his son, and though the boy certainly deserved it, he hoped he wouldn't take it too far and force him to intervene.

McCoy walked to the small wood frame house, which needed a coat of paint, and opened the door. "Bill Junior, if you're in here, you get your ass outside right now!"

There was no answer, so he walked around the side of the house to a garage that had seen better days and opened the door. His other son was cowering behind a rusted out old Ford pickup that looked like it wouldn't hold together long enough to be towed to the junkyard.

"What the hell you doing hiding back there, boy? I know you heard me calling you."

"I'm sorry, Daddy. I was scared."

"You damn well better be scared. Why aren't you two in school, anyway?"

"I don't know."

"How long have you two had that motorcycle, and where did it come from?"

"I never saw it before in my life, Daddy."

"Don't you lie to me, Bill Junior!"

"I swear Daddy, I ain't!"

"Then why were you hiding?"

"Because I was scared when I heard the siren on the police car. I thought he was here to take us in for skipping school."

"Is that the way I raised you, boy? Is it the way I raised either one of you, to not show respect for the law and for other folk's things?"

"No sir."

"You say neither one of you ever saw that motorcycle before today, but I know that's not true," John Lee said.

"We didn't!"

"We've had reports of you two running that thing up and down the road clear to midnight. And it's been going on for a while now."

"Wasn't us," Leonard said.

"Yeah, it was you," John Lee said. "I talked to someone who saw you both riding it."

"Who said that? It ain't true!"

"Yeah, it's true."

"John Lee, you got a nightstick in that police car of yours? Because if you do, I'd like to borrow it and bust these boys' heads wide open. I'm working double shifts at the dairy keepin' the trucks running so I can put a roof over you boys' head and keep you fed, and this is what you two are doing behind my back?"

Leonard started to open his mouth to deny any involvement again, but the look his father gave him made him clamp his jaw shut and keep quiet.

"You two park your asses on the tailgate of my pickup, and don't you move or say a word," McCoy ordered. He turned to John Lee and asked, "Is there any way to know where that motorcycle came from? If there is, I want to return it to its rightful owner, and I'll pay for any damage that's been done to it."

They walked over to the motorcycle and John Lee inspected it, looking for a vehicle identification number. The machine had seen better days. The seat was rotted away, there were no lights, the gas tank was dented, and the tires were so thin and cracked that he was amazed they had not disintegrated while the boys were riding it.

"Looks like it might've been a Honda at one time," he said, straightening up. "I'll call it in to see if there's any reports of it being stolen, but I doubt we're going to find out anything, Bill. If there was ever a serial number on it someplace, I can't find it. Look here, the frame's all bent and twisted to hell, and it looks like that happened a long time ago. I don't doubt it's a junker somebody dumped somewhere and your boys found it."

"Even so, this bullshit of running from you, and both of them lying like they did, there's no excuse for that. I try, John Lee, I really do. We're shorthanded at the dairy and I'm working twelve to sixteen hours a day. I had no idea this stuff was going on or I'd a put a stop to it. Ever since their Mama died two years ago those boys have given me fits."

John Lee remembered Margie from their school days, a friendly and intelligent girl with a real talent for art who always had a smile for everyone and passed up a chance for a scholarship to marry her high school sweetheart. She worked at the post office as a substitute mail carrier on the rural routes around Somerton County and it seemed like every dog on every route knew when she was filling in for the regular mail carrier. They all waited at the side of the road in front of their homes for her to come by and give them a treat from the big bag of dog biscuits she kept in her vehicle. Margie had always seemed like one of the happiest people he knew, but when she discovered the lump in her left breast, it began a long journey down a dark path for her. Radiation, chemotherapy, surgery, none of it had worked, and in less than a year she was gone.

"Can you tell me who reported it? I want to take those boys to them and make them apologize."

"Well, Bill, there's kind of a problem there. The person who reported it really didn't want his name used."

"Why's that? I get along good with all my neighbors. 'Least I try to."

"Well, maybe not all of them."

"I have no idea... wait, was it Arley Dawson?"

"Why do you think that?"

"I don't know, we used to be friends, then he got a bee in his bonnet about something a year or so ago and we haven't said a word to each other since."

"What did he get mad about?"

"Hell if I know! He just stopped talking me, so I stopped talking to him. I don't go pushing myself on someone who don't

The Gecko In The Corner

want nothing to do with me. Truth be told, I miss old Arley. He's a pretty good old boy."

"You know what? That's funny, because that's pretty much what he said about you. Said you're a fine man. I'm thinking that since neither one of you seems to remember what the problem is, or was, maybe the two of you ought to just sit down on the porch and have a couple beers and talk. Good neighbors and good friends are hard to come by, Bill."

"Ain't it the truth, John Lee? Ain't it the truth? Arley was one of the pallbearers at Margie's funeral. Him and Gloria was there for us every step of the way."

"I think if I had a friend like that, I'd do whatever it takes to mend fences."

Bill nodded. "You're right. I think before I beat their asses, maybe I'll take those two worthless boys of mine into town and stop and see Arley. I think all three of us owe him an apology."

"I think that's a good idea," John Lee said.

"Now if you want to take Leonard to jail for running from you, I got no argument with you about that, John Lee. Might teach him a lesson."

"I could, Bill. But I've got a feeling the kindest thing I can do for that boy is get him away from you right now. And to tell you the truth, I'm just not feeling all that kindly towards him."

They shook hands and John Lee got in his Charger and started to back out of the driveway when he noticed something and stopped. McCoy looked at him curiously, and John Lee pulled forward again and put his window down.

"Bill, do you have a riding lawnmower?"

"No I don't. Why?"

"I didn't see it before, but as I was backing out I saw there's a riding lawnmower back there behind the corner of your garage."

"There can't be. I got an old push mower that I need to rebuild the engine on. Damn thing hardly runs. That's it."

John Lee got out of his car and they walked behind the garage.

"Son of a bitch!"

"I hate to tell you this, Bill," John Lee said, looking at the Toro riding mower, "but I think your boys have been up to more than just skipping school and riding a motorcycle around bothering the neighbors."

The Gecko In The Corner
Chapter 28

JOHN LEE WAS HALFWAY THROUGH his shift by the time he brought the McCoy brothers to town, booked them, and lodged them in the segregated cellblock that once held black prisoners but was now used for minors and female prisoners. Then he returned to the McCoy house, where Bill had already loaded the Toro onto a trailer hitched to his pickup truck, and they drove to Rafe Peterson's house.

"You got my lawnmower back! I thought I'd never see it again! That's fine work, John Lee. Was it them two guys that broke into your house?"

"No sir, it wasn't," John Lee told him. "Rafe, this is Bill McCoy. He lives over on Wildflower Road."

"Yeah, I know Bill. How you doin'?"

"Not too good right now," McCoy said. "Turns out it was my two boys that swiped your lawnmower. I wanted to bring it back myself and apologize to you."

John Lee did not know what to expect, given Rafe's quick temper, but the man just shook his head and said, "Damn, I'm sorry to hear that, Bill. I know you've had enough troubles, what with losin' Margie and everything."

"Life is full of troubles," McCoy said. "I looked it over real good and I don't see any damage to it, Rafe. But if there is, I'll be more than happy to fix it, or pay whatever it costs you to get it fixed, or whatever suits you."

Rafe looked the machine over and shrugged his shoulders. "Don't look any worse than it did before."

"Those boys of mine are sittin' in the jail, and I told John Lee here they need to stay there for a while. I'm really sorry about this, Rafe."

"Don't you pay it no mind. Bill. I done some hell raising when I was a youngster, too. And I imagine you and John Lee here did some of it yourselves. We're good."

The men shook hands, and John Lee left them there and drove back toward town. He was almost to the high school when Ramon's cell phone rang. He pulled to the shoulder of the road and looked at the Caller ID. "M" was calling.

"Hello."

"Deputy Quarrels?"

"That's me."

"You have something that belongs to me."

"If you mean those two thugs you sent to break into my house, they're locked up in a jail cell."

"I don't care about them. You know what I'm talking about."

"No, I don't. But I sure wish you'd tell me what the hell's going on."

"Where is your father?"

"Who are you?"

"I am somebody your father stole a lot of money from."

"Then I believe your problem is with my father, not me."

"I think maybe my problem is with both of you. I want my money. All of it."

"You never did tell me your name."

"My name is not important. What is important is that you understand that I want my money and if I don't get it back immediately, I will make you very sorry you were ever born."

"You talk real big for a man who doesn't have the balls to even tell me his name," John Lee said. "So let me lay it on the line for you. Until he showed up at my house a few nights ago, I had not seen my father since I was a baby. You or some of your people had worked him over pretty good, but he wouldn't tell me anything about what happened to him. Then he disappeared again without a word. The next thing I know, you've got Frick and Frack or whoever the hell those two guys are showing up at my place. I warned them the first time not to come back, but they did anyway. I could have easily shot them last night, and I would've been within my rights. I won't be so kind the next time around. Whatever it is you're looking for, I told you, I don't have it. And I don't know where my father is. End of story."

"No, the story is far from over," the other man said. "I want my money and I will have it. The only question is how much you will have to suffer before I get it."

With that he ended the call.

***

John Lee's stomach was turning over, soured by all of the coffee and the two Red Bulls he had downed to get enough caffeine in him to stay awake and alert. But he still knew he felt better than Greg Carson when he stopped by the deputy's parents' house to check up on him.

Greg's face was even more bruised and swollen than it had been the night before, and between that and the many bug bites, his eyes were little more than slits. Still, he managed to smile when he saw John Lee.

"How you doing, buddy?"

"I've had better days," Greg admitted.

"Well, I have to say, you're not quite as pretty as you used to be."

"I heard you and Maddy caught a couple burglars at your house."

"Yeah, it was a long night," John Lee said.

"D.W. was here a little while ago, and Andy and Bob, and some of the other guys. They said your house got pretty messed up."

"Yeah, but I was never much of a housekeeper anyhow. It probably didn't look much better before they broke in."

"John Lee, I'm really sorry about what happened."

"Hey, it's not your fault. You didn't tell them to break in."

"No, I mean out there on the highway with me. When that guy took off running I just started chasing him without thinking. Then we got in that brush and he come up behind me out of nowhere and the next thing I know he's all over me. I didn't have a chance to get to my gun or anything. Once he took off running again I managed to get on my radio and call for help. That's the last thing I remember until Maddy and Andy were there. I know I really screwed up. "

"Shit happens," John Lee said. "All that matters is that you're okay."

"No, that's not all that matters," Greg said, shaking his head. "I could've gotten myself killed out there. But worse than that, you guys could have gotten hurt going after him because of me. I really let you guys down."

"Stop that," John Lee said sternly. "You screwed up, okay? Life goes on. You can't change the past, Greg, but you can learn from it. I bet you won't make the same mistake again."

"John Lee, do you think I'm really cut out to be a deputy?"

"Hell yes I do! Don't even start thinking that way, Greg. We all screw up sooner or later. It happens. But you're a good deputy. I've worked a lot of shifts with you, and I'll tell you right now, if I need backup, there's nobody I'd trust more than you. I mean that. Now you get some rest and get back on your feet again. We need you out there. Got it?"

Greg smiled and nodded his head. "Yeah, John Lee, I got it. Thanks."

***

As he was pulling out of the Carson driveway his cell phone rang. The Caller ID said it was Shania Jones.

"Hey there, pretty lady. What's up?"

"I've been tied up in a conference all day. We just took a break and I heard on the news about Greg being hurt. How is he?"

"He's banged up a little bit, but he'll be okay," John Lee assured her. "In fact, I just left his place."

"What happened, John Lee?"

"He stopped to help somebody with a flat tire, and it turned out to be a doper in a stolen car. The perp took off running and

Greg went after him. The guy jumped him, beat him with a tire iron, and then left him there."

"The news said you guys caught him. Were you there?"

"Oh yeah, I was there. We caught up to him when he was standing in a swamp whining that he had seen an alligator and was afraid it was going to eat him. Damn city boys ought to stay where they belong and not come out here and get in trouble."

He heard Shania sigh, then she said, "I'm sorry about Greg getting hurt. But I have to tell you, John Lee, when the newscaster said the next story was something about a Somerton County deputy being injured, my heart just stopped. I was afraid it was you."

"Oh, so you really do love me, huh?"

There was silence for a moment, the first time he could ever remember her not having some witty comeback. Then she said, "Seriously, John Lee, I was terrified something had happened to you."

"Because you love me, right?"

"I don't know about that, but I think my father might. He keeps asking me when you're going to come around for another visit."

"That's because the man knows quality when he sees it," John Lee told her.

"Yeah, I can tell you're okay, same line of BS as always."

"What can I say? I am what I am."

"Well, I'm just glad you didn't get hurt. I really was worried about you."

"No need to be, I'm fine," he assured her. "It's part of the job, Shania. I know what I'm doing out here."

"Still... look, just be careful, okay?"

"Okay."

"Promise?"

"I promise. Now what else is going on?"

"Just this stupid conference. It's all about budgets and ways to work more efficiently and save money, and all the while I keep thinking we've got 60 people sitting here wasting time rehashing the same stuff over and over that's just common sense anyway, and wondering how much taxpayer money is being wasted in salaries and transportation for everybody to be here when we could be doing something productive instead."

"Bureaucracy is a beautiful thing, isn't it?"

"No, it's not," she replied, "it's a pain in the rear end."

"This too shall pass," he told her.

"Not soon enough. Sorry, John Lee, I've got to run. We've still got one session left. Call me and let's see if we can get together in the next couple of days."

"Maybe we can sneak away and meet in the middle and grab lunch someplace, if nothing else," he suggested.

"Or we could just meet in the middle and grab each other," she teased.

"Is that an offer or are you just pulling my leg?"

"Well, for now it's just your leg I'm pulling on. Talk to you later, John Lee."

In spite of the fact that he was worn out, his stomach was on fire, and his fatigued body felt like someone had beat him with a rubber hose, he couldn't help but smile. If nothing else, Shania knew how to keep him on his toes.

The Gecko In The Corner
Chapter 29

JOHN LEE MANAGED TO MAKE it through his shift and spent the last hour at the office writing up reports on that morning's traffic accident, the vandalized mailboxes, his encounter with Leonard McCoy, the theft and recovery of Rafe Peterson's lawnmower, and the arrest of the McCoy brothers. Then he wrote a secondary report on the burglary at his home and the arrest of the two suspects. He didn't have much to add, leaving his previous encounter with them and the subsequent telephone conversations with the mysterious "M" out of it.

With that done he walked down to the cellblock to check on the prisoners. The McCoy brothers were both sitting on one of the cots in their cell looking frightened and pitiful.

"You boys having a good time in there?"

"No, sir," Leonard said. "Do you know when we get to go home?"

"Might as well make yourselves comfortable," John Lee told them. "You're going to be in there overnight and tomorrow you get to see the judge. After that, it's up to him."

"Please just let us go home. I promise we won't get in any more trouble."

"Sorry, boys, you had plenty of chances to do the right thing and you didn't take them. I don't think you boys know how good you've got it. Yeah, your mother passed away, and that was a terrible thing, no doubt about it. I knew her and she was a fine lady. But your dad busts his ass every day trying to take care of you two, and you don't appreciate it at all. Neither my mother or father were ever around when I was growing up. Neither one of them had time for me. Your dad could've done the same thing, but he didn't. He's buried under a mountain of bills from your mom's medical expenses and he's working himself to death to pay them and to do right by you boys. He deserves a lot better than what he gets from you two. You should be ashamed of yourselves. You sit there and think about that."

John Lee left them and went to the adult cellblock, where Ramon and his companion were in separate cells, one on each side of the cell Jamie Bowers occupied. The two men he and Maddie had arrested at his house were both silent and refused to answer any of his questions, but Bowers was just as belligerent as he had been all along.

"I want to talk to the sheriff! You tell him to get down here. My rights are bein' violated."

"The sheriff doesn't usually take orders from me, and I don't think he really gives a rat's ass what you want," John Lee told him.

"Yeah? Well you just wait and see, mister. I'm goin' to file a federal lawsuit against him and you, and everybody in this place. Time I'm done with you guys, you'll be the ones sittin' behind bars!"

"You know what, I wish we would've left your sorry ass out there for the alligators," John Lee told him. "Only reason we didn't was because we didn't want them to eat you and then be puking all over the swamp."

"That right there is verbal harassment! I'm keepin' track of all this. Yes sir, I am. That's another nail in your coffin, buddy."

John Lee ignored him and stopped in front of Ramon's cell again on his way out. "I don't know about you, but if I was in your place I'd be telling everything I know just to get away from that loudmouth in the next cell."

"I heard that," Bowers shouted. "More verbal abuse. I'm keepin' track of all this!"

Ramon didn't say anything.

Back upstairs, John Lee saw Flag and asked if they had an identification on Ramon's companion or any more information about either one of them.

"Nothin' on that Indian or whatever the hell he is. But the other guy, that Ramon Sainz, Stringer was right about him having done time before. So besides the burglary charge, we've got him for bein' a felon in possession of a firearm."

D.W. came out of his office and saw them talking and walked up to where they stood, looking to head off another confrontation. He seemed relieved when it was apparent there wasn't going to be one.

"That was good work you did, recovering that stolen lawnmower," he told John Lee.

"I just got lucky. But I really feel sorry for Bill McCoy. He's carrying a lot of weight on his shoulders."

"Bill's a good man," Flag said, one of the few times John Lee could ever remember the chief deputy having something good to say about anybody. "Damn shame the cards he's been dealt. First losin' his wife like he did, and then those two maggots he's raise'n. Only a matter of time 'till those two get put away."

"Well, I like to think everybody's capable of turnin' their lives around," D.W. said. "Who knows? Maybe gettin' in trouble now might be the best thing ever happened to those boys. Might be a wake-up call for 'em."

Flag snorted and said scornfully, "Don't hold your breath."

"Probably not," the sheriff said, "but there's always hope. John Lee, you look dead on your feet. Go ahead and go home and get yourself some rest."

"Yeah, I need it," he admitted. "I'll see you guys tomorrow."

***

Herb Quarrels was startled when he saw his face in the bathroom mirror. The bruises had faded away, but he looked like he had aged at least twenty years. And he felt like it had been more like fifty.

This couldn't go on forever, moving from one cheap motel to another, jumping every time he heard a door slam, sleeping in catnaps day after day because he was afraid if he fell into a deep sleep he wouldn't hear them coming for him. He had no appetite and his pants fit so loosely that he had to punch two more holes in his belt just to cinch it tight enough to keep them up.

He had to do something. But what? He could turn himself in and face the consequences of what he had done, but he knew that if he did that Torres would find a way to get to him. How much would it take to convince some convict to slit his throat? Probably not much. But what other options did he have? Until this mess had begun he had lived a quiet suburban life. He was not cut out for a life on the run.

But at the same time, things had gone so far that he knew he could never go home again. And really, what had there ever been for him back there? Whatever affection there might have been between him and Karen years ago had long since disappeared, drowned in bitterness and recrimination. Nothing he ever did was good enough for her. He worked too many hours, because he preferred the comfort of his small office and the numbers he dealt with to the hostility that greeted him every time he walked in the front door of his house. And while she complained about his hours, when he was home Karen complained that he was underfoot. If he sat down in his recliner to watch television she ran the vacuum through the living room, drowning out the sound. If he opened a book to read, she turned the television on loud to some inane talk show or reality program. Home had not been a refuge for him for longer than he could remember. It was just a place to endure every night until he went back to work the next morning.

And Jason? He was his mother's son to the very bone. The boy had never shown him any respect growing up, and every time Herb tried to discipline him because he had ignored his schoolwork or his chores, or had gotten into trouble, Karen had gone on the attack like a mother bear protecting her cub. No wonder he turned out the way he did.

He pulled the suitcase out from under the bed and stared at it. Most people would see it as the ticket to a brand-new life. All Herb saw was a ticking time bomb. One that was going to blow up in his face sooner or later.

He had been over this a hundred times in his mind, trying to figure out what to do, and he always came back to the same thing. Talk to John Lee, lay it all out for him, and see what he had to suggest. But he couldn't do that. It wasn't fair. It hadn't been fair to go to him in the first place and Herb regretted it. He stared at the cheap prepaid telephone on the nightstand, and started to reach for it like he had a dozen times before. And like every time, he stopped himself. No, he had to figure this out on his own.

***

John Lee turned into his driveway, wondering if he would have the energy to park his car and then walk all the way to the house. Then he saw the vehicles waiting for him and stopped. Maddy's car was there, as well as Beth Ann's ten year old blue Ford Focus and his grandfather's old rattletrap Jeep Wagoneer that had been built sometime in the early 1960s and seen a lifetime of hard use.

"This can't be good," he said aloud, and was tempted to back out onto the road and drive away from whatever awaited him inside. But he was just too damn tired to do so. He took a deep breath and parked in his usual spot and got out of the Charger.

"Well, hey there," Beth Ann said when he came through the door. She had a dust rag in one hand and a spray can of furniture polish in the other. John Lee looked around the living room and could not believe what he was seeing. The couch and loveseat and his recliner were in their places, their slit upholstery covered with sheets, The room had been cleaned to the point where there was little evidence of the damage the intruders had done the night before.

Maddy came out of the guest bedroom and said, "I don't think it's ready for one of those beautiful home magazines, but we did the best we could and I think you can live with it for now."

"You two did all this?"

"Well, most of it," Maddy told him. "Paw Paw took your truck into Perry and bought new mattresses and box springs for the beds, and Mama Nell is at the grocery store now buying stuff to replace what we had to throw out."

"How? Why?"

"What can I say, John Lee? For some stupid reason, I guess a lot of us love you," Beth Ann said. "When Daddy told me what happened here I came over to see if I could help straighten the place out a little bit, and Maddy was already here clean'n away. Turns out we make a pretty good team. Then the next thing I knew, Paw Paw and Mama Nell showed up. She was mighty pissed that you didn't take a day off and get some rest, what with everything happenin' on top of you have'n the runs and all that a couple days ago. She took one look at the kitchen and started throwing stuff in trash bags, sayin' she wasn't gonna have you eatin' food that those burglars had touched. Said there's no tellin' what kind of cooties they might be carryin'."

John Lee was blown away and didn't know what to say.

"Here, you sit yourself down and just relax," Beth Ann said, leading him to his recliner.

As he sat he heard hammering coming from the direction of the kitchen and looked that way.

"That's Paw Paw hanging a new door," Maddy told him. "He said the old one was too messed up to try to fix."

John Lee started to get up and Maddy pushed him back into his chair. "Just sit, John Lee," she ordered. "You're dead on your feet."

"I'm okay," he protested, trying to rise again.

She pushed him back a second time and asked, "Do I have to handcuff you to make you behave?"

John Lee tried to think of a smart reply, but he just didn't have it in him. He closed his eyes and fell sound asleep.

Chapter 30

THE SOUND OF MAGIC BARKING and a vehicle in his driveway woke John Lee up just as his nostrils picked up the delicious smell of frying bacon and coffee. How did he get in his bed? The last thing he remembered was sitting down in his recliner. No, wait, he had gotten up sometime in the night and gone to the bathroom, then crawled into his bed. He looked at his bedside clock and saw it was a little before 7 AM. Pulling on underwear and jeans, he went into the living room and noticed a pillow and blanket on the sofa.

"Good morning, sleepyhead," Maddy said, poking her head in from the kitchen.

"Did you stay here all night?"

"Yeah, I slept on the couch. I think Beth Ann and I were trying to outlast each other, but you were snoring away so loud that I guess she decided nothing else was going to happen anyhow, so she left around 10 o'clock."

"I don't snore."

"Well then somebody built a railroad track right through the living room when you weren't looking, because *something* was making a lot of noise in here!"

"You didn't have to stay," he said. "Christ, Maddy, you didn't have to do any of this. Not that I don't appreciate it, but... "

"I did it because I wanted to, John Lee. Besides," she said with a wink and a smile, "this is all part of my master plan. I'm thinking this'll be two days in a row I made you breakfast. Who knows? You might decide you like being spoiled and keep me around for a while."

He heard more noise from outside and looked out to see a ladder going up from the front deck. "What the hell?"

He opened the door to see his grandfather climbing up the ladder with a tool belt around his waist.

"What are you doing, Paw Paw?"

"Oh, hey, Morning, John Lee."

"Good morning. What are you doing?"

"I'm fixing this place of yours up so that nobody can come sneaking around again."

"How about you come down off that ladder before you break your neck?"

"What's it with you and ladders these days? I told you the other day I never broke my neck climbing up power poles in the rain and the wind and everything else for more than thirty years. Don't reckon I'm going to fall off a ladder at this point."

"Maybe not, but if you do I'd rather you not do it on my deck. I've got enough stuff to clean up around here."

Paw Paw might have argued with John Lee, but Maddy came out on the deck and said, "Coffee's hot and bacon's ready. Are you two going to help me eat it or do I have to do it all by myself?"

They followed her into the kitchen, where she started serving thick buttermilk pancakes, crisp bacon fried to perfection, and mugs of coffee.

"Damn, now this is the way to start the day! A man don't get fed like this everywhere. If I were you, John Lee, I'd keep her around."

"I'm trying to convince him that's a good idea," Maddy said, bumping John Lee with her hip as she moved to her chair and sat down.

Trying to change the subject, he asked, "Now tell me again, Paw Paw, why are you climbing a ladder up the side of my house at 7 o'clock in the morning?"

"I told you, I'm going to fix this place up so nobody can come sneaking up on you again. Look here." He pulled yellow sheets of notebook paper from the pocket of his bib overalls and smoothed them out on the table. "I'm gonna put motion detection security lights up all the way around the house. I'll have them staggered and aimed in such a way that most of the yard is covered. I'm going to install switches inside the front and back door, and one in your bedroom, so you can control them without even getting out of bed. By the way, do you know there's a lizard in your bedroom?"

"Yeah, it's a gecko."

"If you know it's in there why don't you throw it out?"

"I don't know," John Lee said. "They're supposed to be good luck or something."

"After seeing what those guys did to your house, I think you need to get yourself a new gecko. The one you've got ain't working."

"Look, Paw Paw, you really don't have to be doing all this."

"Yes, I do. I don't want you getting caught with your pants down if those two goons come back. Literally or figuratively."

"I appreciate that, Paw Paw, but I wasn't even home when those guys showed up."

"I know it. But those lights coming on would've scared most people away if they were up to no good."

John Lee wanted to tell him that Ramon and his partner were not *most* people, but before he could, Paw Paw said, "And that's not all. Look at this." He laid out a brochure for a home security system. "There are gonna be cameras mounted outside covering the entire property, and inside, too. And an alarm system with sensors on every door and window. I was gonna go with motion detectors inside, but that wouldn't work with Magic being in here. But don't worry about that, you really don't need them. The way I'm laying this out, if somebody comes in, an audible alarm is going to sound, and there's going to be a transmitter that will send a message and video to your cell phone and to mine. And I've got a bunch of rebar out in the back of your pickup truck to make bars for your windows."

"You're not putting bars up on my house."

"Don't worry, I'll paint 'em black and they'll look fine."

"Forget it, Paw Paw. I spend enough time putting people behind bars at work, I'm not going to live behind them at home."

"Okay. If you say so. That's probably just overkill anyway. Electronic security will do the job."

"That's gonna cost a lot of money," John Lee objected.

"Not nearly as much as you'd think. I can buy most of the components dirt cheap online and rig it all up myself. And you're not going to have to pay any kind of monitoring cost, which is where those burglar alarm companies really get you."

"Paw Paw..."

"I know what you're thinking, but you don't have to worry about that," his grandfather assured him. "I can't be looking at what you're doing here from my phone unless you arm the system. So whatever you and your lady friend here are up to, you're safe. I won't be peeking."

"Paw Paw, it's not like that. Maddy and I are just friends."

"Um huh. I believe you, John Lee. I believe everything you tell me."

"He's telling you the truth," Maddy said. "Don't get me wrong, Paw Paw, I've been trying to get him to let me jump his bones from way back when I first learned about things like that. But he just keeps resisting me."

"Really? I thought you were smarter than that, John Lee."

"You'd think, wouldn't you?" Maddy asked. "But it's probably just as well you can't spy on him with that fancy security system you're putting in. The way I hear it, John Lee has a *lot* of slumber parties, if you get my drift."

John Lee felt his face redden, and Paw Paw and Maddy both enjoyed his discomfort.

"I guess when this boy was growing up, I somehow forgot to teach him that there's quantity and then there's quality. Hard to believe he's going for quantity instead of quality." He smiled and winked at Maddy.

In another attempt to change the subject, John Lee asked, "Where's Mama Nell? Does she know you're over here climbing up and down ladders?"

"Your grandma is headed for some casino in Biloxi," Paw Paw said. "They got some kind of Elvis impersonator over there this weekend who's supposed to be so much like the real thing that if you close your eyes you can't tell the difference. Of course, Mama Nell can tell, but she had to go see for herself."

That was Mama Nell. She made an annual pilgrimage to Graceland, and if there was an Elvis impersonator or tribute artist performing anywhere from Miami to Biloxi, you would find her in the front row. Mama Nell didn't like to fly, but she earned a lot of air miles going back and forth to Las Vegas. She never gambled, but Sin City had some of the best Elvis revues anywhere.

"Mama Nell was the one that said I needed to install some kind of security around here," Paw Paw said, then his face grew serious. "Look, John Lee, I'm not dumb. We all know it wasn't a coincidence, this happening so soon after your father showed up. Those weren't just burglars. Mama Nell and I are both going to sleep better knowing you got some kind of protection."

"Protection? I've got enough guns to start World War III. And did you happen to notice the big German Shepherd sitting there next to you hoping you'll give him a piece of bacon."

"Yeah, I know all that. I also know Maddy spent the night here to back you up in case somebody else came. This is just one more layer of security, John Lee. And I'm not taking no for an answer. I don't know what your father got himself mixed up in, but whatever it is, I think that's what's behind what happened here."

"Look, Paw Paw, if you insist on putting this system in, at least let me pay you for the parts and wait until my next days off and I'll help."

"I'll have the lights up and most of it wired by the time you get off duty tonight. I'll order the sensors and cameras and transmitter and such and it will be here in a couple of days. If you're around you can help me with that. And I'll tell you what, instead of you paying me back, how about you just let me dance with this pretty girl at your wedding, and you two name your firstborn son after me?"

"You've got a deal," Maddy said sticking her hand across the table to shake Paw Paw's.

"You two seem to be jumping to a lot of conclusions," John Lee said. "Don't I get a say in any of this?"

"Hush up and eat your breakfast," Maddy said. "We both have to be to work soon."

Paw Paw smiled broadly from across the table and said, "Yep, she's gonna make you a fine wife someday, John Lee. She's already got ordering you around down pat!"

The Gecko In The Corner
Chapter 31

His cell phone rang again, and Miguel stared at the display on the screen. What should he do? Esteban was no fool. He knew something was amiss, and the longer Miguel tried to stall him, the worse it was going to be. But then, how much worse could it get? Miguel shuddered. He did not want to think about that. Reluctantly, he pushed the button to answer the call.

"Good morning, Esteban."

"It pleases me to learn you are not dead, Miguel. But I am confused. If you are not dead, why were you not here yesterday as I expected?"

"I apologize. There has been a... a complication."

"A complication?"

"Yes, but nothing I cannot handle."

"Was this complication so great that you could not call me and tell me you would be delayed? I may be an old man, Miguel, but I do not have time to sit here waiting for you to call me. Do you think I am some foolish schoolgirl sitting at home waiting hopefully for someone to call and offer me a date? Is that what you think I am, Miguel? A foolish girl?"

"No, Esteban. Of course not."

"Then maybe you think I am a feeble old man who is no longer capable of taking care of his affairs?"

"No, Esteban. I assure you, I think nothing like that."

"Then why is it you are avoiding me, Miguel? What is this great complication that is so important that you have forgotten your obligations to your benefactor?"

"Oh no, Esteban. I have not forgotten. I would never do that."

"This is what you tell me, but that is what you did. I am concerned, Miguel. First you cancel our regular appointment because you are sick. And then I hear only silence from Orlando. When we talked the last time, you assured me that this illness of yours would be past and we would be back on schedule. But now you tell me there is some sort of complication which has caused you to miss our meeting. Our *second* meeting. Tell me about this complication, Miguel. I will be interested to know what is so important that you have let me down."

"It is my nephew, Ramon."

"What about him?"

"He has... gotten himself into some difficulty."

"That is too bad. But what does that have to do with me? What does it have to do with you not honoring your commitments to me?"

Miguel's mind was racing, trying to come up with something that Esteban might believe, even if it was only long enough to buy him a little more time. "While I was sick, his poor wife died."

"That is unfortunate. But these things happen. People die every day, Miguel."

"I know that. But the timing was very bad."

"Is there ever a good time for something like that?"

"No, of course not. But I was sick, and Ramon was helping to manage things for me. After Gabriella died, I guess the shock was too much for him. He just disappeared. I learned just yesterday that he is in jail in a place called Somerton in the northern part of the state."

"In jail for what?"

"There was some difficulty with a sheriff's deputy. I don't have all the details yet, but apparently he has been accused of breaking into this man's home."

"Why would he do that? A man loses his wife and he travels out of town to break into a policeman's home? That makes no sense, Miguel."

"At times like these, maybe sometimes a man's mind leaves him for a while. I don't know what his reason was, but I am worried that he might say something foolish while he is locked up."

"Foolish? What are you saying to me, Miguel?"

"Only that I hope he would not betray our confidence about things that happen in our day to day business operations."

"I see. So you are telling me that this nephew of yours, this man who shares your blood, this man who you entrusted to help fill your position when you were sick, would talk to the police to save himself from such a small charge as burglary?"

"I would hope not. But still, it is a possibility. So I felt I must go to Somerton and deal with the situation before anything like that could happen. That is the only reason I was not able to make it to our meeting. I felt it so urgent that I neglected to call you. For that I apologize. But I assure you that the situation will be dealt with today and things will be back on track by this time tomorrow."

"Your promises mean nothing to me at this point," Esteban said bitterly. "What I'm hearing, if this story of yours is even true, is that you placed your trust in someone who cannot be depended upon. Someone who could expose you to the authorities. That is what I'm hearing, Miguel. And that makes me wonder about you. Maybe you cannot be trusted either."

"Oh no, Esteban. You know me. You know my loyalty to you. You have been like a father to me. You know my ability to keep things flowing well on my end. I am very disappointed in Ramon for doing such a foolish thing. And maybe I am just overreacting in my fear that something could leak out about our business. But as they say, it is better to be safe than sorry. That is why I took this upon myself. Even though Ramon is my own blood, as you said, he is nothing to me when it comes to our business affairs."

"That is comforting to know," Esteban replied. "Sometimes one has to eliminate problems, even if one shares the same blood with them."

"It is unfortunate, but what you say is true."

"Yes. And sometimes... sometimes one has to eliminate problems even if those problems do not share your blood, but claim to be like a son to you."

Miguel felt a chill run down his spine and he had to swallow twice before he could reply. "Please, Esteban, I beg of you your patience. Let me handle this situation and then we can meet and put this little difficulty behind us and be back to the way things should be."

"I would like to see that happen, Miguel. I truly would. But in the meantime, what about your obligations to me? What about certain things that are owed to me? Am I supposed to just forget about them?"

"Of course not! I take full responsibility for all of this. Instead of the usual percentage due to you, I will make sure that there will be more as compensation for your patience."

"That's very generous of you," Esteban said. "You are offering to let me have more of my own money. Now it seems you are becoming *my* benefactor. Maybe you think I'm just a foolish old man who needs somebody like you to take care of him."

"No! No, not at all, Esteban! My apologies if that is the way it sounded. I only meant..."

"Enough of this," Esteban shouted. "My patience is exhausted with you. Deal with this problem quickly and then come to see me. But I am warning you now, Miguel, do not waste any more of my time! Every hour I wait for this to be resolved will only make it worse for you."

Miguel started to acknowledge the old man's words, but he was speaking to a dead telephone. Esteban had broke the connection and ended the call. He looked at his bodyguard and said, "Drive faster. We need to get there as quickly as we can."

The Gecko In The Corner
Chapter 32

WHILE THE DAY BEFORE HAD been busy, this one took a slower pace. The first two calls of the day had been minor issues, one a report of a dog killing the neighbor's chickens, and the other an out-of-town motorist who had locked her keys in her car after stopping at a fruit stand to purchase oranges and grapefruit to take back home to her family in Indianapolis. John Lee had told the owner of the dog to keep it chained up and suggested that the neighbor who had lost his chickens take civil action to be compensated if the two of them could not work out some sort of equitable arrangement between them. He had used a thin strip of metal called a slim jim to unlock the tourist's car.

Just before lunch he was in the courtroom when the McCoy brothers were brought before the judge. Their father had already talked to them and they pled guilty. Judge Taylor knew Bill McCoy, and like everyone in Somerton County, respected him and was aware of his hardships.

"The easy thing to do would be to give you boys a fine, but that's just going to be one more expense your father has to pay," he said, looking sternly at the boys. "So this is what I'm going to do, I'm going to put you both on one year's probation, and I'm going to give you each 500 hours of community service. I will let Sheriff Swindle decide what that will be, and his department will handle scheduling and things like that. But my suggestion to him is going to be that you boys use an old-fashioned non-powered push lawnmower to keep the lawns mowed at the courthouse, at the school, at the park, and anywhere else in town he thinks needs it. In addition, both of you are going to apologize to your father, you're going to go to each neighbor up and down your road and apologize in person for disturbing them with that motorcycle you were riding around on, and you are going to go to Mister Peterson's house and apologize to him for stealing his lawnmower.

I'm also going to have my court clerk contact the school and let the folks there know that anytime either one of you boys is absent, I want the school to call me. And believe me, if you're not in a hospital or sick in bed under a doctor's care, we are going to revisit your situation. Maybe a year or two in juvenile detention might make you wake up. Do you understand me?"

Both boys nodded their heads dejectedly and the judge repeated loudly, "Do you understand me?"

"Yes, sir," they replied in unison.

"Good. Now get out of here."

John Lee shook Bill McCoy's hand and left the courtroom. As soon as he stepped out into the hall he was approached by two men wearing suits.

"Deputy Quarrels?"

"That's me. What can I do for you?"

They both showed him gold badges and identification cards. "Special Agents Thalman and Barber with the Federal Bureau of Investigation. We need to talk."

***

Special Agent Ron Thalman had dark hair and looked to be in his mid-40s, an average looking man in every way except for a very noticeable crescent-shaped scar under his left eye. Terry Barber was younger, had closely cropped blonde hair, and looked like he had just graduated from Quantico. They were seated in an interview room at the Sheriff's Department, and John Lee was sure that Sheila Sharp had already alerted half the town that he had visitors from the FBI.

"What's this about?" John Lee already knew the answer, but felt like he had to ask anyway.

"When was last time you saw your father, Deputy?"

When they approached him in the courthouse, John Lee had to decide quickly how he was going to handle things. Not letting D.W. and Flag know about his father's visit was one thing, lying to the feds was something else entirely. And besides, he suspected they already knew a lot more about whatever his father was involved in than he did. And while he didn't know all that was going on, he was smart enough to know that he was in over his head.

"He showed up at my house about eight days ago in the middle of the night," John Lee told them, and then gave them a full account of his father's mysterious visit, the injuries he had suffered, his evasiveness, and how he had just as quickly disappeared without a word.

"Before that, when was the last time you talked to him?"

"I don't remember ever talking to him before that."

"What do you mean?"

John Lee told them about his parents' divorce when he was very young and about how Herb Quarrels had never been a part of his life.

"That's very interesting," Special Agent Barber said.

"I don't know if it's really that interesting," John Lee replied. "It's been my experience that a lot of fathers aren't involved in their children's lives after a divorce."

"That's true. But most of them probably don't put over a million dollars in a bank account in their kids' names."

"A million bucks? Not in my account, he didn't. Last time I looked, I had somewhere around $900 in the bank."

Barber opened a file folder and slid a sheet of paper across the table to John Lee. He looked at it and shook his head in shock. It was a statement from a bank in Cincinnati, Ohio showing a balance of $1,125,000 in an account with his name on it.

"I have no idea what this is all about. But I never heard of this bank and I never knew anything about this until just now. What the hell is going on?"

"That's what we're trying to figure out," Special Agent Thalman said. "Have you ever heard of a company called Zelina Acquisition Services?"

"The name's familiar, but I don't know where from," John Lee told him

"How about a man named Miguel Torres?"

"I don't know that name, but I think I may have talked to him yesterday," John Lee told him.

"You talked to Miguel Torres?"

"I won't swear to it," John Lee said, then told them about the burglary at his house, about calling the mysterious "M" the night he and Maddie caught the burglars, about keeping the cell phones, and about "M" calling him back the day before on Ramon's cell phone claiming that John Lee had something that belonged to him and saying that Herb Quarrels had stolen a lot of money from him. When he was done he said, "Okay guys, I'm not holding back on you. How about you tell me what's happening?"

He had expected to be stonewalled. He had always heard that the FBI played their cards close to the vest and never wanted to share information with local police agencies. So he was surprised when Thalman said, "I think maybe you'd better tell the dispatcher you're going to be tied up for a while yet. It's a long story."

Chapter 33

Herb stared at the laptop's screen in horror. He had bought the computer at one of the big box stores, paying cash, and logged on to the Internet with the motel's Wi-Fi. A Cleveland news station's site was showing photos of the shell of a burned house. *His* house! He read the story quickly, then read it a second time. According to the report, there had been an explosion just before the fire erupted. The fire marshal said that no one had been injured and the cause of the blaze was under investigation. When asked if he thought it might have been a gas leak, he said it was possible but that he would not know until more details were available. The news report said that the woman who lived in the house had left to go shopping just minutes before the explosion. The report said that she was unavailable for comment, but added that a missing persons report had been filed on her husband, Herbert Quarrels, a few days earlier when he had disappeared without a trace. The report said that at the present time there was no evidence to connect the two incidents.

Herb went to two other local news station websites and they all carried basically the same story. The only additional information was that windows had been shattered at houses on both sides of his from the force of the explosion. One report said that in addition to the fire marshal, the Bureau of Alcohol, Tobacco, Firearms, and Explosives have been called in to assist in the investigation.

Typing in the bank's website address, Herb entered his password. ACCESS DENIED in large red letters. Although he knew it was futile, he tried a second and then a third time with the same result. He logged onto another account. ACCESS DENIED. And a third one. ACCESS DENIED.

He wasn't surprised to have been locked out of the company's regular accounts, given his sudden disappearance. But how had they discovered the special accounts he had set up so quickly? Everett must have called in some kind of emergency auditor.

In desperation, he logged onto a different bank to check on one of the other dummy accounts he had set up, one that had no connection to the dealership. He breathed a sigh of relief when he was allowed in and could view the account balance of $600,000. He tried a second of those accounts and could access it. Between the two accounts there was a little over $1 million. It still wasn't enough, not even close to being enough. And he had no idea how long that money would be available before they found it, too.

Maybe there was still a chance. He could not approach Miguel again, he knew how that would turn out. No, there was only one thing to do. As much as he hated to drag him any further into all of this, maybe John Lee could help in some way. He looked at the cell phone on the nightstand again, then shook his head. No, he wasn't going to drop all of this in his son's lap with a telephone call. He would go back to Somerton County and talk to John Lee in person. He deserved that. If nothing else, he needed to know that he, too, might be in danger.

***

"Wait a minute, you're telling me my father is some kind of drug runner?"

"We don't think he is involved in the transportation or sale of drugs directly," Thalman said. "But it looks like he was laundering money for Miguel Torres."

"Okay, and just who the hell *is* Miguel Torres?"

Special Agent Barber showed him a picture of a Latin-looking man who appeared to be in his early 50s. He had a round face, a thin mustache, and his dark eyes looked lifeless.

"Miguel Torres is the top man in the drug business in the Orlando area," Barber told him. "He controls everything that goes in or out of the city. He's also involved in prostitution, and is a suspect in close to a dozen homicides over the years. But it doesn't end there. Torres is part of a much larger organization run by a man named Esteban Muñoz. Have you ever heard of him?"

"Yeah, I have," John Lee said. "I think every cop in Florida knows who he is. He's supposed to be a major player in the drug business in the southern part of the state. So far no one's been able to touch him."

"That's right, so far. Torres is big, but Muñoz is at the top of the heap."

"And you want to get to Torres and use him to get to Muñoz."

"That's how the game is played."

"So why haven't you busted him yet?"

"Oh, we've tried," Thalman assured him. "The FBI and DEA have been watching his movements for a long time, but he's sneaky as hell. He's got a big organization under him and just trying to unravel it so we can get something that actually ties back to him has been more frustrating than you could ever believe. We've hit one stonewall after another. He's got a bunch of different shell corporations that all insulate him from anything we can find. One of those corporations is Zelina Acquisition Services. The SUV that you reported the night your house was broken into is registered to Zelina."

"That's where I remember it from," John Lee said.

"That's what first got our attention. That report popped up because anything to do with Torres or any of his corporations or operatives is flagged. And then your father's boss up in Ohio contacted us and said you had called asking all kinds of questions."

"I'm just a small town boy," John Lee said. "What does any of this have to do with me?"

"Your father is, or was, the accountant for a big automobile dealership in Ohio called Everett Automotive Group. We noticed a while back that a subsidy corporation connected to Everett was making large deposits, and then money was being transferred to Zelina Acquisition Services and a couple of other dummy corporations that are associated with Torres. On the surface, it looked like just everyday business. Supposedly Zelina deals in exotic cars, which they were selling to this subsidy company of Everett Automotive Group. Only problem is, we looked closer and there is no such company, except on paper. And there isn't any record of any vehicles actually being transferred. Not to mention the fact that Everett deals in everyday cars, minivans, and SUVs, things like that. Not collector cars and custom cars like what the records show were being purchased from Zelina."

"When I talked to Anthony Everett he said something about finding an extra $5 million in the bank account or something. Is that money my father was putting in?"

"Looks like it," Barber said.

"And nobody got suspicious that there's that much money sitting there?"

"No offense, but like you said, you're a small town boy," Thalman replied. "Do you know anything about how the automobile business works, Deputy?"

John Lee shrugged his shoulders. "No, I guess I've never really thought about it. Dealers sell cars."

"Yes, but those dealers don't normally own the car sitting on their lots," Thalman said. "The manufacturers and the banks work together on basically what is a very elaborate consignment program. The dealer pays a monthly flooring fee, which is basically an interest payment, on the inventory. When a new vehicle sells, he pays the bank the wholesale cost of it. So it's not uncommon for a dealership to have a lot of money in a flooring account. And for a big place like Everett Automotive Group, we're talking big, big money."

"So my father gets this money from the drug dealers, runs it through these bank accounts and back to them, and now they've got legitimate income, right? Why go to all that trouble? I mean, most people buying drugs don't use checks or credit cards, do they? As far as I know, it's always been a cash business."

"Oh, trust me, a lot of it stays in cash," Thalman said. "But Miguel Torres lives in an estate valued at over $2 million. He drives a new top of the line Mercedes and has a fleet of half a dozen expensive vehicles. That money has got to come from somewhere. On paper he's an investor and consultant, so he can justify his lifestyle to the IRS. Which is where your father and all those dummy corporations come in."

"And something went wrong?"

"Obviously," Barber said, "but we don't know what, yet."

"You're saying my father pulled this disappearing act out of nowhere," John Lee said. "But that doesn't make sense. I mean, if he was going to take the money and run, why leave $5 million sitting there? Why didn't he transfer it to one of those secret offshore accounts or something first?"

"That's a good question. And we don't know the answer to it. Do you know much about psychology, Deputy?"

"About as much as I do about the automobile business."

"Oh, you probably know more than you think you do. For example, would you agree it takes a certain kind of person to be a deputy? That a deputy needs certain traits to be successful? Self-confidence, a certain amount of aggressiveness to be able to take control of a situation, but also enough restraint not to go overboard?"

"Yeah, for the most part I think that's right."

"I think it's the same for any profession," Thalman said. "For example, I don't see a guy like you being comfortable spending his life sitting behind a desk in an office somewhere."

"No, that would probably drive me nuts."

"Right. Or if a guy really craves a lot of people contact, he's probably not going to make a good over the road trucker who spends all his time alone in the cab of a semi. Being an accountant is the same way. People who are drawn into that kind of work are very organized and they usually don't like to vary from a set schedule and things like that. What I'm saying is, they're not spur of the moment people who just take off on a whim. Yet, it looks to us like that's exactly what happened with your father. Why?"

"I have no idea," John Lee said, shrugging. "Like you said, a person in that line of work is usually pretty well organized. So if my father is that organized, and I'm assuming he had to be to get to the position he was with that big car dealership up north, why just disappear? And again, if he was going to disappear, why leave so much money sitting around instead of taking it with him or making it accessible to himself somehow or another?"

"That may be where you come in," Barber said.

"What do you mean?"

"This bank account that you didn't know about. Regular payments have been going into it for a while now. Your father is also a signer on that account, so he could transfer money back out anytime he wanted to."

"And did he? Was it just another account set up to launder money?"

"Not that we can tell. Money has gone in but nothing has ever come out of it."

"Okay, but still, a million bucks is a lot of money to me. A lot of money to most people. But it's not five million. Why leave more than four times that amount just sitting there when he took off?"

"Maybe because he didn't think he was going to take off?"

"I'm not following you," John Lee said.

"Maybe something went wrong that he didn't expect. Or at least didn't think it was going to go as far wrong as it did. Maybe he thought it was going to continue along, business as usual, but he was wrong for whatever reason."

"Guys, this is so far over my head I don't know what to say," John Lee told them. "Where do we go from here?"

"Well, as I understand it, you have a couple of people sitting in a cell that might be able to tell us something. How about we see what we can get out of them?"

"Good luck with that," John Lee said. "We can't get a word out of either one of them."

"No disrespect intended," Thalman replied. "But we've played this game before. We may have a trick or two up our sleeves that you folks here in Somerton County don't know about."

The Gecko In The Corner
Chapter 34

THEY MAY HAVE KNOWN A lot of tricks, but none of them worked with Laurencio. The FBI agents tried simply asking for information, and when that didn't work they tried bluffing, demanding, and even cajoling. But the big man just sat silently, ignoring them.

"Look, at least tell us your name," Thalman said. "Maybe we can work out something to our mutual benefit. I've got a feeling you're here illegally, but we don't care about that. We can move you someplace safe and you can start all over with a clean slate. No more worries about immigration or anything else."

There was no response, so Barber tried the bad cop routine.

"We know you work with Miguel Torres and sooner or later we're going to get a hit on your fingerprints. We've already got you for two felonies. Why make it worse on yourself?"

Finally there was some response, but it wasn't what they had hoped for. Laurencio simply turned his head and looked at the FBI agent with no expression on his face or in his eyes, then he looked away again. They kept at it for another 45 minutes with no luck, then had Laurencio returned to his cell.

"Do you think we'll have any better luck with the other one?"

"Hard to say," Thalman replied. "At least we know something about him. That's a starting point."

Deputy Obediah 'Obie' Long returned with Ramon, saying, "Hope you don't take as long with this one. Going up and down the steps all the time is bad on my back." Obie was a sandbagger who never did anything more than he absolutely had to, and what little effort he did put out was always accompanied by a myriad of complaints. For months now he had been claiming post-traumatic stress after being ambushed and enduring a fusillade of shots fired at his patrol car. The fact that his attackers had been no more than mischievous boys armed with fireworks and that he had become the laughing stock of the town didn't matter. Obie had suffered, damn it, and he was going to milk it for as long as he could. He had reluctantly gone back to work after the psychiatrist they had sent him to said there was no reason for him not to return to duty. Flag had put him to work in the jail, where he could keep an eye on the reluctant deputy, since Obie was known to spend as much of his on duty time as possible parked under a shade tree sleeping when he was supposed to be on patrol.

When Obie left, Thalman introduced himself and Barber, and added, "I understand you've already met Deputy Quarrels."

Ramon started out with the silent routine, but at the same time he was considering all of his options. He knew sooner or later Miguel was going to get to him. If his uncle couldn't extract his revenge for Ramon's failures personally, he would have someone else do it. Too much had happened and too much time had passed to even entertain the thought of ever going back to Orlando. He would have liked to recover the money and just disappear, but he was a realist and knew that wasn't possible any longer. So he knew his only option was to take the best offer he could get. Maybe if they gave him a new identity and sent him someplace far away Miguel would never be able to find him. Sure, he might have to work as a bus boy in a restaurant or a clerk in a convenience store, which was no life compared to what he had lived, but it was still better than what he would have had back home in his little village, and it *was* a life. With Miguel, there would only be pain and suffering for as long as his uncle could inflict it before life ended.

Barber started the interview by laying out everything they knew about him and had against him. "You're a felon already. Between the burglary and the possession of a handgun, you're going away for a long, long time. You know it and I know it." He let that sink in for a moment, then added, "And we also both know that you work for Miguel Torres, and we both know what he does for a living. How do you think he's going to feel about one of his guys doing something so stupid as to get popped for a burglary? So how do you want this to turn out?"

Ramon remained silent for a few moments longer. The only sound was the ticking of the clock on the wall. Barber started to say something else, but the more experienced Thalman subtly shook his head, signaling that it was better to wait him out.

Ramon tried to think of any other way. He wanted to see Gabriella again, but he quickly pushed that thought out of his head. She was the past. There were other women in the world. He knew that no matter what kind of deal the feds might offer him, sooner or later Miguel might find him, and if that time came, his only option was to go on the run. A woman would only slow him down. No, it was time to make a deal. If nothing else, it would get him away from the silence of Laurencio, and from the constant complaining of the junkie housed in the cell between them.

Then another thought came to him. Who knew? Maybe there was a way for this to work out after all. Maybe he could play both ends against the middle to his benefit. He wondered if there was some way he could take whatever they offered him, but then agree to try to arrange a meeting with Quarrels under the pretense of convincing him to reveal the details of his end of the operation. Maybe he could still get the money Quarrels had and disappear. It was what the gamblers called a long shot, he knew that, but it might be worth a try. He sat back in his chair, looked at the FBI agents, and asked, "What kind of deal can we make?"

***

Paw Paw didn't know why John Lee always worried so much about him being up on a ladder. He had no fear of heights, and even at his age he was still active and loved a challenge. Hell, this wasn't work, it was fun. A hell of a lot more fun that traipsing off to that damn casino with Nell to see another make believe Elvis.

He'd never say it to her face or there'd be hell to pay, but Paw Paw had never thought Elvis the Pelvis was all that great anyway. Yeah, the man could sing, but Paw Paw found all that gyrating he did on the stage distracting. He acted like he had ants in his pants or something. More than once he wanted to yell "just stand still and sing, damn it!" at the TV screen when Nell was watching an Elvis movie or performance from her collection. Of course, his wife's obsession with Elvis did have its benefits. When she took off to go to a concert by one of those impersonators she was always going off to see, he had the house to himself and could play some of that good old hard rock music that Nell hated so much. Everything in life was a tradeoff.

As he hung the electrical conduit and strung the wire along the outside of John Lee's house, he was thinking that maybe he could take this even further. All an intruder had to do was cut the power to the property and none of this would be any good anyway. But if he powered the whole thing with solar panels they could cut every damned power line in the county and still not disarm the security system. Yeah, that was a good idea. It wouldn't take a big panel or big battery bank to do it. He had everything he needed right at home. Damn, John Lee was gonna be impressed when he saw this.

He was at the back of the house when he heard Magic barking and looked at his watch. No, it was too early for John Lee to be off duty yet. Maybe it was that insurance fellow that was supposed to be coming by to look at the damage the burglars had done. Good, he wanted to be here when that bird showed up. Paw Paw knew how those insurance people were. Oh yeah, they wanted that premium paid on time every month, but if you had a claim they didn't want to know you.

Look at the way they treated him after that accident of his, claiming that if he had maintained his Jeep better the brakes wouldn't have failed and he wouldn't have missed the stop sign and hit Harry McDermott's tractor. Those brakes were just fine, you needed to pump them a little bit! And Harry was 87 years old. He didn't have any business driving that damn tractor down the road anyway. Yep, it was a good thing he was here. He'd let that insurance adjuster know right up front who he was dealing with so they wouldn't try to pull any of their shenanigans. He climbed down off the ladder and called to Magic. The dog came to him and Paw Paw locked him in his dog run.

The Gecko In The Corner

"I know you hate being in the slammer, buddy, but I don't want you eating this guy before he approves John Lee's claim in full." With the dog secured, Paw Paw went around to the front of the house, ready to give that insurance guy what for. But as soon as he saw who was getting out of the car, Paw Paw knew it wasn't anybody from the insurance company.

John Lee Quarrels Series

The Gecko In The Corner
Chapter 35

"Overall, I think it's a good deal for both sides," Barber said once Obie had taken Ramon back to the cellblock. "But, I need you to sign off on it, Deputy Quarrels."

"Me? Why do you need my approval?"

"You're the victim here. It was your place Ramon and his buddy trashed."

"What the hell, why not?"

"We appreciate that," Thalman told him.

"Did I really have any choice? If I objected would you have canceled the deal?"

"To be honest with you, no. Getting your house torn up is a violation, whether you're Joe Citizen or a cop. But as they say, this is for the greater good."

"I think they told the kamikaze pilots that just before they stuffed them into the cockpit of their airplanes," John Lee said.

Thalman chuckled and said, "Probably so. But still, we understand where you're coming from and we appreciate all of your cooperation."

"On another note," Barber said, "You probably didn't think about this, but the Internal Revenue Service is going to expect you to pay taxes on that money in that account up in Cincinnati."

"What? No, I never thought about that. I mean, I just assumed the money was going to be seized as evidence."

"It will be," Barber told him. "So don't go on any spending sprees. As for the IRS, this is going to be an identity theft case officially, with you as the victim. So don't worry about that, we'll keep them off your back."

"I appreciate that. So what happens now?"

"Now we put a call in to our supervisor and update him on what's going on. He'll make arrangements for transporting both prisoners out of here. Ramon will go to a safe house and we'll start interrogating him about Miguel Torres and his operation, and the silent one will go into a cell. Who knows? Maybe we can get him to break, too, given enough time. But I'm not holding my breath on that. If nothing else, I'm sure Ramon will give us plenty of information to indict his pal with."

"And what happens with me in the meantime? I don't think Torres is going to back down on wanting whatever he thinks I have of his just because these two are in federal custody."

"Don't worry, we're not going to leave you hanging," Barber promised.

"Not at all," Thalman agreed. "We'll hang around here as long as we can, and hopefully get this resolved quickly."

"Hopefully. Define hopefully."

"I'm not going to bullshit you, Deputy Quarrels. Just because we've got those two guys in lockup doesn't mean we're going to be taking Torres down overnight. But hopefully, finding out we have them will give him enough to worry about that he'll forget about you. But the same time, you need watch your back."

"And what about my father?"

Barber shook his head. "Sorry, he doesn't get a pass on all of this. He's in too deep. If he has any sense at all, when we locate him he'll cooperate with our investigation. That will go a long way in helping his case. If you hear from him, you might want to tell him that."

"I doubt I'll be hearing from him," John Lee said. "And that's just fine with me. I don't want anything to do with the man."

***

Obie locked Ramon back in his cell, then checked on the other two prisoners. Jamie Bowers seem to be going through some kind of withdrawal and was sweating and shaking as he paced his cell.

"Man, I need to see a doctor or somethin'. What you guys are doin' to me to just ain't right!"

Obie ignored him. If there is anything a chronic complainer loathes, it is another complainer. Who's got time to listen to all that nonsense when you've got plenty of problems of your own? He stopped in front of the other prisoner's cell and sneered at the big man with the ponytail. That one really irritated Obie. Who did he think he was, ignoring anything you said to him? Oh yeah? Well, Obie had a thing or two to say to *him*!"

"Man Kemosabe, you are one dumb ass! Sittin' in there like ya'll some kind of statue while your buddy down there is makin' a deal with the feds. That's right, while ya'll are rottin' away in a cell somewhere, he's goin' to be livin' the good life in the Witness Protection Program while the taxpayers pick up the bill. I was listenin' through the door and I heard it all. Ya'll are goin' down, and so is that boss of yours, that there Michael Torres!"

Obie started to turn away, not expecting an answer. Why should today be any different? So he was surprised when the prisoner said, "I'm entitled to a phone call. I want to make it now."

***

Miguel watched Jorge spit blood and then wipe his face with the back of his hand. Miguel had to give the old man credit, he had put up a pretty good fight. He had never seen anyone land a blow on Jorge before. And it had been a good one, nearly knocking the bodyguard down. It had taken three men to subdue him, and as he watched Jorge glare at the old man he had no doubt that he would die a painful death. But not yet. Right now they needed him. But that was okay, let him live for a while longer. A man that brave deserved that much.

Seated on the floor in John Lee's living room, his hands tied behind him with some sort of heavy-duty zip tie and his feet bound the same way, Paw Paw was silently cussing himself. He never should have locked Magic away in that pen. Between the two of them they might have had a chance. If not, at least these bastards would've known they had been in a fight! Not that he did too bad on his own. Look at that big son of a bitch spitting blood all over John Lee's floor. He clocked that one pretty good, didn't he? Of course, he had taken his own licks, too. One eye was swollen nearly shut and he had a throbbing headache from when one of them had conked him on the head with a club or something just before the lights went out. Paw Paw may have been hurting, but he sure as hell was not going to let this crowd of assholes see it. No way! He wouldn't give them the satisfaction.

"Hey, are you the man in charge?"

Miguel, sitting in John Lee's recliner, looked at him and said, "Just keep your mouth shut. You will live longer that way."

"How about you tell that big ape of yours to quit spitting on the floor?"

"Don't worry about the floor, there will be a lot worse than spit on it before too long."

"Yeah I bet there will be. Because when my grandson shows up you guys are all going to be shitting your pants."

"Shut up, old man. If you behave I'll let you watch me cut his heart out before I turn you over to Jorge."

"You talk big now, but you just wait and see. Your messin' with the wrong man when you take on John Lee. When he's done with you, you ain't going to be nothing but a big fat greasy stain on the rug."

"Shut him up," Miguel ordered, and Jorge walked over to the old man. He bent over and punched Paw Paw in the face, rocking his head back and causing it to slam into the wall behind him. Blood streamed from his mouth, but Paw Paw just grinned at him.

"Is that all you got? Jesus Christ, my old lady hits harder than that!"

Jorge grabbed him by the throat and jerked him upright. There was a metallic click and the blade of his knife pressed into Paw Paw throat. "I'm going to enjoy killing you, old man."

"Not yet," Miguel ordered. "We need him alive for a little longer. Then you can have him."

Paw Paw wasn't intimidated by the big man or his knife. He just grinned and said, "If you think you're scarin' me, you'd better think again, Jack. I've wiped my ass with better men than you."

Jorge punched him in the stomach, knocking the wind out of him, and he would have collapsed if the bodyguard hadn't been holding him up. Jorge followed up with a second and then a third blow before Miguel shouted, "Enough! You can have your fun with him later. But not yet."

Jorge let go of the old man and stepped back and Paw Paw fell to the floor with a thud. Before turning away, Jorge gave him a sharp, vicious kick to the kidney, causing a groan of agony, and then the old man was silent.

***

John Lee had given the FBI agents the two phones he had taken from the burglars at his house and Barber was studying them while Thalman talked to their supervisor on his cell phone. John Lee was still sitting at the table, waiting to hear what the results of that conversation were going to be when the door burst open and Chief Deputy Flag Newton asked, "What the hell is goin' on in here? Why aren't you out on patrol, Deputy?"

Barber stood up and showed his identification. "Myself and Special Agent Thalman here needed to ask the deputy some questions about a case we're investigating."

If the FBI agent thought Flag was going to be impressed by who he was, he was sadly mistaken.

"You come into my Department and start talkin' to one of my people and to my prisoners without informin' me or the sheriff ahead of time? I don't know how you boys do things up there in Washington, but that ain't the way we do it 'round here. And that fancy gold badge of yours don't mean nothin' to me!"

Thalman ended his call and tried to soothe Flag's ruffled feathers. "We certainly meant no disrespect to you, Chief Deputy. But this is a sensitive matter and things are kind of on a need to know basis."

"Hey. Newsflash," Flag said belligerently, "whatever happens in this county *is* my business and I need to know what's going on."

"I think you need to take that up with Sheriff Swindle," Thalman replied. "We touched base with him when we got here."

"Are you sayin' D.W. knows about this and he didn't tell me?"

"Apparently not. Now, if you don't mind, just give us a few more minutes here. We're wrapping things up now."

"Oh, I mind," Flag told him. "Yeah, you can bet your ass I mind!"

He stormed out of the room and Thalman got up and closed the door. "I bet he's a lot of fun to work with on a daily basis."

"Don't let that gruff exterior fool you," John Lee told him. "That's just to put you at ease when you first meet him. Inside, he's one hundred percent asshole."

"I hope we didn't cause you any problems. We did touch base with the sheriff first. He's the one who told us you were in court and where to find you,"

"No sweat. Flag's one of those people who seem to wake up pissed off every day and spend their time looking for someone to tangle with. He's the least of my worries. What did you find out?"

"They're dispatching a team and a helicopter to pick up the prisoners. They should be here within the hour."

"Wow, you guys move fast."

"Like I told you, this investigation's been going on for a long time. It's a top priority."

The Gecko In The Corner
Chapter 36

Upstairs, Flag was beating his fist on the sheriff's desktop. "Damn it, D.W., this ain't right! How dare you shut me out like that? There's no excuse for that. No excuse at all!"

"Just calm down, Flag. It ain't no big thing."

"No big thing? The god damn FBI is here interviewing our prisoners and one of our deputies behind our backs, and you say it's no big thing?"

"Nobody's doing nothin' behind our backs. I told you, they talked to me ahead of time."

"They talked to you! But nobody said a word to me."

"How 'bout you lower your voice? I bet folks can hear you across the street."

"Why wasn't I informed about all of this?"

"They said it was some kind of need to know basis, and I didn't figure you needed to know, that's why."

"That's bullshit! That's bullshit and we both know it."

"Sorry you feel that way, but that's the decision I made. And I'm stickin' with it."

"And what the hell does John Lee have to do with all this stuff anyhow? What's he got himself mixed up in?"

"I don't know," D.W. replied with a shrug. "I imagine we'll find out what it's all about soon enough. Now meanwhile, why don't you go someplace and kick puppies or scare pregnant women or somethin' and get out of my office? I've got work to do."

Flag was so angry he felt like his head might explode at any moment. Damn D.W., and damn John Lee, and damn the whole freaking FBI. Well they weren't going to get away with it. No, sir, he wasn't going to take this lying down!

He slammed the door to D.W.'s office behind him and as he marched down the hall to his own office, Obie Long was coming in the opposite direction.

"Get the hell out of my way," Flag ordered, pushing the deputy aside.

"I need to ask you somethin'," Obie said, looking around to see if anybody had observed the shove. Unfortunately nobody had, which was too bad, because he could have used a witness in his claim that the assault by the chief deputy had injured his back. But that was okay, it was still going to be worth at least a month, and maybe six weeks recuperation time.

"I don't want to hear about the god damn prisoners, I've got enough to deal with right now," Flag said, interrupting his scheming.

"I know, but..."

"No buts, damn it! Are you deaf or somethin'? I said I'm busy. Whatever it is, get the hell out of my sight and deal with it. Act like you know what you're doin' for a change instead of needin' somebody to take you by the hand all the time. Could ya do that, Obie? Could ya?"

Smarting from the chief deputy's harsh words and not knowing what to do about the prisoner's request to make a phone call, Obie thought he should at least tell somebody the guy had finally said something. But when he got to the sheriff's office door it was closed and he knew from experience that no matter what was going on, that meant D.W. was not to be disturbed. Probably sittin' there at his desk sleeping, but when Obie did it everybody acted like it was some big crime. Well the hell with both of them, D.W. and Flag, too! He wasn't going to screw up the assignment at the jail and be stuck out there in the street again. No way! At least with this job there was nobody breathing over his shoulder all the time, and except for making sure the prisoners got fed when their meals were delivered from the Southern Star diner across the street and escorting them back and forth to see the judge or to be interviewed when needed, nobody expected much out of him. And that was just fine with Obie.

He went back to the cellblock and told the prisoner to back up to the bars and put his hands through so they could be shackled, then he led him around the corner to a small cubbyhole where a phone hung on the wall. One end of another pair of handcuffs was attached to a sturdy steel bar bolted to the wall. Obie attached the other end to the prisoner's left wrist next to the handcuffs he was already wearing and said, "Make it fast, I ain't got all day."

***

Miguel was not a patient man under the best of circumstances. He had grown bored waiting and was tearing John Lee's house apart once again. He didn't expect to find anything that Ramon and Laurencio had missed, but at least it kept him from dwelling on his situation with Esteban. Every time he thought about that, he felt his stomach clench and wasn't sure if he was going to throw up or lose control of his bowels.

He was staring at the gun safe, which was as big as a refrigerator. It's five-spoked steel handle was bent and the combination dial was missing, all the result of Ramon's earlier assault upon it. What kind of fool thinks he can beat such a fine safe open with a hammer? Thinking about Ramon made him angry again. He wished Gabriella was still alive. At least she gave him *something* to work his rage out on. He was tempted to go back to the living room and beat the old man just to relieve some of his anger. But when he approached him, instead of showing fear, the old man just grinned. Something about his insolence both enraged and awed Miguel. Never in his life, from his days as a boy on the streets of his village stealing what he could to survive to his rise to power in the drug trade, had he ever met a man with such courage. Everybody knew what he was capable of and feared Miguel Torres! But not this old man. Maybe he was crazy. Maybe that's why he acted the way he did. No, he wasn't crazy. There was something about him, something that Miguel had never encountered before. The old man made him feel like even with all of his money and his hired gunmen and enforcers, he had no power. Why would a man in his position act like that?

***

Special Agent Thalman had been right, John Lee could have never handled a career that required him to sit at a desk all day long. With the interviews over and the arrangements to transfer the prisoners into federal custody made, he was getting fidgety. He wanted to get back on the road. He wanted to do anything but sit where he was. He didn't think the FBI really needed him any longer and was tempted to ask if it was okay to leave.

Thalman had gone down the hall to use the bathroom, and Barber was across the hall making copies of the preliminary agreement Ramon had signed that granted him a new life in the Witness Protection Program in exchange for helping to bring down Miguel Torres and Esteban Muñoz. Before he left to empty his bladder, Thalman had said, "If you think this guy is going to be living the good life sleeping his days away in a hammock, that's not going to happen, Deputy Quarrels. WITSEC doesn't support them for the rest of their lives. He'll get a small stipend, but it isn't much and won't last forever. He's going to wind up someplace cold and nasty, working in a warehouse or driving a cab, or something like that. And just looking at this guy and talking to him, I can tell you that he's a schemer. He's not going to be content with a life like that, and sooner or later he's going to do something stupid. Once we're through with him, I really hope he does. And when he does, he's screwed. Part of the agreement is that he not violate any laws of any kind. If he does, all bets are off."

That was some consolation, but John Lee didn't really care what happened to Ramon or to his partner. Miguel Torres was still out there somewhere, and no matter what the FBI said, John Lee had a feeling that he was going to do something long before their investigation progressed much further. As if on cue, Ramon's telephone rang. John Lee looked at the Caller ID, looked at the door to make sure nobody was coming, and then answer the call.

"Now what do you want?"

"I want the same thing I have wanted all along. I want my money."

"And I told you, I don't have anything that belongs to you. Your problem is with my father. Find him and deal with it, and leave me out of it."

"It is not that simple, my friend. Your father seems to have disappeared."

"Yeah, well, he's good at that. He disappeared from my life a long time ago. How about you do the same?"

"I don't think so. I want what is owed to me."

"That's fine, I don't blame you at all. But like I said, I don't have anything that belongs to you."

"And that is the difference between you and me."

Instantly John Lee was wary. "What do you mean?"

"I mean I have something that belongs to you. Perhaps we should make a trade."

A moment later he heard Paw Paw's voice. "John Lee, tell this greaser to stick it up his ass! Don't worry about me, these guys ain't nothing."

There was the sound of a thud and then a groan and John Lee squeezed the telephone tight.

Miguel came back on the line. "As you see, my friend, the situation has changed."

"Let him go. He doesn't have anything to do with this."

"Oh, but he does. He is my, how you say, bargaining chip."

"I keep telling you, I don't know where my father is and I don't have your money."

"That is unfortunate."

"Please, just let him go. I'll meet with you wherever you want, I'll do whatever it takes to help you get your money back."

"Oh, so you do know where my money is?"

"No. No, I don't. I swear I don't! But I'll help you any way I can."

"If you don't have my money, as you claim, and you don't know where it is, how can you help me?"

"I'll find my father. I'll do whatever it takes. Just don't hurt Paw Paw."

"Paw Paw. That is an endearing name, but it doesn't fit such a strong old man. I wonder how strong he really is? Maybe when we start cutting his fingers off we will find out. What do you think?"

"Take me," John Lee said. "I'll trade myself for him."

"And what good would that do me? If you don't know where my money is you are worthless to me."

"If you have me, maybe it will make my father come out of hiding."

"But you say you do not know where he is. So how would he know that I have you?"

"I don't know," John Lee admitted. "I really don't. I've told you over and over, we don't have any kind of relationship."

"I don't care about your family troubles. All I care about is my money."

"How much? How much do you need?"

"I want all of it."

"I understand that," John Lee said. "But how much is all of it?"

"Ten million dollars. Do you have that much money?"

"No, of course not."

"Maybe it is in this big safe of yours?"

"I keep telling you, I don't have your money."

"I think you should open it and we will find out."

"I wish I could, just to show you. But those idiots you sent beat it up so bad that I don't even know how to open it."

"You are the son of a thief. I don't believe anything you tell me. But you listen to me, and you believe what I tell you, John Lee Quarrels. If my money is not in that safe and you don't have it, as you keep saying, you do whatever you have to do to find your father and you bring him to me. If you do that and if I get my money back, this old man lives. But time is running out. Do not make me wait much longer."

The call ended and John Lee stared at the phone, his hands shaking. When he heard the door knob turning he quickly set the phone down.

John Lee Quarrels Series

Chapter 37

"Boy, for somebody who's supposed to be such a big shot, you're not very smart, are you?"

"Shut up old man, before I cut your tongue out."

"You can cut off anything you want, but it ain't gonna make any difference."

"I said shut up!"

"John Lee can't open that safe. I looked at it the other day. Any fool can see the dial's busted off. So how can he turn the combination to open it?"

"Shut up," Miguel roared, jerking Paw Paw to his feet and shoving him forcefully against the wall. "You have already served your purpose. I can kill you right now."

"Go ahead," Paw Paw said defiantly. "I'm not afraid of you or any of these losers you brought here with you. But if you had half a brain, you'd realize that I can solve your problem for you."

Miguel had drawn his arm back to punch the old man, but he stopped. "And how can a worthless old man solve my problem?"

"I thought you were gonna hit me. What's the matter? Afraid of breaking one of those pretty manicured fingernails of yours?"

"I will do worse than that to you before this is over."

"Then go for it and get it over with," Paw Paw said with a shrug. "Because this shit is getting boring. It's your loss"

Miguel dropped his arm and stared at the old man. "What are you saying? Do you know where my money is?"

"Nope."

"Do you know where Herb Quarrels is?"

Paw Paw grinned and shook his head. "Nope, strike two."

"Stop playing with me old man. I don't have time for your nonsense."

Paw Paw shrugged his shoulders. "Like I said, your loss."

"I'm done with you," Miguel said and turned to Jorge. "Give me your knife," he demanded, "I'm going to do this one myself."

He took the knife, pushed the button to pop the blade out, and pushed the point into the skin of Paw Paw's neck. Bright red blood flowed out.

Paw Paw ignored the pain and the insolent grin never left his face. He acted like they were just two men discussing the weather or the baseball scores instead of something much more lethal. "Like I said, I don't know about your money or where Herb Qarrels is. But I can open that safe."

***

Now that he was back in Somerton, Herb wasn't sure what to do next. Should he drive by the house and see if John Lee was there? If he was on duty and not home, should he wait for him? How safe would that be? He had dumped the Hyundai and purchased an ancient Ford Tempo for cash, but who knew when some of Torres' men might show up looking for him? Maybe he should go to the Sheriff's Department and ask for John Lee. But he was sure that there was some kind of a bulletin out for him, especially after the missing persons report had been filed and his house had been bombed.

No, he decided the best thing to do was to drive by the house and see if John Lee's patrol car was there. If not, he would just keep driving around and come back and check later. Yes, that was what he would do.

He drove down John Lee's road and saw two vehicles in his son's driveway, the pickup truck and an old Jeep, but no patrol car. He was tempted to stop and knock on the door anyway, in case John Lee *was* home. No, that wasn't what he had planned. He would just drive around a little bit and come back. If John Lee was home and had company, he would just as soon avoid seeing them. He wondered if it might be Maddy, that pretty deputy who had helped clean him up and who had been back to check up on him. John Lee had said they were just friends, and he had made it very clear that he didn't want his father snooping into his business, but there was definitely something between the two of them. Herb had been able to pick up on it even in the pain and drug haze he had been in while they treated his injuries.

***

"We're going to need all the windows open for ventilation, and somebody's gonna have to be stand by with those fire extinguishers," Paw Paw said. "And we need to run a garden hose inside to keep the safe cool as I'm working. It ain't gonna do much good to get the safe open if we burn the house down in the process."

"Are you sure you can do this? This is not some trick?"

"Hell yes I can do it! Piece of cake."

"Then get busy and do it."

"Just hold your horses," Paw Paw told him. "I said I can do it. I didn't say I can do it just by snapping my fingers or twitchin' my nose. This here safe's a big heavy son of a bitch and it ain't gonna open up like a tin can. It's gonna take some time. There's a lot of thick steel to cut through."

"The longer you stand there talking, the longer it will take. Stop wasting time."

"You know what? Just forget it. Just go ahead and kill me if that's the attitude you're gonna take."

"What is your problem, old man? Why do you play these games with me?"

"I ain't playing any games, asshole. But doing something like this takes some time and takes a little bit of planning. If you don't want to give me the time to do that, get one of these bozos you got working for you to do it."

Miguel looked around at his men, but they all shrugged their shoulders or shook their heads, indicating they had no idea how to open the safe.

"What do you have to plan? Just open it!"

"Well, for starters, like I said, there's a lot of thick steel I have to cut through. And we have to be sure we don't set fire to the place while I'm at it. And something else you have to think about, mister, there's a lot of guns and ammunition in there. If I go too fast with this cutting torch, things could get real noisy around here real fast. That's why I've got to cut a little bit at a time."

"Fine, do what you must. Just get started."

Miguel's cell phone rang. He took it out of his pocket and read the Caller ID. Somerton County Jail. He stared at the phone, not sure what to do. It rang eight times and then stopped. A moment later, it began ringing again with the same Caller ID. He pushed the button to answer, but didn't say anything.

"Ramon has made a deal with the FBI. They are coming to pick us up soon."

He recognized Laurencio's voice and said, "Do what must be done."

And with that, the call ended.

The Gecko In The Corner
Chapter 38

SHERIFF D.W. SWINDLE LIKED GOOD press and took advantage of every opportunity he could to get his face in front of a news camera. So he was disappointed when Special Agent Thalman told him there would be no news conference and no press coverage of the transfer of the prisoners. That was too bad because it would have looked good for the voters. Sure, he understood that they needed to keep a lid on things so they didn't tip off that drug organization.

The sheriff was somewhat placated when Thalman had promised him that once the big bust happened and they took down Torres and Muñoz, he would make sure that D.W. was included in the press conference announcing the end of the investigation, and that the Somerton County Sheriff's Department would be credited for capturing two important individuals associated with the drug ring.

Still, he wished he could say *something*! At least to Dixie Landrum. The auburn haired young reporter from the local newspaper could always be depended on to make him look good. In spite of what Thalman said, he was tempted to call Dixie anyway. He couldn't reveal anything about what was actually happening, but he might drop a hint or two that if she stood back in the distance she might get a good photo op to use at a later date. Of course, he planned to put himself in the middle of that photo op. A picture of him with the FBI and the two suspects would sure look good on the front page of the local newspaper when the story did break. Yeah, that was a good idea. He trusted Dixie to keep it under her hat until he told her to. A scoop like that didn't come along every day for a small town newspaper reporter. Or for a small town sheriff either, for that matter. He picked up the telephone and made his call.

A few minutes later D.W. was coming down the hall to talk to the two FBI agents when he encountered John Lee heading in the opposite direction at a rapid pace.

"Where you goin' in such a hurry?"

"Got to run," John Lee said, never breaking stride.

"You got the runs again? That's too bad. You need to see a doctor if that keeps up, John Lee." But his advice was unheard. John Lee was already gone.

He pushed open the door to the room where the FBI agents were waiting for him and said, "I think that helicopter's goin' to be here pretty soon. They're goin' to land at the baseball field at the high school. I sent a couple deputies over to make sure nobody was on the field and to take care of traffic. You all about ready to go?"

"Yeah, we're ready," Thalman said. "But where did Deputy Quarrels go in such a hurry? He just asked if we needed anything more from him and when I said no, he was gone."

"Well, he was probably embarrassed to say anything," D.W. said, "but that boy's been dealin' with a bad case of the trots for over a week now. I imagine his bunghole's gettin' pretty sore 'bout now."

"He didn't say anything about that before," Barber said.

"Like I said, he was probably embarrassed. Let's go get those two guys out of their cells and head over to the football field."

***

As soon as he was out of the building and away from anyone who might hear him, John Lee pushed the speed dial on his phone. Maddy answered on the third ring. "Where are you?"

"Out on Settlers Lane, headed back to town. Dispatch said that D.W. wanted me to go to the baseball field at the high school and help clear it because a helicopter's coming in."

"They've got Paw Paw!"

"Paw Paw's in a helicopter?"

"No, Miguel Torres has him."

"Back up, John Lee, you're talking a mile a minute and not making any sense. Where does Torres have Paw Paw, and what does a helicopter have to do with any of it?"

He took a deep breath, feeling his heart pounding in his chest. When he spoke again, he tried to do it slowly enough to be understood. "The FBI is bringing in a helicopter to take those two guys we busted at my house away. And Torres called me and said he had Paw Paw."

"Do you think he's bluffing?"

"No," John Lee said, "They put him on the phone. It was him."

"Shit! Where do you think they're at?"

"I don't know. Maybe my house. That's where he was last time I saw him. He was going to be working on that damned security system."

"Don't go out there, John Lee!"

"I have to, Maddy. It's Paw Paw!"

"I know, but if you go rushing out there you're playing right into their hands. You can't help Paw Paw if they kill you, too."

"They won't kill me. Torres needs me alive to try to lure my father in."

"So what do you think he's going to do with Paw Paw if you show up there? Just let him leave so he can go call for help? There's no way they're going to let him walk out of there until they have what they want."

"Torres said they're going to start cutting his fingers off!"

"John Lee, it's time to get some serious help. Go talk to those FBI agents. They can bring in a SWAT team."

"I don't want Paw Paw in the middle of a shootout!"

"No, and you don't want him cut to pieces a little bit at a time, or just blown away once he's not useful to them anymore. You know I'll back you all the way no matter what you want to do, John Lee. I'll head for your house right now and meet you there if that's what you want. But what are we going to accomplish besides getting Paw Paw and ourselves killed? Face it, we're in over our heads. Those FBI guys are trained in this kind of thing."

John Lee wanted nothing more than to go to his house or wherever Torres was keeping his grandfather and kill the drug dealer and all of his henchmen on sight. But he knew that what Maddy was telling him made sense. He didn't know how many people Torres had with him, but the two of them were no match for whatever awaited them at his house. And while he was more than willing to sacrifice himself to save Paw Paw, he did not want Maddy harmed in the process.

"Go talk to those FBI guys, John Lee. That's the only chance Paw Paw has."

"Okay. You're right. I'll do it."

"I'll be standing by."

John Lee stuck the phone in his pocket and went back inside. The interview room was empty and he went across the hall to Dispatch. "Where did those FBI guys go?"

"They went to the cellblock with D.W.," Sheila said. "I guess there's a helicopter comin' to pick up those two prisoners or somethin'. What's wrong with you, John Lee? You look white as a ghost. Is your diarrhea kickin' up again? My brother Clifford said about the time he thinks it's all over, it comes back around again."

But John Lee didn't answer her, he was already on his way to the cellblock. He was just reaching for the heavy steel entry door when he heard shouting and then gunshots exploding from inside.

The Gecko In The Corner
Chapter 39

IT HAD BEEN AS EASY as Laurencio had expected. When he finished his phone call and said that he was done, the lazy jailer had made him sit there for a few moments, just to show him who was in charge. When he did saunter up to the cubbyhole he sneered at Laurencio. "I'm sure goin' to be glad to see your ass gone. You wait until they get you in that prison, boy. Or guess I should say girl, with that damn long hair of yours. Yep, I guaran-damn-tee you that some big old con's goin' to see that hair of yours and make you his bitch. You may think yer somethin' with the silent treatment and that crap you been given us 'round here, but you mark my words, yer gonna be face down and squealin' pretty soon. Squealin' real loud!"

Obie bent down to unlock the handcuff securing the prisoner to the bar on the wall, and when he did Laurencio slammed his other fist into his temple with such force that the jailer's head hit the block wall with a dull thud. Before Obie could fall, Laurencio wrapped his arm around the unconscious man's neck and pulled him upward, squeezing tight to cut off his oxygen and blood flow. When he was sure the jailer was dead he let go and used Obie's keys to unlock the handcuffs.

"What the hell you doin'? How'd you get loose?" Jamie Bowers asked when he saw Laurencio come around the corner unshackled and alone.

Laurencio ignored him and unlocked Ramon's cell door.

"Hey man, get me out of here, too!"

Laurencio ignored him and spoke to Ramon. "Hurry, we don't have much time."

"What did you do?"

"I said hurry. They will be here soon."

Ramon's heart was pounding and he began shaking. "You go, do whatever you want to do. I'm staying here."

"Stop wasting time, we must go," Laurencio said.

Ramon shook his head and backed into the far corner of his cell. "No! No, I'm not going anywhere with you!"

Laurencio came into the cell as Ramon tried to shrink even further into the corner.

"Please, Laurencio, don't do this! I beg of you."

There was no expression on the big man's face as he wrapped his strong fingers around Ramon's neck. Horror filled Ramon's eyes and he flailed out with his hands, striking Laurencio's face and arms with no apparent effect. He began seeing bright yellow and red spots as he fought for breath. The sharp smell of urine filled the cell as his bladder released.

"Hey man, stop that! Come on, stop," Bowers said from the next cell, but Laurencio ignored him. He increased the pressure on Ramon's throat, and continued even after the other man went limp.

Suddenly there were shouts and he looked up to see three men with guns pointed at him. The fat sheriff who had tried to interview him before and the FBI agents. He needed to get past them and outside. Once he was out the door, he knew he was free. It would be easy to elude any kind of pursuit the small town's police could muster quickly. He would steal or hijack a car and be back in Orlando by nightfall.

Laurencio pulled Ramon's body in front of him as a shield and rushed for the cell door. He knew they wouldn't expect that and that they would hesitate to shoot to avoid hitting Ramon, in the hope that the traitor was still alive and could give them the information they wanted. All he had to do was get outside the cell door and get his hands on one of them. The fat sheriff was the one to grab. He would have less training than the others. Get out of the cell, push Ramon's body at the other two to distract them while he got behind the sheriff and took his gun away. The sheriff was soft and out of shape and would present no challenge for a man like Laurencio. Use him as a shield while he killed the FBI men and got out the door, then kill him, too. The rest would be easy.

He had not counted on the older FBI agent. Thalman was a combat veteran and had close to 20 years in the Bureau under his belt. He had seen more than his fair share of dead bodies in his time, and one look at Ramon Sainz told him their star witness was gone.

"Freeze," he ordered, knowing it would do no good. He also knew that there was no way he was letting Ramon's killer out of that cell. By the time the man took another step Thalman was squeezing the trigger. The first 165 grain bullet from his .40 pistol was traveling at over 1,000 feet per second when it hit Laurencio high in his left shoulder, shattering his collarbone. It would have put a lesser man down, but all it did was force Laurencio backward a step or two and cause him to drop Ramon's body. Then he charged for the door with nothing to lose. Thalman fired twice more, and Barker two times. All five bullets struck home. Even before he stepped into the cell and leaned down to feel for a pulse alongside the big man's neck, Thalman knew he was dead.

Sheriff D.W. Swindle had not fired a shot, but when the door to the cellblock jerked open and John Lee ran in with his gun in his hand, the sheriff thought it might be someone coming to assist the escape and almost shot him. When he realized who it was he dropped his gun hand down to his side.

The air was hazy with gun smoke and everybody's ears were ringing from the sounds of the shots fired in such a confined space. The FBI agents were in Ramon's cell, crouching over his body and Laurencio's, while D.W. stood outside the cell looking like he was in shock.

Two more deputies crowded into the cellblock, with Flag close on their heels. Everybody was shouting at the same time. Barber was on his cell phone reporting the shooting to his supervisor, a finger stuck in his other ear to try to block out some of the noise. Howls of shock and anger were added to the din when someone found Obie's body stuffed into the telephone cubbyhole.

"What the hell happened?" John Lee asked D.W., but the sheriff did not answer him.
"I'll tell you what happened," a shocked Jamie Bowers said from his cell. "The shit just hit the fan!"

John Lee Quarrels Series

Chapter 40

"This is crazy," Maddy said when John Lee called her and told her about the shooting at the jail. "What do we do now, John Lee?"

"I don't know. But we can't wait. We need to get Paw Paw away from Torres. Who knows how long it'll take the FBI to do something now?"

"Meet me at Perkins store," Maddy said.

Clyde and Thelma Perkins ran a small convenience store at the intersection of two country roads a mile from John Lee's house. Their establishment was a small place with a single gas pump out front and a counter inside from which they sold beer, soft drinks, snacks, and other items that nobody wanted to run all the way into town to purchase. They were good people who put in long hours and lived in a mobile home next door to the store. Everybody around knew that even if the store was closed, all you had to do was knock on the door if you needed milk or gas or whatever, and they would open up. Well, anytime but Sunday morning. Come rain or shine, on Sundays you would find Clyde and Thelma at the Maranatha Baptist Church, where Thelma played the organ and Clyde helped pass the collection plate.

John Lee drove there with his lights and siren on and ground to a stop in the dirt parking lot in a cloud of dust.

"The radio's going crazy," Maddy said. "Everybody's talking at once and nobody can be heard."

"I know, it's nuts."

"How are we going to do this, John Lee?"

"I don't know," he admitted. "I just want to go in there and kill all of them."

"Like I said before, that's only going to get Paw Paw killed, too. But I've got an idea. Let me go first."

"No way, Maddy! They'll shoot you on sight."

"Hold on and hear me out," she said. "We need to know what's going on in there. We need to know how many men Torres has with him."

"Forget it! Getting you killed or taken hostage, too, isn't going to help anything."

"You're right, they'd kill a cop as soon as they saw me. But I'm not going there as a cop. I'm going as a Bible thumper."

"What the hell you talking about?"

***

Thelma Perkins wasn't sure she understood what John Lee and Maddy were telling her, but the looks on their faces and the urgency in their voices told her there wasn't any time to waste, asking a lot of questions. Five minutes after they came in the store Maddy was dressed in one of Thelma's long skirts and a modest blouse and was climbing into her old Dodge Omni.

"I don't like this, Maddy. I really don't."

"Trust me, it's going to be okay, John Lee."

"I'd feel a lot better if you took a backup gun with you," he told her.

"I'm not gonna need it. It's gonna be a quick in and out, I promise."

"Please be careful," he said, his concern for her evident in his eyes and in his voice.

"I will. You just sit tight and monitor the radio so we know what the hell's going on in town." She gave him a final smile, started the Omni in a cloud of blue smoke, and drove out of the parking lot.

Watching her go, John Lee wanted to wave his arms and shout for her to come back. But he knew she was right. They needed to know what they were going up against before they took any further action.

***

The Gecko In The Corner

Orange sparks flew as the bright blue flame Paw Paw was using slowly cut its way into John Lee's gun safe.

"Keep that water trickling down as I cut," he ordered the one they called Armando, who was holding the garden hose. "Yeah, just like that. Keep it just a few inches above where I'm cutting, just like you're doing. Good job."

Paw Paw knew he could have gotten into the safe quicker, but the big boss man had taken his word for it about having to go slow so the ammunition inside the safe didn't explode, killing them all. So far he had cut a nine inch long slice in the door.

Miguel impatiently watched him work. Twice his telephone had rang and it was Esteban. He didn't answer. He didn't know what to say. He knew that it had taken too long to recover the money and that things had gone too far to hope for redemption. Even if he gave Esteban all of it, he knew the old man would never trust him again. And when Esteban did not trust somebody they disappeared.

So that's what Miguel would do. Just disappear. It would be hard to leave everything that he had built up, but there was no other way. Once he got the money back he would find himself some quiet place and live out his life in leisure. Maybe in South America, or some island someplace. Yes, that might work. He would have enough money to live well. Who knows? He might even get some more whores and go back into business. But he would stay away from the drugs. Yes, there was big money in them, but so many problems. Sure, the whores could present problems, too, but they were easy to control if they got out of hand. Or to replace, if it came to that. But still, he knew Esteban would never rest until he found him.

Then another thought came to his mind. One he had considered before. Esteban was a sick old man. He could not live forever, and *someone* needed to take his place when the time came. Why not himself? And why wait? Maybe Esteban needed to go away now. It wouldn't be easy, the old man had a small army of bodyguards. But they worked for money. Would they really care if that money came from Esteban or from him?

His thoughts were interrupted when Ignacio called him on his telephone. "A woman is coming."

***

The sentry had watched as she made her way toward the house, stopping at every place along the road. There were only a few, but she knocked on each door. If someone answered she spoke to them for a few moments, and if not she left some piece of paper on the doorknob. Watching from where he was hidden in the dense brush alongside the road, Ignacio thought she might be some kind of salesperson.

She started the old car, which belched smoke and sounded like it might collapse into a pile of steel and oil and gasoline and rubber at any moment, and backed out of the driveway. There was one more house to go before they got to where Miguel and the rest were trying to break into the safe. He raised his phone to call Miguel and tell him she was coming.

***

The radio traffic was still out of control. It sounded like every Somerton County deputy, the four officers from the small city police force, every highway patrolman in the region, and the dispatcher were all talking at once. Twice John Lee heard his unit called, but when he tried to respond he couldn't break through the noise. That was just as well. He was too busy to account for where he was or what he and Maddy were up to.

He was too fidgety to sit inside his patrol car, so he was standing outside of it by the door, looking down the road that went to his house, waiting for any sign of Maddy returning. A couple of vehicles had come and gone, people stopping at the store, and he had not paid attention to any of them. So he didn't notice the old blue Ford Tempo passing by on the road until the driver hit the brakes, reversed, and pulled up beside him.

"I'm so glad to see you. I've been looking for you, John Lee," Herb Quarrels said.

John Lee Quarrels Series

Chapter 41

THE WOMAN HAD BLONDE HAIR tied back on top of her head in some sort of bun, and even with the long skirt and the blouse that looked like it was too big for her, Miguel she could tell she was very attractive. In another time and at another place he would have looked enjoyed talking to her. But not now. There was too much happening to waste time with a puta. Even one who looked like she had as much potential as this one did.

He opened the door when she knocked and said, "What do you want?"

"Oh, I have everything I could ever want or need right here," the woman said with a smile, holding up the Bible in her left hand. "Jesus gives me everything I need. I'm here to share the Word with you."

"This is a bad time," Miguel told her. "I'm sorry, but we are busy with a house repair."

"Oh, I'm sorry to hear that," the woman said. "I know how those things can go. But could I just have a moment to tell you about the Lord's love? He really does love you, you know?"

She was nodding her head earnestly. Behind him he heard the torch start up again and wished the old man would just get it done with instead of stopping to let the safe cool so many times. But Miguel knew he was right, making all the ammunition inside explode would only add to his troubles, and probably burn up the money inside.

"Something really smells in there," the woman said, waving her hand in front of her face. "Is something burning?"

"The pipes. They are welding a pipe or something, I don't know exactly," Miguel told her. "Really, I must go."

The woman held her hand over her mouth and coughed. "I'm sorry, I didn't mean to take any of your time." She coughed again.

Miguel started to close the door and she said, "Can I just leave you this pamphlet? Maybe you could read it later on, when you're not so busy."

"Yes, thank you," he said, taking the paper she offered him. She coughed again, harder this time, and said, "I'm really sorry, but could I trouble you for a glass of water? Something has set my asthma off. Maybe that smoky smell from inside."

"No. We had to turn the water off to do the welding. I'm sorry. Now I must go."

He closed the door as she started to say something else. Miguel watched from inside as she climbed behind the wheel and started the old car, making a wide U-turn in the yard before driving away. The back end of the clunker was festooned with Honk If You Love Jesus and God Bless You bumper stickers.

Just his luck that a woman who looked so good would show up when he was so busy, and she would be in love with the Lord. If he wasn't so preoccupied with his present problems, he would have taken her and shown her a very different kind of love. One like she never knew existed.

***

"You've got a lot of explaining to do, mister, and I don't have time for any bullshit. So start talking," John Lee said.

"I'm sorry I ran off like I did," Herb said. "And I'm sorry I got you involved in all this in the first place, son."

"I'm *not* your son. You don't have the right to call me that. What the hell have you done to cause all of this? And I'll tell you something right now, don't you lie to me! People are dead because of you, and Maddy is in danger right this minute. I want to hear it all right now."

"It's a long story, John Lee."

He shoved his father against the side of his patrol car and said, "Make it short, because I'm about ready to break you in half."

The Gecko In The Corner

"Okay, okay! I've got another son, his name is Jason. I swear I didn't know it, John Lee, but he was running drugs for a man named Miguel Torres. Three years ago he ripped Torres off and they were going to kill him. He came to me begging for help, and I scrounged up $25,000 and went down to Orlando and met with a guy named Ramon Sainz, who is a middleman for Torres. I was hoping that would settle the debt, or at least buy some time, or something. But he just took the money and laughed in my face. He said Jason owed his boss four times that much. I was begging him not to kill Jason. I said I would do anything. I told him I handle the books for a big company and I had access to money, but I just couldn't walk into a bank and walk out with $100,000 in cash. He said he would talk to his boss. So we worked out an arrangement."

"Yeah, I know about your arrangement. You were laundering money for Torres. How did it all go bad and lead to this?"

"I set up a bunch of dummy companies and kept the money moving. If it all would have gone into one account and back out it would have gotten the attention of the feds. The way I was doing it, a lot of it made its way into different companies I set up for Torres."

"A lot of it? What happened to the rest?"

Herb looked away, and then back at him. "Everybody got greedy."

"Keep talking."

"Besides the money that we were shifting around, that money was making a lot of interest. A *lot* of interest, John Lee. And I was skimming some of that interest off the top. Ramon and I worked out a deal on the side, where I'd give him a percentage of it. Every two weeks I would send Jason back down here with a briefcase full of money for Torres and a second smaller package for Ramon."

"And Torres found out about it?"

"No, it was more than that. You have to understand, John Lee, I had a job and I had to keep things looking normal. That's what allowed me to move so much money around. The banks all knew me and assumed it was just part of my job. A lot of businesses, even legitimate ones, have a bunch of subsidiary companies under them. But I couldn't be everywhere every time, so I had Jason help me."

"I can see where this is going," John Lee said. "You were ripping off Ramon, Ramon was ripping off Torres, and Jason decided he might as well join the party, right?"

Herb nodded. "Yeah. I didn't know it, but he was taking some off the top of every cash shipment that I sent down. And he was moving some of the money out of the different accounts. Not a lot, and not often, but it all added up. A couple of weeks ago Ramon showed up at my house. He said Torres wanted to know what had happened to the last two shipments. I assumed he had figured out they were light, but that wasn't it. Jason never showed up with either one of them."

"How much money are we talking about?"

"The shipments? $1 million each. But then when I started looking at the different accounts there was another three million missing."

"And Jason took it?"

"He was the only one who could have. When Ramon showed up, he disappeared."

"Where is he?"

"I wish I knew. His mother claims she hasn't heard from him, but I don't believe her."

"Your son sounds like a real prince. First he gets you involved in this bullshit, then he leaves you holding the bag. You know he can't hide forever, right? They'll find him sooner or later."

"I know. Like I said, I can't just draw everything out of the banks at once. We'd have auditors and IRS people swarming over us. But I managed to get a little over two million and I brought it down. I was hoping to buy time again. But Torres wanted all of it. Every penny, from every account. When I met with Ramon, he had a couple of guys with him. He left and they started beating me, wanting to know where Jason was and wanting to know where the rest of the money was. They did this," he said, holding up his hand with the missing finger.

"How did you get away from them?"

Herb looked down, then back up at his son's face again. "I killed them, John Lee. I couldn't believe I did it. Still can't believe it. They had this ammonia thing that they were pushing into my nose to wake me up every time I passed out. But one time I managed not to pass out. I just acted like I did. And when the one came up to wake me up again, I grabbed the gun out of his belt and I shot him. I shot him, and then I shot the other one. I hadn't shot a gun since I was in the Navy, but I did it. And then I got the hell out of there as fast as I could."

"And you came up here?"

"I didn't know where else to go. I'm sorry."

"Tell me about the money in my account. What's that all about?"

"I don't know," Herb said, shaking his head. "I felt like I owed you something for all those years I ignored you. So I started putting some money in, a little bit at a time. I guess maybe I thought it might make up for being such a bad father to you."

"So you thought you could buy me?"

"No, that wasn't it," Herb protested. "I swear, John Lee. I just wanted to be able to help you somehow."

"Well, you've helped a lot. My house is trashed, Miguel Torres thinks I have his damn money, one of our deputies is dead, along with your buddy Ramon and another guy, and Torres is holding Paw Paw hostage to try to force me to give them the money you ripped off from them. Which, by the way, Torres claims is $10 million."

"With the money Jason stole and all the money sitting in the different accounts that's probably about right."

"You said you brought money down to try to buy them off. A couple million dollars. Where is it?"

Herb nodded at the Tempo. "In the trunk."

John Lee was surprised that so much money could weigh so little. The currency was mostly banded stacks of $100 bills, with a few stacks of $50 bills. It all fit into a large valise that didn't look much different than a laptop computer bag and probably weighed about 25 pounds, bag and all. The overall package seemed rather insignificant compared to all of the suffering it had caused. He closed the Tempo's trunk.

"I'm so sorry I dragged you into all of this," Herb said once again.

John Lee held up his hand to silence him. "Just stop, okay? Just stop. I don't want to hear it. You need to know that no matter how this all works out, the FBI is going to throw you in prison for a long, long time."

Herb hung his head and said, "I know that. And I deserve it. And I also know that it won't take long for Torres to get to me in there. But I just don't care anymore, John Lee. I'm tired of running and tired of hiding and tired of... I'm just tired of it all."

John Lee thought he should feel some empathy for the broken man standing in front of him, but he didn't. If his father went to prison, so be it. And if Torres managed to have him killed there, there was nothing he could do about it. All John Lee cared about at that point was Maddy returning safely, and rescuing Paw Paw. From there, the chips could fall wherever they wanted to.

"What do you want me to do now?"

"Can you back up time? Because that's about the only thing I can think of that would help right now. Just back it up enough that I'm not mixed up in any of this bullshit of yours."

"I wish I could," Herb said. "Believe me, I really wish I could."

Before John Lee could reply he heard a car pull in near them and Maddy called his name. When she got out of the Omni he felt a sense of relief like he had never experienced before and it took all he could do not to rush to her and pull her into his arms.

Chapter 42

"They're there all right," Maddy said.

"Did you see Paw Paw? Is he okay."

"I didn't see him." she said, shaking her head. "But he's there. I heard him talking."

"Run it down for me, Maddy. What did you find out?"

"There's a big SUV parked in the trees behind your place. It was half hidden, but I saw it. And there's a guard hiding in the bushes at each side of the property, watching the street. They're city boys and didn't do a very good job of hiding. Hell, one of them was smoking and I could see the smoke before I got to where he was. There's at least three or four of them in the house with Paw Paw. I get the feeling that the one who came to the door is the big boss man. And they're doing something in there, John Lee."

"What do you mean?"

"I never got inside, I just stood at the door talking to the one guy. But I kept seeing a reflection of a real bright light coming from down the hall where your guest bedroom is and it smelled like something was burning. He said they were welding pipes."

"There aren't any metal pipes in the house," John Lee said, "it's all PVC or whatever they make things out of these days."

"So what were they welding?"

He thought for a minute and said, "They aren't welding anything. Paw Paw's cutting my gun safe apart."

"Why?"

"Because Torres thinks that's where his missing money is. He said he wants me to come and open the safe."

"So what are we going to do?"

"I'm going to give the man what he wants," John Lee told her.

***

John Lee parked his patrol car on the side of the road a hundred feet from his house. He got out slowly, keeping his hands visible, and turned around to show that he had taken his gun belt off.

"I know you're around here somewhere," he said loud enough to be heard by the hidden sentry. "Tell Miguel I'm here."

He stood there for two or three minutes that seemed like hours, then a man came out of the brush pointing a pistol at him.

"Stay in front of me and keep your hands up where I can see them or I will shoot you," he said.

John Lee did as he was ordered as they walked to his driveway and up to the house. A heavyset Latino man stepped outside with a gun in his hand and said, "John Lee Quarrels. I've been waiting for you." He looked past John Lee to the sentry and asked, "Did you search him?"

"Not yet, Miguel. You said to get him here, so I did, as fast as I could."

"Do it now. Do not move, John Lee Quarrels, or I will kill you where you stand."

John Lee remained motionless, his hands in the air, as the sentry patted him down. The man took his wallet and cell phone away and handed them to Miguel.

"That's everything."

Miguel motioned with the gun and said, "Get inside."

As soon as they were inside the door, Miguel slammed him in the side of the face with the barrel of his pistol. The blow was hard enough to rock John Lee, but not enough to knock him out. He knew it was punitive and not intended to render him unconscious. Miguel needed him awake.

"Smells like you're burning the place down."

"Don't talk unless I tell you to."

"Whatever you say, you're the man with a gun."

"That is correct, and don't you forget it for even one minute."

He could see the bright flame from the cutting torch and said, "So you figured out how to get into my safe after all."

"I told you not to talk."

"Then why do you want me here? I told you I couldn't open the safe and you seem to be doing it anyway."

"Shut up." Miguel waved the barrel of the gun at him menacingly.

"If you were going to shoot me, you'd have done it by now."

"Maybe I will, just to shut you up."

"No you won't. You need me alive. Because once you do get in that safe and find out I've been telling you the truth all along and there's no money in it, you're going to need me to get my father to come to you."

"Than you do know where he is!"

"Maybe, maybe not."

Torres backhanded him and John Lee could taste blood in his mouth.

"Do not play games with me! I don't have time for this."

"You're right, you don't. Your man Ramon is dead, and so is that big ugly ape who was with him. The FBI is in town and they're going to be crawling all over you any minute now."

Torres jammed the gun under his chin. "Then you had better give me my money fast, because you will be the first to die if they come here!"

"Okay, write this down, because your memory seems to really suck and I'm tired of repeating myself over and over. I don't have your damn money! I never did have it! Got it?"

Torres hit him in the face with the gun barrel. "I will kill you right now!"

"Then do it! What have you got to lose? One way or another, you're a dead man already. The only question is if you're going to die in prison or if Esteban Muñoz does the job."

John Lee saw something in the other man's eyes at the mention of Esteban's name. "That's right, the feds know all about you and your buddy Esteban. They also know that you have been ripping him off on his weekly payoffs. And I bet by now he's figured that out, too. The way I see it, your best chance is to hand me that gun and give yourself up right now. You know that

Ramon was going to rat you guys out to the FBI. That's why you had him killed. But you could tell them a lot more than anything he could. Take the deal they offered him, it's your only chance."

Torres laughed at him. "Do you think I'm such a fool to believe anything you tell me? Do you think I do not have plans in place for this sort of situation? I can disappear just like that," he said snapping his fingers.

"You can, but not without that money. The feds are shutting down all those offshore accounts my father set up for you right now. All you have is the money that my father took. And like I said, I don't have it. So you're screwed, buddy!"

"Then I have nothing to lose, as you say. I can at least have the satisfaction of killing you."

"Yeah, you can. But you won't live long enough to enjoy it. Or..."

"What? Or what?"

"I can't get you all the money, but I know where a couple million of it is."

"Where. Where is it?"

John Lee shook his head. "Not until you let my grandfather go."

"Give me my money!"

"We can stand here playing this silly-assed game all day long if you want to," John Lee said. "But the more time you waste, the sooner the FBI is going to be here."

Torres grabbed him by the back collar of his shirt and pressed the gun into his left cheek. "You want to see the old man? You can see him."

"That wasn't the deal," John Lee said. "You let him go and you get your money."

"He is going to die with you if my money isn't in that safe!"

He marched John Lee into the guest bedroom, where Paw Paw was working on the safe. The air inside the living room was bad enough, but here it was a thick smog of smoke and fumes. A man stood beside Paw Paw with a garden hose trickling water down the safe's door, and two others held fire extinguishers. One of them was a big man with a ponytail who could have been the twin of the prisoner who had been shot at the jail.

"There. There is your beloved Paw Paw. Now before I put a bullet in him, tell me where my money is."

"Whoa! Stop right there, Paw Paw," John Lee screamed when he saw the cutting torch's progress. "The safe is booby-trapped and you're about to blow us all up!"

The ruse worked. Every eye turned toward Paw Paw and the safe at his outburst. Every eye but John Lee's. He took advantage of the momentary distraction to jam his hand into the crotch of his pants and pulled out a small Sig Saur Equinox .380 pistol, never feeling the pain as the duct tape holding it in place peeled the hair from his body. There were no time for niceties, John Lee jammed the little gun into Miguel Torres's face and pulled the trigger twice.

Bedlam erupted with the gunshots. Jorge turned and threw the fire extinguisher he was holding at John Lee, then reached for the pistol in his belt. His hand never touched it because Paw Paw raised the cutting torch he had been using on the safe and sent a burst of 3,500° flame into the side of the man's face, melting his flesh and one eye instantly. Jorge screamed in agony and tried to run away, but made it only three steps toward the hallway before he collapsed.

The other two men in the room seemed frozen in place. John Lee scooped up Miguel's pistol from where he had dropped it and pointed in their direction. "Both of you, hands in the air," he ordered.

Paw Paw turned off the torch, looked at his grandson and said, "Well, it took you long enough!"

***

As soon as she heard the screams and gunshots from the house, Maddy rose up from where she had made her way to a hiding place less than 50 feet from the sentry who had returned to his post after bringing John Lee to Miguel. "Freeze! Hands in the air or I'll shoot you."

He took one look at the Remington shotgun she was pointing at him and quickly obeyed. Maddy ordered him facedown and handed Herb her handcuffs. Once he had the man's hands secured they searched him and took his pistol, then pulled him to his feet.

"Let's go!"

Staying in the trees, they marched the prisoner to the edge of John Lee's property. Maddy handed his pistol to Herb and said, "Keep him here." She wasn't sure if there was a guard at the rear of the property, but she knew there was one on the other side and planned to circle around and take him down. But he saved her the trouble as he came running into the yard with his gun in his hand.

"Police. Freeze! Drop your weapon!"

This one didn't give up as easily. He raised his gun and fired twice at her, the shots cutting into the trees behind her. Maddy fired once, and even though she was at the outer limits of range with a short barreled shotgun, two of the shell's eight double-aught balls hit their target, taking him down. She jacked another round into the chamber and approached the guard cautiously, with her eyes moving all the time between him and any other potential threat. If there was a guard hiding somewhere at the rear of the property, he deserted his post and was gone.

Maddy kicked his weapon out of reach, then checked the man on the ground. One ball had hit him in the left leg just above the knee and the other was lodged in his pelvis. He was bleeding but didn't look like he was going to die anytime soon. She handcuffed him and approached the house, ready to take on whatever threat lay in wait there.

"Don't shoot, Maddy," John Lee shouted from inside, "we're coming out."

Chapter 43

THEY COULD HEAR THE SOUND of sirens approaching quickly. John Lee left Maddie and Paw Paw to guard the prisoners while he went for his father and the other sentry.

"Are you okay, son?"

"I'm not your... yeah, I'm okay."

He took the sentry back to his yard to join the rest of Torres' men just as the first police cars arrived. Soon the area was swarming with deputies, FBI agents, state troopers, and emergency medical personnel. Six deputies began searching the woods around the house for any strays who might be hiding. The paramedics were tending to the man Maddie had shot, and Chief Deputy Flag Newton was on the attack.

"You're going down for this one, John Lee! Yep, you can bet your ass, you're going down. You're history."

John Lee was coming down off the adrenaline high and felt like he could close his eyes and fall asleep right there with everything happening around him. "Shut up, Fig, I don't want to hear it today."

"Listen to me, you punk," Flag said, grabbing him by the collar of his shirt. "It don't matter how hard you kiss D.W.'s ass, I've got you now."

John Lee wasn't a gambler, but a minute before he wouldn't have taken any bets on his ability to even walk back up onto his porch. Looking back later he didn't know where he got the energy, but it came out of nowhere and traveled through his entire body to his right fist, which he swung as hard as he could into Flag's jaw. The chief deputy was bigger than him, and heavier by close to fifty pounds, but the blow staggered him a step backwards and then he landed on his back, out cold.

More cops and more paramedics arrived. Sheriff D.W. Swindle, still shocked by the violence that had taken place in the cellblock, took charge of the situation and did an admirable job of it. All weapons involved in the incident were taken into custody for ballistics tests, the whole area was quickly cordoned off to keep the crowd of curious neighbors and others who had heard about the shooting on their police scanners or by word of mouth away from the scene, and an FBI SWAT team joined the hunt for anyone else who might have been with Torres and fled, but found no evidence of anyone.

John Lee watched as two paramedics brought out the body of Miguel Torres on a gurney, and heard someone shout from inside, "We've got one alive in here!" Another gurney was rushed into the house and soon another pair of paramedics came out with Jorge. The man looked like something out of a horror movie, one side of his face blackened and disfigured, bone showing through. John Lee did not know how anybody could have survived the injuries he had sustained. He turned away to keep from throwing up.

"You should have told us what was going on," Special Agent Barber chastised him.

"I was going to," John Lee said. "That's why I was coming into the cellblock just as everything went to hell in there. Then it was so crazy that I just had to get out of there and here to save my grandfather."

"You could have gotten yourself killed in the process."

"At that point, I wasn't thinking about myself. With Ramon and the other one dead, I knew I was running out of time."

"Procedure says..."

"Okay, let's just take a step backward," Thalman said. Only a few people in the Bureau knew about the Silver Star he had earned as a Marine in Kuwait, but Thalman knew a thing or two about loyalty, and he understood why John Lee had done what he did. "This isn't the time or the place to point fingers and say who did what. It'll all come out in the wash. The important thing is that you're okay, Deputy Quarrels. You and your grandfather."

"And our whole investigation is screwed," Barber said sarcastically. "With Ramon Sainz dead and Torres dead, what have we got?"

The Gecko In The Corner

"We've got a lot, Thalman said. We closed down a major money-laundering operation, and that's going to hurt Esteban Muñoz right in the pocketbook. We've got a couple of his major players out of the game for good, which is going to shut down much of his Orlando operation. And who knows? Maybe those guys over there can tell us something," he said, nodding toward the prisoners. He turned back to John Lee and added, "And then we've got your father. Where is he?"

"To be honest I don't know. He was here a minute ago." John Lee wondered if his father had run off again.

"I'm right here," Herb said, stepping out of the trees. "Sorry, I had to take a leak and I can't get in the house. I told you, I'm tired of running. Do whatever you have to do to me, I deserve it. I'll tell you everything I know."

"Before you say another word, I have to formally arrest you and read you your rights," Thalman said.

"Okay, have at it."

Before the FBI agent could say anything else, there was a scream of shock and pain from one of the paramedics. If John Lee could not have believed anyone could have survived the injuries Jorge had suffered, how could he believe what was happening right before his eyes? But there it was. The big man had somehow managed to get his switchblade knife into his hands and stabbed the paramedic attending to him in the stomach. Then, in what witnesses who had seen it happen would later describe as some sort of superhuman strength, he jumped off the gurney and charged toward John Lee with the bloody knife. He was only ten steps away and closed the distance quickly. It was a scene John Lee would relive in his nightmares for many years to come. He instinctively reached for his gun, forgetting that he had locked his gun belt in his patrol car when he had surrendered himself to Torres. Both FBI agents drew their guns, but by then Jorge was almost on top of John Lee, the knife swinging down in a vicious arc.

"No!" Herb shouted and threw himself between his son and the nightmare who was trying to kill him. The blade sank deeply into his chest, but he managed to pull Jorge down with him as he went. The big man rolled away and somehow started to get to his feet, but never made it as a fusillade of bullets tore into him.

John Lee dropped to his knees beside his father. Herb managed to flutter his eyes open for a second or two and smiled weakly as the son he had never known cradled him in his last seconds of life.

Epilogue

THE INVESTIGATIONS SEEMED TO GO on forever. John Lee and Maddy were interrogated by agents from half a dozen different federal agencies, the Florida Department of Law Enforcement, two US Attorneys, and other people whose names they could not even remember. They turned down requests to speak to the press, deferring that to Sheriff D.W. Swindle.

In the end they were exonerated of any wrongdoing for their actions, even though they may have strayed quite a ways from accepted police procedure. Then again, there's not much in the police procedural manuals that covers having a family member in immediate danger of death from a gang of drug dealers known for their propensity toward violence.

The FBI and Sheriff Swindle held a joint news conference in which the Bureau credited the Somerton County Sheriff's Department with helping to bring down a major drug operation in Central Florida, and specifically mentioned Deputies Madison Westfall and John Lee Quarrels for their help in the investigation, and Deputy Quarrels for recovering nearly $2 million in laundered drug money.

Chief Deputy Flag Newton fumed while the feds were making John Lee look like some kind of damned hero. He attempted to file a formal charge against John Lee for assaulting him, but every witness on the scene said they believed the deputy was defending himself and that if anybody should be brought up on charges, it was Flag.

He knew when he was beat, so instead Flag turned his attention to the events leading up to the death of Deputy Obediah 'Obie' Long. He said that if the jailer had followed proper procedure and informed a supervisor before moving Laurencio out of his cell, he would still be alive. "Everybody knows that when you've got a dangerous prisoner, you have another deputy there before you do anything with him. But Obie always was a lazy dumb ass, and it got him killed. If he'd a taken the time to come and find me or D.W., he would still be alive today and none of this would have happened."

A lot of deputies had been frustrated by Obie's lack of effort over the years, but putting a dead man down didn't fit well with any of them. Obie may not have been much of a deputy, but he was still one of them. Flag's outburst only lowered him in their eyes, if such a thing was possible.

***

Shortly after the investigation wrapped up, Bill McCoy finished a double shift at the dairy and climbed into his old pickup truck, aching in every joint. When he started to push in the truck's clutch pedal he felt something in the way. He got out and reached down to investigate, and found a thick manila envelope with the words For Hospital Bills scrolled across the front with a black felt marker. Bill opened the envelope and began to shake as he looked at the $75,000 inside. It was life-changing money.

***

"So are you still bald down there?"

"That's for me to know and you to find out."

"Now you know what it feels like for us girls when we get our lady parts waxed," Maddy said.

"I'm not sure I'd ever want to do that. The duct tape was bad enough," John Lee said.

"Well at least I had fun putting it on you. I'm just glad we didn't blow your weenie away in the process."

"Yeah, I appreciate that, too."

"I still can't believe they didn't find that gun when they searched you."

"I was pretty sure it would be okay," he said. "You got to keep in mind these guys weren't trained like we are. And I know some cops that would've missed it, too. Guys have just got a thing about not grabbing someone else's junk."

"Still, I don't know if I would've done that."

"Oh yeah? Where would you have hidden it, Maddy?"

"Uhh... no comment."

" Did I tell you I heard from Thalman today?"

"No. Please tell me that they don't have more questions!"

"No. He wanted me to know that they arrested Jason, Herb's son. He was sitting on a beach in Jamaica with a drink in one hand and a hot redhead in the other."

"He didn't get far."

"Nope. Herb said he was a mama's boy and I guess he was right. They were listening in when he called his mom and nailed him."

"Good. So I guess that wraps it all up."

They were sitting on a redwood bench on the back deck of his newly remodeled home, wrapped in a blanket and drinking beer in spite of the chilly night air. Magic got up from his position at John Lee's side, walked down to the yard and relieved himself against a tree, then roamed the perimeter of the property.

They sat in comfortable silence for a while, two friends who had shared so much over the years. Maddy looked up at the sky and said, "I like to think that what we call stars are really the souls of people who have passed on. Like my daddy and brother and all the people we loved and who loved us are up there watching over us. And maybe when we see a falling star, it's one of those souls coming back to earth to give it another try."

John Lee didn't reply, just sat looking up at the night sky. It was an hour later and Maddy had fallen asleep leaning against his shoulder when he saw the shooting star streaking across the sky and said, "I hope things work out better for you next time around, Herb."

****

Author's Note: Thank you for reading *The Gecko In The Corner*. I hope you enjoyed it and will consider leaving a review.

You can follow me on my page Facebook at https://www.facebook.com/NickRussellAuthor/ for updates on my writing projects and news about my upcoming books and those of my author friends. If you would like to be added to my free mailing list, Nick Russell's Writing Life, with more information, short stories, and links to some great reading, please send me an e-mail at editor@gypsyjournal.net.

Turn The Page To Check Out A Sample Of Badge Bunny,
The Third John Lee Quarrels Book, Coming Soon!

The Gecko In The Corner
Badge Bunny
Chapter 1

Nobody in Somerton County took much notice when Leona Darling went missing. Not her mother, Mary Lou, who was obsessed with daytime talk shows and primetime reality programming, and seldom left the couch except to nuke a TV dinner in the microwave and pour another glass of sweet tea. Not her father, Curtis, who spent most of his time at the American Legion hall reliving his glory days as a cook at Fort Sill, Oklahoma. And certainly not her younger sister Jessie, who had recently discovered the thrills of bath salts, a synthetic drug that gave her an effect much like cocaine but was cheaper and easier to obtain. Jessie didn't notice much of anything these days.

But really, who could blame them? Ever since Leona had developed boobs she was gone a lot to who knows where.

It was only after she failed to show up for court on a charge of driving on a suspended license and having no proof of insurance that anyone started looking for her. And that someone was Deputy John Lee Quarrels, the arresting officer.

Judge Harrison Taylor had been on the bench for over 20 years and had earned a much deserved reputation for fairness and honesty. But he had little patience for those who flaunted the law. When Leona missed her court date the judge told John Lee to find her and bring her to him immediately. But finding Leona was not easily done.

He tried calling her cell phone but got a message saying her voice mailbox was full. Next he tried her last known place of employment, where he learned she had been dismissed for showing up for her shift drunk. Then John Lee drove out to the Darling home on Sugar Maple Road. It was a doublewide mobile home that looked like it had not seen a power washer or a paintbrush since it had been set in place back in the late 1980s. A huge satellite TV dish stood next to the house, and two large dogs chained to it barked at him when he got out of his patrol car. John Lee climbed the rickety stairs and knocked on the door.

Jessie Darling opened it and look startled to see a police officer standing there. One look at her told John Lee that the girl was spaced out on something. She asked what he wanted and he told her he needed to talk to Leona.

"She ain't here," Jessie said, slamming the door in his face. Lately Jessie had been feeling depressed and paranoid, a result of her bath salts addiction, and the last thing she wanted was to find a cop standing at the door.

Mary Lou Darling tried to ignore it when John Lee pounded on the mobile home's door again, but when he didn't stop, she finally heaved a heavy sigh and picked up the remote control to pause *Dr. Phil* and opened the door again.

"I need to find Leona," John Lee told her. He wasn't the first man who had shown up at the door looking for her oldest daughter, and he certainly wasn't the ugliest.

"Ain't seen her in a while," Mary Lou said. "Did you check at Hog Wild Barbecue? I think she's workin' there."

"She got fired two weeks ago," John Lee replied.

"Maybe at the Fillin' Station?"

He shook his head. "Lester canned her when she got in a fight with his daughter and called her a fat sow."

"Well, Nancy *is* a pretty big ol' gal."

"Yeah, she is," Johnn Lee acknowledged, "but Lester didn't feel that gave Leona the right to be saying things like that right there in the middle of the restaurant."

"Leona's got a mind of her own," her mother said, shrugging her shoulders. "Look, I got things to do. If I see her I'll tell her you're lookin' for her."

John Lee drove back to town and stopped at the Legion Hall to ask her father if he had seen Leona, but instead of an answer he got a long lecture about how nobody appreciated the soldiers who worked behind the scenes. "It ain't all guns and hand grenades and glory," Curtis Darling said. "They say an army moves on its stomach. Well, who the hell do ya think fills those stomachs? But does anybody ever build a statue to the cooks? Hell no!" John Lee left about the time Curtis began telling him how keeping his hands immersed in all those greasy pots and pans over the years had caused arthritis. But would the VA give him a disability for that? Hell no! "It just ain't right," Curtis was saying as the deputy walked out the door. "It just ain't right a'tall!"

And so it went all day long. Nobody John Lee talked to had seen Leona or the old blue Mazda pickup she drove. No one in her family, none of the regulars in the bars where she hung out, not her aunt or uncle, and not Mary Lou Nelson and the other three women who worked at the Cute-Z Cuts N' Curl, where Leona had a standing appointment every other Thursday afternoon to get her hair styled and her nails done. He talked to several other deputies and the officers of the tiny Somerton police force. Leona was a familiar face to all of them, but nobody knew where she was or could recall the last time they saw her. John Lee even struck out with her two favorite drinking buddies, Crystal Tobins and Holly Griggs. And if *they* didn't know where she was, nobody did.

As it turned out, only one person in all of Somerton County knew where Leona Darling was, and they weren't saying anything.

Made in the USA
Middletown, DE
19 May 2017